IT'S ALWAYS HALLOWEEN HERE

MATT FORGIT

This book is a work of fiction. Any reference to historical events, real people, or real places are used fictitiously. Other names, characters, places, and events are products of the author's deranged imagination. Any resemblance to actual events or places or people, living or dead or undead, is entirely coincidental.

ISBN 979-8-9853874-7-6

First edition published September 2025

Cover design and artwork by Matthew Keller at matthewkellerart.com

Copyright © 2025 Morgan Meadows Hall Publishing. All rights reserved. In accordance with the US Copyright Act of 1976, the scanning, uploading, and electronic sharing of this book (both in part or in its entirety) without the permission of the author constitutes unlawful piracy and theft of the author's intellectual property. No parts of this publication may be reproduced, stored in a retrieval system, or transmitted in any form or by any means, without the prior permission in writing by the publisher, nor be otherwise circulated in any form of binding or cover than that in which it is published and without a similar condition including this condition being imposed on the subsequent purchaser. If you would like to use material from this book (with the exception of review purposes), prior written permission must be obtained by contacting mattforgit@gmail.com.

To Grandma, for being the best, always encouraging my writing, taking me to my first PG-13 movie, taking me to get Madonna's *True Blue* cassette tape, and for the time she found me waiting on the couch at one a.m. for *Student Bodies* on HBO to start, then sat down to watch it with me

To my fellow kindred spirits who grew up during the glorious, magical era of VHS horror movies, made-for-TV thrillers, practical special effects, plastic Halloween costumes, Jason taking Manhattan (well, a cruise), 1-900 numbers to call Freddy, and Mom-and-Pop video stores; got their spooky television thrills and chills from USA Network's *Up All Night* and *Saturday Nightmares, Scooby-Doo, Friday the 13th: The Series, Monsters, She-Wolf of London, Freddy's Nightmares, Twin Peaks, Sightings, MST3K, Unsolved Mysteries, Tales from the Darkside, The X-Files*, and *Buffy the Vampire Slayer*; and grew up reading *Scary Stories to Tell in the Dark, Fear Street*, Christopher Pike, Point and Scholastic YA Thrillers, *Choose Your Own Adventures, Bunnicula*, Jan Harold Brunvand's urban legends, *Weird N.J.*, Time-Life's *Mysteries of the Unknown*, and Nancy Drew mysteries

And, as always, to Matt, my number one movie date—The Hansel to my Zoolander, MC Skat Kat to my Paula Abdul, Jo to my Blair, Wayne to my Garth, Wilson to my Phillips, Ernie to my Bert, Marcia to my Jan, and Andy to my Ellie

"Every shadows were they then—
But to-night they come again;
Were we once more but sixteen
Precious would be Hallowe'en."
    —Joel Benton, "Hallowe'en"

"We have no title-deeds to house or lands;
Owners and occupants of earlier dates
From graves forgotten stretch their dusty hands,
And hold in mortmain still their old estates."
    —Henry Wadsworth Longfellow, "Haunted Houses"

"A haunted house is a house with ghosts in it. The spirits of people who died. But the spirits living in a house possessed never existed in human form. They've only existed in spirit form. They're pure evil. They're demons."
    —*Night of the Demons* (1988)

"My victims walk in the land of the dead. They are all my children, and I am their ultimate lord."
    —*Spookies* (1986)

IT'S ALWAYS HALLOWEEN HERE

At the end of Farel Street in Doran, Massachusetts, stands The Faulkner House.

It is the last house on the street, hidden behind locked gates, a mile from the main entrance.

No one in the neighborhood has ever seen or met the Faulkner family.

The house is always dark.

Except on Halloween night, when the front porch light is lit.

Every year, on Halloween night, the gate is left open.

Every year, there is one person who waits at the front door to give candy to trick-or-treaters.

Every year, it is someone different.

Their age and appearance vary.

Sometimes, it's a woman. Sometimes, it's a man.

Sometimes, it's someone dressed in costume.

People in town say that if the greeter invites you inside, you must decline.

People in town claim that those who go inside are never seen again.

CHAPTER ONE

You can't go home again.

But Loretta Ward had done just that. Temporarily, at least. Summoned by her cousin Tiffani-Amber to be a bridesmaid at her upcoming wedding, scheduled to take place in the backyard of said cousin's childhood house. Loretta's mother could barely contain her excitement over the impending nuptials, unable to resist making asides and comments that her oldest child—Loretta, almost fifty—had never given her a wedding or grandchildren.

Loretta was happy for her cousin but even happier to see her old friends. She had been living in Boston for the past twenty years, two hours away from her hometown of Doran. Even better, Tiffani-Amber's wedding date was Sunday, November 2nd, which meant she would be in town for Halloween, her favorite holiday.

She smiled as she recalled her Halloween traditions with her hometown friends. Scary movie marathons at the drive-in, movie theater, or on VHS in someone's basement-turned-family room. Trick-or-treating in costume with younger siblings, nieces, and nephews. Bonfire parties and keggers in the woods. It was a simpler time, when life felt full of possibilities and hope.

Her trip down memory lane was suddenly interrupted by her phone. Kristen had texted to tell her something she never thought she'd hear. The Faulkner House was going to open for tours on Halloween night. The very same house that terrified her in her youth. She grew up several streets down from it, in the same neighborhood, filled with tall tales and ominous warnings from residents and her parents. The folktales and urban legends told at campfires about who lived there and their mysterious origins. The way her parents exchanged fraught glances when any of them brought up the subject of Faulkner House.

Loretta was aware that every neighborhood in every small town had that one house. The one that people whispered about and avoided, though there was never any factual evidence to back up any claims or horror stories told about its existence. The one that came with its own mythology and ever-expanding lore, meant to keep kids afraid and provide a cautionary tale. Don't poke your nose where it doesn't belong.

The number of people allowed to tour the house was limited. Kristen already had tickets for everyone. Her friends were going to celebrate Loretta's return by demystifying a childhood legend and finally getting to see what the inside of Faulkner House looked like.

Even though the whole thing was a bit silly, Loretta was excited.

CHAPTER TWO

Kristen Iasillo picked Loretta up in a Jeep covered in dog hair, blasting a playlist of '90s hits like they were still teenagers. She'd barely changed. Same deep red curls, same big laugh that filled up every room. Kristen had stayed in Doran her whole life, working as a school librarian and volunteering at the historical society.

"You look tired," Kristen said, with that disarming smile. "Like Boston's been sucking the soul out of you."

"Hello to you, too!" Loretta laughed "I work in an E.R. I work long hours and can't follow a strict bedtime beauty regimen, you judgy cow."

Kristen chuckled. "You look wonderful. Tired but wonderful."

They drove past the old stone buildings, past the general store with the broken E in "Market," past the shuttered bakery where Loretta had worked her first job. Most of the strip malls, restaurants, video stores, and assorted buildings that Loretta remembered were now empty vessels. Time and progress hadn't touched Doran. It had only gathered dust.

They met the others at The Pickle, the town's only real bar. Virgilia Dain was already on her second gin and tonic, leaning over the jukebox in a vintage leather jacket she'd probably owned since high school.

Frannie Scott was dressed in heavy winter clothes, typical of a New England resident. Her face was painted completely green.

"I chaperoned my kids' Halloween dance at school and went as The Wicked Witch of the West from *The Wizard of Oz*," Frannie explained, her expression turning woeful. "The makeup stained my face!"

"You look like Genie on *Pee-Wee's Playhouse*," said Virgilia.

Bruce Magliochetti and Drew Gionta arrived together, still inseparable after all these years. Bruce ran a mechanic shop and was still who Loretta called if she needed Mr. Fix-It advice. Drew, the ever-struggling artist, still painted eerie landscapes that nobody bought but everyone respected.

They hugged, laughed, and caught up with all the years between them. It was easy, for a little while, to pretend that nothing had changed. That so much time hadn't passed. That they weren't completely different than they were thirty years ago. That they hadn't all grown up near something wrong.

"You're the only one who escaped this place," Virgilia said to Loretta.

"How does it feel to be back in this dinky, nowhere town?"

"Oh, it's just different than the city," said Loretta. "It's quieter here. More trees and farms."

"So modest," said Virgilia. "You worked hard and got your medical degree, like we always knew you would. The rest of us got married—some of us, divorced—and had kids. You save lives every day."

"Yes, I am a hero," Loretta said. "No autographs, please."

"No special someone in your life?"

"Did my mother tell you to ask me that?"

"You don't ever miss it here?" asked Frannie.

"Well, I miss you guys," said Loretta. "I miss the way everything here looks in fall. I'm in the city. We don't get the same scenery when the seasons change."

Loretta was only half truthful. If she were being honest, she would have told her friends that she would have withered and died being stuck in Doran. She would have felt suffocated and unfulfilled in the doldrums of suburbia. She pictured what her life would've looked like had she stayed in a town without forward thinkers, ruled by homogeny and small-minded citizens, whose biggest excitement every week was going to the same bars, chain restaurants, and churches. She wanted more for her life than that.

She wanted more than to be married, popping out a bunch of children, and owning a generic house with a white picket fence. She did not judge her friends for choosing, or settling for, that life, but she knew it would come across as snobby, rude, and judgmental if she expressed that opinion. Like she looked down on them for their choices. She didn't. Loretta was happy for whatever path in life made her friends happy.

She worried that if she talked too much about her life in Boston, it would come across as bragging and condescending to their lives in a small town.

"It's great to see you again. Like old times." Virgilia clinked her drink against Loretta's.

"To the memory of our beloved karaoke nights and late-night diner hangs," Frannie said.

It didn't take long before someone brought up the history of the Faulkner House.

"I have never found any proper paperwork on who currently owns the place," said Kristen. "If the state owns it, or some family, but the taxes and bills for it get paid every year, like clockwork."

"Can you believe it?" Virgilia said, leaning forward, eyes bright. "They're opening it up tonight. For the first time ever. Self-guided tours."

Drew's eyes narrowed. "Seriously? That's not a joke?"

"Not a joke," Kristen said. "I saw the sign. Hand-painted. Just said *'Come See What Waits Inside.'* There was a roll of tickets at the gate. I grabbed a whole bunch."

"It was just a roll of tickets?" said Loretta. "That doesn't seem suspicious at all."

"Sounds like a trap," Bruce muttered into his beer.

"So, you brought us all here under the guise of seeing Loretta again, when in reality, you're dragging us to what inevitably will be a cheesy, boring tour of some old house?" Virgilia said.

"Yes," laughed Kristen.

"Not any house," said Bruce. "The Faulkner House. The fabled nightmare house of our childhoods."

"Did you invite the rest of the old gang to the festivities?" Drew asked.

"Of course," Kristen said. "They'll meet us there."

"Why did you tell them that we were going there, but not us?" Frannie asked Kristen. "Were you afraid we wouldn't join you?"

"The short answer is, yes," said Kristen. "And I forgot."

"God, remember all the stories about that place," said Virgilia. "Every time anything happened, we blamed it on the Faulkner House. Missing kid? Check the Faulkner House. Teen runaway? The Faulkner House. Never an ounce of proof. Just an old, creepy house that kids with vivid imaginations were afraid of."

"I mean, it's weird that no one in the neighborhood ever saw anyone there," Bruce said.

"Rich people," said Drew. "They want privacy and to be away from people. Can you blame them? Think they'd buy one of my paintings?"

"It's wild to me how, if you're rich, you're eccentric," said Kristen. "But if you're poor, you're crazy."

"It's probably got a serial killer basement," Virgilia said.

Loretta felt a chill creep up her back.

The Faulkner House. She hadn't thought about that place in years, but even the sound of it made her feel uneasy.

CHAPTER THREE

The crunch of gravel under tires broke the stillness just as Kristen's Jeep clicked into park. A few porch lights blinked somewhere distant behind the black iron gates, but otherwise, the end of the long dirt driveway might as well have been the edge of the known world.

Kristen, Loretta, Virgilia, Frannie, Drew, and Bruce spilled out of the car with varying degrees of enthusiasm.

"Agh," Drew said, stretching. "I felt like a sardine."

"Can I just say," Bruce said, shoving his hands in his jacket pockets, "that I already hate this."

"Put your big boy pants on," Kristen chirped, slamming her door. "We haven't even gone inside yet. Save the existential dread for the inside horrors."

Drew adjusted his scarf. "This driveway is longer than most relationships I've had."

"No one's arguing with that," Virgilia said.

They turned toward the gates, where a ragtag group had already congregated. Eleven figures lit by the yellow haze of an old lantern that hung from the top of the gate. When the lantern swung in the breeze, a muffled cackle followed.

"Look who decided to show up uncommitted," Donna Seeley called out, raising an accusatory finger clad in a sequined green glove.

"Oh, God," Loretta muttered. "Here she goes."

"You're not even wearing a hat," Donna continued, stomping forward, her massive mermaid tail slapping the gravel with every step. The shimmering scales clung to her legs, forcing her into an aggressive waddle that didn't exactly inspire sea-bound majesty.

"I told her the tail would be too much. She wouldn't let it go," Kristen whispered.

Donna stopped inches from them and planted her hands on her hips. "It's Halloween. The one night of the year we're all allowed to dress like lunatics and pretend our aging joints don't exist. And what do I see? A group of literal buzzkills in North Face and regret."

"We're dressed as tired adults," Bruce said. "It's a very niche horror genre."

"Oh, look," said Angela Cressler, sidling up. She wore a giant foam

IT'S ALWAYS HALLOWEEN HERE

costume shaped like a garlic bulb, complete with cloves on the shoulders and a sign pinned to her chest that read, "Certified Vampire Repellent." "Bruce is trying sarcasm again. It's cute when he fails."

"Where's your matching onion suit?" Drew asked.

"Next year," she winked. "Gonna be a whole soup course."

Next to her, Judy Bryan adjusted the massive foam dice strapped around her shoulders, each cube bigger than her head. Every time she moved, they clacked together like ill-tempered castanets.

"I made these myself," she said proudly.

"Did they come with a neck brace?" Virgilia asked, raising a brow.

Judy grinned. "It builds character. And back problems."

Marti Valbiro wore a Gothic-inspired, low-necked, red-ruffled, lantern-sleeved dress, with a Victorian-lady cameo brooch around her neck.

"I may need to steal someone's hoodie by the end of the night," Marti laughed. "This is colder than our usual Halloween."

She stood beside Phyllis Denning, who was dressed as Alicia Silverstone's character from *Clueless*. Yellow plaid blazer and mini-skirt, white crop top, over-the-knee socks, and Mary Jane heels.

"Loretta!" Phyllis pulled her in for a hug. "I had to come when I heard you were going to be here."

Suzanne Aspinall and Jerry Bartalos had been high school sweethearts. There was never a time the friends hadn't known them as a couple. Loretta marveled at how happy they always seemed. If there was evidence of soulmates being a real thing, Jerry and Suzanne were living proof.

Suzanne was dressed as '80s Cyndi Lauper. Bright, tousled red-and-blonde wig and heavy make-up, puffy and vibrantly-colored dress, along with lots of jelly bracelets, thrift-store necklaces and jewelry, and scuffed high-heeled shoes.

Jerry was dressed as Kiefer Sutherland's character, David, from *The Lost Boys*. Spiky, bleached blonde mullet. Black overcoat and gloves. Shit-kicker boots.

"Nobody better have garlic bread in their pockets," he said, laughing at his own joke. Everybody else groaned. "Who wants to touch my mullet?"

"Why does that sound so dirty?" said Virgilia.

Jerry noticed Angela in her vampire repellent costume and faked an overexaggerated hiss, showing off his plastic fangs. "Stay away from me, slayer!"

"Frannie, your face," Suzanne said. "I have some cleanser that will get that right off."

"It said water soluble on the label," sighed Frannie. "Lies!" The green make-up was already starting to chip and fray, making her look like a crazy goblin-woman.

Callie Merrill sauntered forward, dressed as a beekeeper. Mesh veil, white coveralls, and an audible buzzing sound coming from a Bluetooth speaker clipped to her hip.

"I bring sweetness and stingers," she said, giving a tiny hip-shake.

"No bees?" Loretta asked.

"I'm the queen. I don't carry bees. I summon them."

"God help us if that thing has a strobe setting," Reuben Lowenthal added, approaching from the side dressed head-to-toe as a disco ball. Not metaphorically. A full sphere of tiny mirrors encased him like a tragic Fabergé egg. His arms barely poked out. "I already blinded myself twice trying to pee."

"Reuben!" Kristen laughed. "Did you glue that on in the car again?"

"Don't judge me," he said. "Hot glue is a lifestyle."

"Not sniffing it, Reuben," said Phyllis.

"Well, I never! I strictly use Elmer's for that."

Helen Friede gave a long, exaggerated twirl, her costume catching the dim lantern light. She was a haunted bingo card, complete with splattered "blood" over the G column and actual plastic markers velcroed to random spots.

"I call her 'Bingo Bloodbath,'" Marti said, nudging Kristen.

"I was going for 'Murder in the Rec Hall,'" Helen replied, deadpan.

"Sold," Virgilia said, nodding.

Last came Ionia Delaney, who was the only one glowing. She wore a bodysuit covered in tiny LED lights that blinked in erratic pulses. On her head was a spinning weathervane. Across her chest was a neon sign that read, "Walking Doppler Radar."

"Too soon to ask what she's compensating for?" Drew whispered.

"Definitely," Kristen said.

Donna cleared her throat again and gestured broadly. "See? This is what effort looks like."

"I wore clean underwear, like Mom always told me to," Bruce offered.

"You have socks on that don't match, Bruce. That's a sign of mental decline," Marti said.

Loretta folded her arms and stepped forward. "Fine. You all look deranged and fabulous. But let's see how those costumes hold up when the weird starts. You think haunted bingo cards scare ghosts away?"

"Please," Helen said. "They respect the elderly. I'm invincible."

"I'm just here to outlive Reuben," Judy said.

Reuben raised his mirrored arm. "You'll have to catch me first, Dice Lady."

"You're literally spherical," Ionia said. "If you fall, we're all going down."

Donna clapped her sequined hands. "Alright, Misfits of Middle Age. Let's get this party haunted."

They all looked up at the gates. Large, looming metal, squeaking slightly in the breeze. Towering over them. Chains and locks in a pile on the ground. A central locking system in place between the two parts of the gates.

There were other people milling about. Other curious looky-loos and travelers waiting for their chance to see inside the infamous Faulkner House.

"I have flashlights if anyone needs any," Donna said, reaching into her bag and handing them out to her friends.

"Donna, how heavy is your bag?" Phyllis laughed. "It's like a convenience store in there."

"I was a Girl Scout," she said. "I'm always prepared."

Behind them, the iron creaked. Just a little.

Kristen took a step closer to Loretta. "You think the house knows we're here?"

Loretta didn't answer. The creak came again. And then, a *click*.

The gates opened.

CHAPTER FOUR

They walked with flashlights bobbing as they made their way past the old, locked gate and down the overgrown gravel path. A mile of walking, just as the rumors had always said. Cars weren't allowed past the gate. Something about preserving the grounds. But everyone knew it wasn't for nature.

It was to keep people from leaving too quickly.

The path to the Faulkner House twisted through the countryside like a forgotten scar, a narrow ribbon of rutted dirt flanked by fields gone fallow and groves of skeletal trees. Under the October night sky, the world seemed hushed, swallowed in darkness save for the cold gleam of the moon filtering through bare branches like fractured glass. Dry leaves skittered across the road in erratic gusts, whispering with every scrape as if conspiring in secret. The earth smelled of damp soil and decaying foliage, rich and heavy, with the occasional sharp tang of woodsmoke drifting in from distant farmsteads. Fences long surrendered to time leaned drunkenly along the path, their posts wrapped in rusted wire and tufts of windblown corn husks.

The property was surrounded towering hedges pruned into grotesque shapes that hovered between the familiar and the eerie. A stag reared on hind legs, its limbs unnaturally elongated, mouth open in a silent, leafy scream. Nearby, a cluster of rabbits sat frozen in mid-hop. Each one carved with unsettling precision, their black eyes made of polished stone that gleamed even in shadow. A swan with a split neck twisted back on itself in an impossible loop, feathers suggested in jagged, curling vines. Further on, a hound crouched low to the ground, its leafy ribs protruding in sharp ridges, jaws parted in a snarl that showed no teeth, only hollows.

Weathered statues reflected the moonlight, giving them a ghostly glow. Flanking the pathway, they stood like mourners in a silent procession; crumbling stone figures whose expressions had been worn into smudged agony. One held its hands over its eyes as if to block out something it could no longer bear to see. Another reached out with fingers snapped at the knuckles, the hand fixed mid-gesture as if pleading. A childlike figure knelt beside a basin cracked straight down the middle, its face featureless except for a shallow hole where the mouth should have been. Vines had begun to creep across the statues, tracing veins across their eroding bodies, binding them slowly to the earth.

Every so often, an owl would call from the trees or a shadow would flit just beyond the reach of perception, quick and silent. The deeper they walked, the more the modern world seemed to fade, swallowed by the eerie, timeless hush of rural autumn. A corridor leading not just to a house, but into another strange world.

There were small groups of people ahead of and behind them on the path. Other curious people, taking their chance to see inside The Faulkner House. Loretta didn't recognize any of them. Not that she would, after two decades away and sparse visits to Doran in between.

The conversation flowed and overlapped as the friends chatted.

"Walking a mile sounded much easier five minutes ago," said Kristen.

"Thirty years ago, this walk would've been nothing to us," Helen said. "Now, we have old, weary bones, back problems, and sciatica."

"We're still strong and vital!" Virgilia said. "Everyone took their pills today, right?"

"Are you scared?" Drew asked Callie.

"Of everything," she responded.

"I'm with you," said Judy. "I always think I love scary stuff until I'm actually confronted with scary stuff."

"This calls for my best *CSI: Miami* David Caruso-patented-dramatic-sunglasses-removal impression," Reuben said. "Trademark."

He put his sunglasses on. "I hope we don't get," Reuben said in a deadpan-serious tone, taking his sunglasses off in one exaggerated motion. "Voted off the island."

The friends stared at Reuben. "Hold for applause," he said.

"Wow, A-plus for the completely outdated reference," Virgilia said. "Reuben, keeping 2006 alive. Maybe next, you can wear some low-rise jeans."

"That didn't even make sense," said Angela. "We're not on an island."

"Nobody gets me," Reuben said.

"This is no different than when we went urban exploring back in the day," said Ionia. "This is probably safer than all the abandoned buildings we used to go looking in."

"We didn't even know it was called 'urban exploration' back then," Drew said. "It was just how we entertained ourselves and passed the time. Another lifetime, I guess."

"Yes, the fearless bravery of youth," Virgilia said. "We thought we were invincible."

"The fearless stupidity of youth," Phyllis laughed.

Donna rustled around in her bag. "I brought snacks for everybody, if you need them! And wet wipes, some extra water, and ibuprofen. Just let me know."

"Mmm, snacks!" said Bruce. "What you got?"

Donna held out a pack of peanut butter and cheese cracker sandwiches. "Yes, please!" Bruce said, tearing into the package.

"Do you believe all the stories about this place?" asked Phyllis.

"There's never been one ounce of proof," said Loretta. "I remember how bad this house scared me as a kid. I could see it from where my house was. But there's not one single news article or any evidence that ties The Faulkner House to anything nefarious or malicious."

"I just want to know how an entire family supposedly lived here and nobody ever saw them," Marti said. "How do you explain that?"

"Nobody actually lives here," said Bruce. "Somebody, somewhere, owns the property. The Faulkner family owned the place way back in the 1800s and it has to be one of those generational wealth, nepo baby things, where it's passed down from generation to generation."

"There's stories of squatters and trespassers coming through here, but nobody knows whatever happened to them," said Frannie. "People say they can hear screams and wails and moans coming from the house."

"The gate was only ever open on Halloween night," said Kristen. "Nobody ever knew why. But nobody ever dared to enter. Well, nobody that ever returned to talk about it. Remember how our parents used to warn us? 'Stay away from The Faulkner House. You'll never come back again!'"

"Our parents were also convinced there were razor blades and drugs in our candy," Bruce said. "As if people were out there, giving out free drugs."

"I mean, I know some people went up to the door on Halloween night and got candy from whoever it was giving it out," Callie said. "Not me, but some kids did."

"In our plastic Halloween costumes," Donna said. "You could barely see out of the eyeholes or breathe through that little slit for your mouth on the masks. Not to mention, it was freezing on Halloween night, so we had big, puffy coats on top of whatever costume our parents bought for us at the local drug store."

"It was never the same person, year after year," Reuben said, in his best spooky voice. "The legend says that every year, a different person stands at the doors of The Faulkner House, waiting for innocent blood."

"Absolutely zero proof or confirmation about any of this," Kristen

IT'S ALWAYS HALLOWEEN HERE

said. "All speculation, hearsay, conjecture, rumors, and town gossip."

"What about Sean Sullivan?" Angela said. "He said he and Murph broke in and saw all kinds of dead bodies and stuff."

"Sully and Murph?" said Virgilia. "They're alive and well. They were on an episode of *Cops* a few years back, busted for trying to rob a Dunkin Donuts. Sully left his kids alone and texted his girlfriend he was going to the packie at three a.m. When the cops asked where his kids were, he said, 'They've seen *Home Alone*. They know how to defend themselves. They're good.' Then he turned to the camera, in his scally cap and Red Sox shirt, and said hello to his ma, his parole officer, and the guys at the bar, and yelled 'Go, Celtics!' Then he asked if he could call his girlfriend so she could bring him a PBR and cigarettes. I don't think Sully and Murph are the most trustworthy, reliable news sources."

"That's scarier than The Faulkner House," Helen said.

"We were just a bunch of bored, townie kids with vivid imaginations," said Bruce.

"You don't have to be a townie, Bruce," Loretta said. "Come hang out in Boston with me."

"I will," he said. "Someday."

Someday. Her friends and family always said that in response to her invitations to the city. She understood. Doran was their home, and they were comfortable and settled there. She tried not to judge their feelings, but she always wondered if they limited themselves by not being open to living anywhere else.

Loretta looked around at her hometown friends. Most of them were married with children now. Moms and dads who owned houses and property, clocked in to nine-to-five jobs, and went to their kids' sports games and recitals.

They weren't the same teenagers who were best friends in school, hanging out at each other's houses and listening to the "Top Nine at Nine" countdown on the radio, calling in to vote for the latest New Kids on the Block song. None of them had been a part of the "cool" clique in high school, yet somehow, they had found each other. Though Loretta had great friends in Boston, who were like family to her, she held a special place in her heart for the people who knew her when she was just a quiet, nerdy girl who loved science and Donnie Wahlberg. She still loved science and Donnie Wahlberg.

She remembered them as teenagers and early twenty-somethings. How Donna was always the group mother, always taking care of everyone, checking on them to see if they were okay, and reminding them to wear their helmets and take their vitamins. Ionia, who made her own clothing and didn't follow fashion trends. Reuben, telling corny jokes and trying to make everyone laugh. Judy, with her perfect attendance and good grades, always cautious and trying to view everything from every angle. Virgilia, outspoken and brash, never afraid to speak her mind.

At their core, Loretta's friends were the same people they once were. Now, they had decades of life experience, pain, trauma, heartbreak, and pathos added on top of the kids they used to be. Sometimes, when she looked at her friends, she saw the people they were so many years ago. Full of hope, wondering what the world would bring them, imagining what their future would be like. Now they knew. They were in their imagined futures, whether it was how they pictured it or not.

It occurred to Loretta that she didn't really know her hometown friends anymore. She loved them, and they always picked up right where they left off every time they saw each other. But she knew who they were, not their day-to-day lives or the people they had grown into.

"A lot more gays in Boston than in Doran," said Virgilia.

"I'm sure there are," Bruce chuckled. "I'm not looking for a life partner."

"Oh, man, remember how all the girls in school had crushes on you?" Virgilia said. "None of them had a clue that you were a flouncy fudgepacker."

"That would be an offensive thing to say if you weren't my friend," said Bruce.

"We all would've thought Drew would've been the gay one," said Virgilia. "The sensitive, tortured artist. But, no, it was Bruce, who fixed all our cars and porches and read books about how to survive in the wilderness."

"That's a terrible stereotype," Bruce said.

"I always knew," Loretta said. "I mean, your favorite singers in high school were Madonna, Debbie Gibson, and Paula Abdul. It wasn't a hard code to crack."

"That's also a terrible stereotype," said Bruce, then quietly added, "Though completely true."

"I would've guessed Drew, too," said Phyllis.

"Hey!" Drew said, turning to Bruce. "Not that it's a bad thing."

"Well, I mean, you live with your mom and everything," Kristen said.

"I don't live with my mom," said Drew. "I have to take care of my mom after her butt lift and help her set up for her Pimps and Hoes party. Every Saturday, we do the Lisa Rinna workout video and watch *Antiques Roadshow* together." His expression turned grim. "Unless her special friend Buck comes over. Then they go to her room and play Scrabble together and I have to guess how valuable someone's great-great-great grandfather's cookie jar is actually worth by myself. Sometimes I hear her yell, 'Triple word score!' from her room. You're not my new dad, Buck!"

Drew's friends exchanged bemused looks, not wanting to mock the ridiculousness of it all.

"Do you think those *Antiques Roadshow* guys secretly blow each other behind the scenes?" said Virgilia. "I definitely get that impression."

"Oh, yes, absolutely," the friends nodded and sounded off in agreement.

Loretta's heart felt full at the moment. She had missed her old friends. The ones who knew her when. She hadn't loved living in a small town and left as soon as she had the chance. She wished she could have brought every one of these people with her. That wasn't how life worked.

CHAPTER FIVE

Jerry was retelling his favorite Halloween story as the group proceeded. They'd heard his story for decades. The Halloween Turkey. A magical turkey that only came around on Halloween night, to spread Halloween cheer and give full-sized candy bars to trick-or-treaters.

Clearly, his parents had raised him with the tale of The Halloween Turkey. No one could tell if Jerry truly believed it or if he was simply kidding around.

"The Halloween Turkey will protect and guide us," he said.

"That's not a thing," said Ionia.

"So, you can believe in The Great Pumpkin, but not The Halloween Turkey? Who guards your house from getting TP-ed and egged? Who makes sure your candy bucket gets filled every year? Who protects you from the boogeyman? You better not let him hear you talk about him like that."

"It's okay, sweetie," Suzanne said, rubbing Jerry's arm. "I'm sure The Halloween Turkey left you lots of Whatchamacallit bars and candy corn under your Jack-o'-lantern."

"If you had told eighteen-year-old me that we'd be seeing the inside of The Faulkner House," Donna said. "My kids were so excited when I told them about it. They wanted to come, but I told them it was grown-ups only."

"Did everybody take their kids out trick-or-treating tonight?" Loretta said.

Lots of nods and affirmations. "Most of our kids are old enough to go out on their own and don't want their moms and dads coming with them," said Judy, almost sadly, then added, as if to convince herself, "It's okay. They're growing up. I'm not upset about it. It's natural."

Loretta smiled. Some of her hometown friends had kids in college. Time had flown by. She didn't have children, pets, or even plants. She felt a momentary pang of sadness that she didn't really know her friends' kids all that well. She was too busy and far away. There was never enough time.

For a moment, she felt melancholy. There was a finality to growing older, to the passing of time, to change. You could never go back to a time and place that didn't exist anymore. There was nothing anyone could do about that.

"There's someone in that window," Frannie said, pointing to the third

IT'S ALWAYS HALLOWEEN HERE

story of the house.

A person's outline, dark and indiscernible, watched the approaching crowd from behind partially opened curtains. A mixture of fear and anticipation ran through the group.

"Probably just one of the scare actors," Phyllis said, though her voice wavered.

"Is it sad that we're this excited about this?" Drew asked. "Like, our lives are so boring and empty that seeing the house of our childhood urban legends is the highlight of our week?"

Everyone paused. Then burst out laughing.

"Yes, yes, it is sad," Kristen said. "But, hey, Loretta is here!"

The group cheered for Loretta.

"That's life in a small town," said Ionia. "You ask someone around here for directions and you get the creepy *Scooby-Doo* villain guy Old Man Willikers saying, 'If you kids insist on still going, take this road all the way down past the abandoned car lot, then past the abandoned rabbit hutches, then the stoop where Mrs. Leeds gave birth to all her kids—the house is gone, but the stoop is still there—then past the rock that looks like Utah, then past the rock that looks like The Rock, then you'll see a big pile of discarded tires. Keep going, under the covered bridge, then past the abandoned sheep farm—you'll smell it before you see it—then another few miles past the abandoned government nuclear testing site and the old silverware factory, then the old RC cola factory, then the black dirt with all the rotted pumpkins and onions, then you'll see the sign for Dead Hope Road. That's the road you want. But don't say you haven't been warned.'"

"I think those are the actual directions to The Faulkner House from town," Callie laughed.

Kristen linked her arm to Loretta's. "The sad truth is, we all don't really hang out as much as you'd think. We're busy and there's never enough time in the day. Everyone got together tonight to see you."

"I'm honored to bring everyone together," Loretta said. She meant it. She was genuinely touched that her friends still cared so much about her, despite time passing and distance.

"We'll make some new memories tonight," said Suzanne, linking her arm with Loretta's free one.

"I expected more of the goth and emo crowd to be here tonight," said Helen.

"Hey, goth and emo are two separate things," Drew said. "Goth is The Cure, emo is My Chemical Romance."

"Listen," said Reuben. "I say there's nothing to fear but fear itself."

"Did *you* say that?" said Marti.

"And dying horribly and painfully," Reuben concluded. "Horror is all propaganda, anyway. Cautionary tales meant to scare us into submission. It all depends on how you look at it. Look at horror movies. *The Texas Chainsaw Massacre*? It's a pro-vegetarian manifesto. *Halloween* is about the need for better mental health care. *Friday the 13th* is a call for learning proper water safety. *When a Stranger Calls* tells us to watch our children while they're sleeping or some maniac will come get them. *A Nightmare on Elm Street*? Sleep less and you'll be more productive. *The Blair Witch Project* says don't go wandering the woods if you have no outdoor experience."

"Don't you think that's a little bit reductive?" Donna said. "The truth is, we can find themes and moral lessons in anything we read or see. It all depends on the viewpoint of the singular audience member."

"It's all perception and storytelling, isn't it?" Virgilia said. "For instance, we're taught that George Washington had wooden teeth. But in reality, he had horse and donkey teeth and dentures made of gold and lead. If he smiled at you in the street, you'd think he was some grody creepozoid who needed a Certs."

"*My Bloody Valentine* looks at the dangers of mining in small towns. *Scream* is about technological reliance on our phones. *I Know What You Did Last Summer* is a driving safety instructional video," continued Reuben. "*Chopping Mall* is about consumerism and the perils of overspending. *Black Christmas* is about the loss of meaning for the holiday season. *The Conjuring* tells us not to buy old houses. *Barbarian* warns us not to trust Airbnb's."

"*The House Bunny* is about how Playboy bunnies make great sorority house mothers," Drew offered.

"You're not good at this," sighed Reuben.

"I just remember all of us going to Kristen's house to watch *Creepshow 2* and I have never fully recovered from the trauma of that movie," Judy said.

"'Thanks for the ride, lady!'" the friends shouted, quoting one of the infamous lines from that film.

"Oh, you guys are the worst," said Judy. "I still can't swim in a lake or look at a hitchhiker because of that movie."

Swish! Crackle!

Something, or someone, skittered past them. Hidden among the trees and darkness. A sudden, rapid movement. Too close to them, yet far enough away that nobody could identify the source.

IT'S ALWAYS HALLOWEEN HERE

Everyone stopped in their tracks.

"What was that?" said Kristen.

"We're in the countryside," said Donna. "It's just a deer or something."

"Deer!" Jerry called out to the woods. "Hey, deer?"

"We're already this freaked out and we haven't even gotten to the house yet," said Drew.

They resumed walking, occasionally throwing glances toward where the noise originated.

"Do you remember Mrs. Tipton, that crazy PTA lady?" said Bruce. "The one who tried to rally the whole town together to ban Halloween, because she claimed it was Satanic? And we were going to Hell by celebrating it?"

The group laughed as they recalled.

"Oh, whatever happened to her?" Helen said. "I was terrified of her. She had those signs, and she protested every Halloween night, screaming that our souls were in danger."

"I'm on the PTA," Donna said. "I see her all the time. She's still a giant nutbag."

"Maybe we'll see her here tonight," Reuben said.

"I remember her telling us that women were meant to serve their husbands and God would punish us if we spoke out of turn," said Virgilia. "And that heavy metal music was from the devil. She would scream at us that we were blasphemers, fornicators, and heretics."

"Crazy, old Mrs. Tipton," Kristen said. "My mom was in a quilting club with her. I thoroughly believe she put poison in the cherry pies she'd leave on her windowsill to cool off."

Without warning, an elderly, grizzled man, dressed in tattered clothes and a ratty fedora, burst from the darkness and lunged toward the group. Some of the friends jumped back in surprise. Ionia let out a small scream.

"You're all doomed!" he bellowed at them.

"Jesus Christmas," Reuben said. "Mr. Cantler. You should be at the assisted living center right now. What are you doing all the way out here?"

Mr. Cantler was the local harbinger of doom. Like every small town in America, Doran had their very own town doomsayer. He was well-known to the townspeople and the local mental health center.

"I tried to warn the others," he continued. "They didn't listen. You'll never come back again!"

"Mr. Cantler, it's late," Helen said, reaching out to help him. He pulled back.

"I am a messenger of God," Mr. Cantler said. He turned away from them and ran back into the darkness, his footsteps receding into the night.

"Well, I nearly crapped myself and almost needed a costume change," said Jerry. "Anybody else?"

The friends laughed, if only to relieve the tension.

"Do you think Mrs. Tipton heard us talking about her and sent him as her messenger?" Virgilia said.

"Should we call someone?" Judy said.

"Like who?" said Drew. "The assisted living home isn't too far from here. He's probably drunk, again. He's just living up to his title of scary, local loony."

"Speaking of scary things," said Reuben. "We're here."

The reunited friends—Angela, Bruce, Callie, Donna, Drew, Frannie, Helen, Ionia, Jerry, Judy, Kristen, Loretta, Marti, Phyllis, Reuben, Suzanne, and Virgilia—stared up at their destination. They couldn't tell if it was dread or excitement they were feeling.

"Good grief, this place is enormous," Suzanne said, as they all looked at the house before them.

"Whose idea was this again?" said Helen.

CHAPTER SIX

The Faulkner House stood alone at the end of the path, a brooding colossus etched against the burnt-orange moonlight. It was vast, imposing, bigger than Loretta remembered. An architectural chimera towering over the landscape. A monstrous fusion of styles collided in its frame. Soaring Victorian turrets pierced the sky like bayonets, while stately Colonial gables jutted outward with stiff, angular pride. Wrapping around the front, a twisting Queen Anne veranda curled like an ornate serpent, its gingerbread trim casting intricate shadows across warped floorboards.

The building was in solid shape, but it wore its years unevenly. One wing gleamed with fresh, ivory paint, the wood still smelling of lacquer, while another sagged under the weight of rot and rain, shingles flaking like old scabs. Iron balconies clung to upper windows, some pristine, others bent and rust-stained. Thorny ivy coiled up the brick chimneys, choking them in a green death grip.

The house was completely decked out for the holiday.

Jack-o'-lanterns of every imaginable expression—grinning, grimacing, ghoulish—lined the serpentine walkway to the house, their flickering innards casting chaotic light patterns that danced like mischievous spirits. The lawn was a fever dream of Halloween exuberance, with plastic skeletons clawing from mock graves, foam gravestones tilted at odd angles with epitaphs both chilling and cheeky, and animatronic witches that cackled when the wind triggered their motion sensors. Crimson floodlights bathed the rotting wing in an infernal glow, while the refurbished side shimmered in eerie purples and greens like a haunted carnival.

Cobwebs, both real and fake, draped every eave and railing, mingling with strings of orange bulbs shaped like bats and ghosts. A twelve-foot inflatable Frankenstein loomed beside the porch, his stitched hands raised in silent greeting. From the shadows near the veranda, a hidden speaker looped a mix of vintage radio horror shows and echoing chains, giving the air a strange, timeless pulse, as though Halloween from every decade had converged here in one sprawling, celebratory haunt.

The house didn't just stand. It loomed, as if it had been wrenched out of time, a relic from a dream too strange to forget.

The windows watched them approach. They were dark, but somehow still full of presence.

23

"What the hell kind of place is this?" Bruce asked.

"It's always been like that," Kristen said, voice hushed. "No one's ever lived here, not really. No mail. No lights. Just here."

"How much do you think this place goes for on Zillow?" Reuben said.

They reached the porch. The floorboards groaned. A single gas lantern flickered by the front door, where a woman in an old-fashioned black gown stood motionless. Her hands were gloved, and her hair was pinned in a 19th-century style. She had no coat despite the biting cold.

She smiled, but there was no warmth in it.

"Welcome to the Faulkner House," she said. Her voice was low and unaccented, like reading from a script. "Please, come in. You may explore at your own pace."

"Is there a tour?" Drew asked.

"The house leads," the woman said.

Virgilia smirked. "Creepy."

Loretta looked at the woman. Her eyes, sunken slightly, too dark. There was something crooked, wrong with her smile. Not sinister. Not aggressive. Just the wrong shape for a human face. She couldn't say why.

"Will you be coming in?" Loretta asked the woman.

"No," the woman replied. "I must remain at the door. To welcome. And to guard."

She held out a bowl of wrapped candies for trick-or-treaters. None were in sight.

No one reached for the candy.

Callie glanced at the bowl, then up at the woman again. "Are we supposed to take one?"

"You may," the woman said, without moving the bowl closer. Her arms stayed unnaturally stiff, elbows locked at an angle too sharp to be casual. "You may take one. Only one."

Judy leaned closer. "What happens if someone takes two?"

The woman's lips pulled back an inch further. A smile, or maybe just teeth. "That would be unwise."

A long silence fell.

Donna cleared her throat, trying to shake off the tension. "Okay. Well. This is definitely the weirdest Halloween party I've ever been to."

"It's not a party," the woman said, in that same flat, emotionless tone.

Reuben gave a small chuckle, but no one laughed with him. He shifted his weight, the porch creaking beneath his boots. "We going in, or just standing here staring at a murder mannequin?"

Kristen gave a short nod. "Let's go. Come on. We didn't walk all this way to chicken out now."

They stepped forward together, a ripple of movement as they passed through the doorway. The woman didn't move, didn't blink. As the last of them, Marti, stepped inside, the door swung shut behind her with a soft click. No one had touched it.

"I didn't close it," Marti whispered.

"No one did," said Drew.

CHAPTER SEVEN

Loretta turned back toward the door. There was no handle on the inside.

"What the hell," she murmured. Her breath fogged in the air. It was even colder now. The kind of cold that felt intentional.

Callie gave a nervous laugh, though it didn't make it far past her lips. "Did she say the house leads?"

"Yeah, she did," Reuben said, his eyes locked on the woman. He didn't blink.

Loretta frowned and tilted her head. Up ahead, a woman wandered by, disappearing into the shadows beyond the open doorway like she'd never been there at all. Her gown didn't rustle. No footsteps. Just gone.

"Okay," Marti said, scanning the porch. "That's not weird at all."

The group hesitated, paused together in the spacious foyer. No one wanted to be the first to cross the threshold into the main hall.

Frannie stepped forward, summoning her bravery. "We walked a mile to get creeped out, right? Let's get creeped out." She flashed her light into the entryway, revealing an expanse of darkness and wood grain, and took a step inside.

One by one, they followed. Drew ducked slightly beneath the warped beam, and Donna brushed her fingers along the carved doorframe. The wood felt warm, though she didn't feel any hot air coming from the multitude of radiators and vents.

The walls were lined with taxidermized animal heads on mounts, antique sconces, and vintage light fixtures. Reuben picked up a dusty candleholder from a table next to the front door.

"Think they get décor at Pottery Barn?" Reuben said. No one laughed. "Home Goods? No?"

"Did anyone else feel that on the wood?" Donna whispered to Suzanne, who gave a vague shake of her head, distracted by the ornate chandelier overhead. It was unlit, but the crystals shimmered faintly, as if catching light that wasn't there.

Inside, the air was thick. Not dusty, like they'd expected, but heavy. Saturated. It smelled faintly of dried lavender and something older. Like forgotten books, old milk, and copper pennies.

Kristen's flashlight cut a swath through the dark foyer. The house swallowed the beam. Walls extended too far, doorways appeared where there hadn't been any seconds ago. Every window they passed was curtained in thick velvet, sealing out the night. Or perhaps sealing something in.

"It's like being inside a giant version of the Clue board game," Bruce said. "You could definitely have an epic murder mystery party here."

"As long as it's not ours," Suzanne said.

"I swear it's colder in here than it was outside," said Callie, hugging herself.

"Maybe it's the ghosts," Ionia teased, though her voice lacked its usual spark.

"Let's not let our imaginations run away with themselves," Frannie said, almost to convince herself as well as the others. "These are scare actors. There's probably some 'Spooky Sounds of the Haunted House' CD hooked up to a speaker system wired throughout the house. The place is rigged to scare us."

"You know, we're at that age where we start getting targeted ads for Depends," said Jerry. "Right now, I wish I had bought some."

"It's not that scary, you big wimps," Reuben said. "Where's your sense of adventure? Your curious, courageous spirit?"

"I left it at home, next to my fiber chewables and reading glasses."

They stood inside the foyer, flashlights lowered, half-forgotten. The air pressed in around them. Heavy and dry, like the inside of a long-sealed crypt. Somewhere in the distance, something creaked. Not the playful moan of an old house. This was deliberate. Like someone testing their weight on a stair tread.

"Well, my cell phone doesn't work in here," said Frannie. "No bars, no reception."

The others checked their phones as well. All agreed, no service for them, either.

"Horror cliché 101," said Reuben. "Have to get the reason why we can't call for help out of the way right away, so everyone doesn't ask, 'Why didn't they call the police?'"

"At least we have flashlights," Kristen said, shining hers around the room.

Ionia shivered and touched Helen's arm. "My hair is standing on end."

Helen nodded. "Yeah. Static. Like the air before lightning."

"It's our minds playing tricks on us," Suzanne said. "Our perception of this house is influencing the reality of it. We expect it to be scary. Therefore, we're scared."

"Houses aren't evil," said Bruce. "People are. Ghosts, spirits, and demons aren't real. People are. Mrs. Tipton is."

"Let's not test that theory tonight," said Judy.

"Think we can get some delivery out here?" said Reuben. "I could go for a pizza."

They didn't speak for a moment. A dull pounding sound echoed somewhere far off, muffled and rhythmic. Not footsteps. A heartbeat maybe, but not theirs.

Loretta stopped and stared down the lengthy, dimly lit hallway. She swore she saw someone peeking around the corner at them. A stark white face, almost inhuman.

"I don't like this," said Callie, gripping her flashlight tighter. "Guys, I—"

A soft rustling interrupted her.

They turned. In the corner of the entry hall stood a coat rack, tall and clawed at the top. It was empty. But one of the hooks had just swayed slightly, as if a heavy garment had just been removed.

"Did anyone else—" Angela began.

"Shh," Virgilia hissed, holding up a hand.

They listened. Nothing. No footsteps. No wind. No voices.

Then, a laugh. Light and childlike, echoing from deep within the house. But warped. Stretched. Like an old recording played too slow.

"Please tell me someone brought a weapon," Bruce muttered.

Kristen elbowed him. "Don't start."

Donna turned in a slow circle. "Where do we go? Are we supposed to just wander?"

"No tour." Drew repeated the woman's words. "The house leads."

"Well, the house better start leading," Judy said. "Because I'm not standing here all night."

As if on cue, a hallway to the left flickered. Just once, a single overhead sconce stuttered to life. A trail of dim lights blinked on in succession, deeper into the shadows.

Reuben swallowed. "Guess that answers that."

They began to move slowly, together, the light growing weaker the farther they went. The walls seemed too close, the ceilings too high. The house groaned in places they couldn't see. The floors sloped subtly, almost imperceptibly, like they were descending even when they weren't.

IT'S ALWAYS HALLOWEEN HERE

Loretta walked near the back of the group, uneasy. She kept glancing over her shoulder. The hall behind them was empty. But something about it felt less empty the longer she looked.

At one point, a door they passed began to creak open slowly, so slowly they almost didn't notice, until Donna caught it and slammed it shut.

"Don't open doors we don't have to," she said, more forcefully than she meant.

"I didn't open it," Marti whispered.

Everyone stopped. No one had touched the door.

Another giggle. This one closer. The hallway lights flickered.

"Okay," Ionia said, her voice tense, "I want it on record that I don't love this idea anymore."

"Same," said Callie. "Seriously, is this place even zoned for this kind of trauma?"

Up ahead, the hall opened into a wide sitting room. Long-abandoned, but not dusty. Clean. Waiting. A grand piano sat silent in the corner, its lid closed. The air in this room was slightly warmer, but not in a comforting way. More like breath from something large and unseen.

They stepped inside slowly, clustering in a loose circle. The lights died behind them. The piano struck a single note, low and discordant.

They jumped. Every one of them. No one was near the keys.

"I want to go home now," Helen said, her voice very small.

Loretta didn't answer. She was staring at a portrait on the wall. A woman, pale and stern, in a black dress. The frame bore no name. But the eyes in the painting were identical to the woman on the porch.

"She's in here," Loretta whispered.

"Who?" Virgilia asked.

Loretta just shook her head, unable to look away. She didn't even know why she said that.

The piano struck again. A second note. A third. The keys began to play on their own. Somewhere behind the walls, something laughed. Not a child. Something much older.

They passed a mirror in the front hall, but no one lingered. Its frame was black, matte, and jagged like volcanic glass. Marti looked once, then quickened her pace. Her reflection hadn't moved quite right.

In the parlor, the fireplace was lit. A soft fire crackled inside, though there was no wood, no kindling. Just flame suspended over ashes. Its light painted the furniture in uneven strokes. The upholstery was floral, red and gold, faded but neat. There were no cobwebs. No dust. As if the house had been expecting them.

"I thought no one lived here," Reuben said, frowning.

"Someone does," Donna replied, glancing at the archways leading deeper into the house. "Or something."

A door slammed far off, somewhere upstairs. Then another. And another. Each one closer. Not hurried. Just steady. Purposeful.

They froze.

"Wind?" Virgilia offered weakly.

"There's no wind," Helen said, her eyes wide. "We shut the door behind us."

The house sighed. Not from the floorboards, not from the settling of age. It was a deep exhale, as if the house had taken them in and now, it was tasting the air.

"Okay," said Bruce, trying to keep the mood light. "This place is definitely haunted. I'm calling it. Who brought the salt?"

"Don't start, you weenie," Kristen said.

Callie drifted toward the grand staircase. Her flashlight flickered. Once. Twice. Then cut out.

"Oh, come on," she said. She slapped the base of her flashlight. Nothing.

"Mine, too," said Loretta.

A chorus of clicks followed. One by one, the flashlights blinked, buzzed, and failed.

Only the fireplace remained. Its flame shrank to a slow, pulsing ember. Red and dim, like the inside of a mouth.

Silence. Deep and watchful. Then a voice. Not from the woman at the door. Not from any of them. From the second floor, directly above.

"*...don't let them leave.*" It was a whisper, but it curled down the walls like smoke.

"Tell me someone else heard that," Marti said, backing toward the center of the room.

"I heard it," Judy said. "But who said it?"

No one moved. No one breathed.

Footsteps. Slow, soft, unmistakable. Crossing the landing upstairs. And stopped. Right above them. They all looked up at once. The ceiling groaned.

"Who's there?" Angela called out. No one answered.

"I think," Ionia said, voice barely above a breath, "we should stick together."

"Agreed," said Jerry.

"Is this supposed to be, like, a haunted house tour?" Donna said. "I thought it would just be a bunch of antiques and historical stuff."

"I don't know," Kristen said. "It didn't specify."

"I don't like people jumping out at me," said Loretta.

Without warning, the lights came on. Every sconce. Every chandelier. Every flashlight. Harsh and sudden. Yellow and flickering, like gaslight. The fire flared again, unnaturally tall for a moment, casting grotesque shadows that crawled along the walls.

"Jesus," Virgilia said. "Jump scare."

When they turned to the staircase, someone was standing at the top. Not the woman from before.

This one was taller. Dressed in funeral black, face hidden by a wide-brimmed veil. She didn't move. Didn't speak. But they could feel her watching.

A low chime rang from somewhere deeper in the house. An old clock, announcing the hour. Twelve slow tolls.

Midnight. Halloween wasn't over.

And the house had just begun.

CHAPTER EIGHT

The friends stood inside the parlor, laughing at themselves for being so easily spooked. Reminding themselves that The Faulkner House was no different than any other house. That there were no such things as haunted houses.

"Courage up!" Frannie rallied them.

As they talked among themselves, Donna peeked out into the hall. The hallway had minimal lighting, yet shadows lay on the floor like thick, twisting cloth. Donna stepped over them, wondering how the effect had been created. At the far end, a door pulsed slowly. Wood expanding and contracting as though inhaling.

She heard someone behind her whisper something, each syllable dragged as if through gravel. When she turned, there was only an empty coat stand, but its hooks were curling downward, bending toward her like the fingers of a drowning hand.

A pale moth floated past, but its wings were too long, trailing behind it like strips of skin, each patterned with a human eye that blinked in sequence.

Somewhere in the walls, teeth clicked together. Hundreds of them, chewing on nothing, faster and faster, until the sound blurred into a thin scream.

Donna looked down and realized her own shadow was missing. She swore she could feel it brushing against her ankle from behind, trying to climb back into place.

"Donna?" Suzanne said. "You ready?"

Donna regrouped, brushing away her fear. "Yes. Let's do this."

CHAPTER NINE

The air inside remained unnaturally still and cold, as if the entire house couldn't retain the smallest semblance of heat. A silence pressed against their eardrums, heavy and deliberate. The polished wood floors gleamed and shone, their reflections distorted like warped glass. The floral wallpaper clung to the walls in faded, peeling strips. Colors leached out like the life had been drained from them long ago.

Portraits lined the hallway. Dozens of unfamiliar faces stared down with hollow, unsmiling expressions. Their eyes were too dark, too deep, like they weren't painted on but tunneled inward. Watching. Waiting.

Somewhere deep within, a grandfather clock ticked. Slow, arrhythmic, like a dying heartbeat echoing through unseen walls.

The layout defied logic. The entryway fractured into three halls, each twisting away in directions that couldn't physically exist. They saw doors through doors, staircases that turned sharp corners before vanishing into shadow, and windows that revealed not the outside, but more rooms. Layered like nesting dolls, each more claustrophobic than the last.

The ceilings rose dizzyingly high in places, only to dip alarmingly low in others, close enough to brush their heads.

"I always wondered what the inside of this place looked like," said Marti. "Now I know. For better or worse."

"Who designed this place?" Virgilia said. "And how much opium did they smoke at the time?"

"This doesn't match the outside," Bruce said, his voice barely above a whisper. The layout of inside of the house's interior made no sense in relation to the structure's dimensions. Though the Faulkner House was a massive beast, the sheer number of rooms, alcoves, and hallways wasn't mathematically possible.

Kristen nodded, her eyes wide. "It's bigger in here."

Loretta stepped closer to a painting, depicting a somber gathering of mourners in front of the very house they stood in. Everyone in the image wore black, their faces gaunt and blurred at the edges, like the memory of a funeral no one wanted to remember. She leaned in. The eyes shimmered slightly, as though something just beneath the surface shifted, fluid and alive.

Ahead of them, a hallway darkened. The overhead light flickered once with an electric crackle. Twice. Then stayed on.

The silence resumed, thicker now, as if the house had noticed them.

"No map," said Reuben. "No tour guide. Unreliable electricity. At least it's free."

"This has to be purposely set up like this, right?" Callie said. "Like one of those extreme haunted houses. It's all trickery and sleight of hand and movie magic, no?"

"Like a funhouse," Loretta said, although it may have been more to convince herself. "Optical illusions and haunted house attractions, like at the fair." She was embarrassed by how unnerved the manufactured creepiness of the house unsettled her.

"It is starting to occur to me that maybe we should have done a little more research before we jumped right into this," Helen said.

"Look," said Kristen. "There are other people here. Other visitors wandering the halls. It's an act. A show. Do you seriously think someone set this up to murder a couple dozen people? How would they even get away with that?"

"Well, whoever set this up did a really good job," Marti said.

"Okay, everybody," Virgilia said. "Stop being scaredy-cats and chickenshits. We're already all a-tizzy, and we just got here. Now, I'm going to open this door and we're going to see what's behind door number one."

Virgilia grabbed the doorknob and threw the door open.

CHAPTER TEN

They stepped into the room and the door clicked shut behind them with a soft finality, muffling the hallway's sounds into silence. The space was windowless, long and rectangular, its musty air thick with the scent of old celluloid and mildew. Rows of tattered red velvet seats sloped down toward a white-painted wall. In the rear, an enormous antique film projector loomed like a rusted sentinel. Its brass reels tarnished, its lens cracked, yet unmistakably alive.

"A little home movie theater," Callie said.

"What's on the home movies?" said Marti.

As if on cue, the machine groaned to life, gears whirring with mechanical breath. A light flared through the dusty lens, casting a flickering beam onto the screen.

The film began.

Grainy black-and-white images stuttered into view. Shaky, erratic, as though the footage had been found in some damp cellar and resurrected for one final showing.

First, a fog-choked street where mannequins walked like people, jerking in unnatural cadence, their faces featureless save for mouths that opened far too wide.

Next, a long dining table in an empty room, the food rotting and steaming with flies, and at its head, a man in a porcelain mask sat perfectly still, until his head snapped toward the camera, revealing two holes where eyes should've been.

Cutaway to a close-up of a blinking human eye submerged in ink.

The film jumped again. A forest of crucifixes jutted from a dry riverbed. Crows perched on each one, but their heads were human, silent, and watching.

Then, a woman in a wedding dress running in reverse, her scream unwinding like magnetic tape, blood soaking her veil backward as though sucked from the ground.

Cutaway to a doll's face melting in extreme close-up, its glass eyes popping one after the other.

Now a schoolhouse, empty and caving inward, its chalkboard filled with scrawled, frantic phrases in a looping child's hand: IT CAME FROM THE WALL. IT CAME FROM THE WALL. Desks rattled as if something beneath the floor was shifting, burrowing upward.

A boy stood in the corner of the room, facing the wall, murmuring a lullaby in reverse. His shadow moved differently from his body. Its arms longer, its head cocked, listening.

Cutaway to a spinning carousel with horses replaced by snarling wolves, their hooves sparking against the floor as the ride sped faster and faster until the images blurred.

The next scene was a narrow hallway filled with hundreds of doors. Each one opened on its own, creaking wide to reveal the same image. A figure standing in total darkness, its eyes glowing faintly red. The figure grew closer with every cut, as though stepping forward through each doorway.

A living room from the 1950s appeared next, frozen mid-family dinner. No one moved. A woman held a fork in midair, a man's smile was far too wide, and a child at the table slowly began to turn her head completely around, bones cracking with each unnatural twist.

Cutaway to a severed hand winding an old phonograph. The record spins, but no music plays. Just the sound of heavy breathing.

The scenes grew stranger, darker. A child sat at the foot of a bed, whispering to something just out of frame. A shadow, long-limbed and writhing, slid from beneath the mattress and crept up behind them. The child smiled.

Cutaway to black horses with no eyes galloping in slow motion through a burning field.

A series of family portraits, one after another. In each, the people's eyes had been scratched out. In the last photo, one face, the tallest figure in the back, was moving slightly. It blinked.

The final reel stuttered, the film warping. Figures in funeral garb turned slowly toward the screen, now staring out as if watching the watchers. One raised a hand.

The projector stopped. Not with a click, but with a gasp.

The projector's gasp faded into a silence that seemed to hum. Dust motes swirled through the beam of light still cast from the lens, though no film played. Then the beam bent, just slightly, like heat rising from pavement. A cold breeze swept through the sealed room, sharp with the scent of mothballs, scorched paper, and something sweeter, like dried blood on old lace.

Someone coughed.

And then he was there.

CHAPTER ELEVEN

The man stood between the last row of seats and the aisle, though none of them had seen him enter. He hadn't walked in. He was simply there, as if the projector had conjured him or remembered him.

He was tall and angular, draped in a long, coal-black coat made of some heavy, outmoded material that glistened faintly like wet velvet, its hem brushing the dusty floor. His boots were unlaced, scuffed and cracking, the soles whispering faintly as he shifted his weight. A cravat, yellowed with age and stained at the corners, sagged at his throat beneath a waistcoat fastened with tarnished silver buttons in the shape of tiny skulls. His skin was sallow, tight as parchment over a frame that suggested bones sharpened by hunger. His fingers, abnormally long and bony, clasped one another like insects resting.

His eyes, milky gray and rimmed with an angry red, looked clouded by cataracts, yet they roamed the room with eerie precision, as though they could see things the others could not. His smile was crooked, lips papery and thin, revealing blackened gums. His teeth were small, like a child's, but filed to points. His nails were long, horn-colored, and clicked against one another when he flexed his fingers.

His hair, slicked back and coal-black, curled in damp coils around his collar, glistening with something that looked suspiciously like tar. A distinct smell drifted off him. Sweet and chemical, like antique makeup mixed with formaldehyde and rot.

Kristen instinctively stepped closer to Loretta, and Bruce muttered under his breath, "They hired a really committed actor for this thing."

The friends were quiet, watching the man. They huddled tightly together, unsure whether to marvel at the theatrics of it all or scream and run away.

The man raised one hand, long fingers splayed, and slowly turned it palm-up. His hand trembled slightly, not with weakness, but with anticipation. As he moved, his shadow split and danced, like there was more than one of him, and the light behind him flickered as though resisting.

"You saw the flickerings," he said, his voice dry and sweet like syrup. "Yes. Yes. Shadows on the wall of the cave, eh? Mouthing what comes next."

Drew squinted. "What are you talking about? Who are you?"

The man turned his head slowly toward Drew, though his eyes never seemed to land fully on him. Always just to the left or just behind. His smile did not falter.

"Who am I?" he echoed, and then chuckled softly, as if someone had told a private joke just beneath his skin. "I am the breath between the reels. The man in the gap. The scratch in the vinyl. The place where things loop backward."

His voice shifted in pitch with each phrase, like an old radio trying to hold a signal. Behind him, one of the velvet seats creaked softly, though no one had moved.

Judy gave an uneasy laugh. "Okay, very cool performance. This part of the house is amazing, by the way."

"You think this is performance," the man said, lips barely moving. "You mistake the cage for the play."

Loretta crossed her arms. "Look, we're just trying to get to the next room. We didn't sign up for a séance."

"No séance," the man whispered. "Not yet. Though the dead are listening."

His eyes flicked to the ceiling. Slowly, everyone looked up. Faint scratch marks marred the plaster, looping and spiraling like frantic messages carved with broken nails.

Callie tilted her head. "Are you dead?"

"'Are you dead?'" Reuben mocked her. "Yes, Callie, he's risen from the grave to give us a speech."

"Are we dead?" Frannie said, half-jokingly.

The man gave a beatific smile, lacking any mirth. "I am borrowed time dressed in a man's coat. And you, you're all passing through pages of someone else's diary, written in ash, bound in bark."

There was a long pause. Donna shifted her weight uncomfortably, eyes darting to the exit, which now seemed farther away.

Helen frowned. "Is there a way out of here or not?"

"There is," he said, drawing out the word like a thread being pulled from rotting fabric. "But not for everyone. The film is always longer than you think. Some of you will stay for the second reel."

Reuben snorted. "This guy's amazing. Give him a tip."

Loretta's stomach coiled. Behind his smile, there was something wrong with the man. Not just the words. Not just the eyes. The aura around him felt older. Like a cellar that hadn't been opened in a hundred years. It smelled like cloves, spoiled fruit, and the faint metallic tang of something recently exhumed.

Behind the man, the seats began to groan faintly, one by one. As though something unseen was sitting down to watch.

The man turned slowly toward the screen. "Watch carefully," he said, "and listen louder. The next part is not silent."

Then, without turning back, he stepped into the light of the projector. And vanished.

A low scratching sound began to rise from the projector. The film started again. The reel caught. The projector shuddered, rattled once, then steadied.

No title screen. No music. Just a hard cut into motion.

A narrow hallway flickered into view, black-and-white and grainy, its wallpaper peeling in long curls like dead skin. The floorboards breathed, expanding and contracting beneath unseen footsteps. At the end of the hall stood a door with no knob, pulsing slightly, like something inside was pressing against it, matching the rhythm of a slow, angry heartbeat.

The camera panned to a girl standing barefoot in the hallway, her back to the viewer. Her nightgown was stained at the hem, one hand twitching at her side as though counting. A voice, offscreen, low and crooning, whispered her name, again and again, but it wasn't the same voice each time. It shifted—male, female, young, old—layered over itself like a nest of snakes speaking in chorus.

Cut to a staircase. Impossibly long, descending into what appeared to be a flooded basement. Water lapped at the bottom steps, but it didn't reflect anything. Not the walls, not the ceiling, not the camera. It was as black as ink and undisturbed, though whispers bubbled up from beneath it, rising like heat.

A room full of portraits. All identical. Each frame held the same image of a man in a bowler hat with his mouth stitched shut. As the camera lingered, one portrait began to smile. Its eyes moved. Its mouth twitched, threads snapping one by one, leaking dark fluid that dripped down the canvas.

Cutaway to a close-up of an open mouth screaming underwater. No bubbles. No sound.

A forest. Trees that moved slightly even though there was no wind. The leaves rustled, but the sound was squishy and leathery, like flayed hides brushing together. Hanging from the branches were chandeliers, their candles burning despite the lack of flame. Beneath them, pale figures in formal wear danced in slow, jerky motion, their limbs disjointed, heads lolling. Some wore masks. Some had no faces at all.

A small boy in a theater seat, staring directly into the camera. His eyes were missing. Just smooth, pale skin. Yet tears poured from where the eyes should've been, carving wet streaks down his cheeks. He began to clap slowly. Each clap made the screen ripple, as though reality itself was thinning.

Cutaway to a skeleton crawling across a ballroom floor, dragging a long bridal veil behind it.

The final scene began to flicker.

A living room, still and silent. A fire burned in the hearth, though the flames were frozen, unmoving. A clock ticked backward. On the couch sat the group—Loretta, Virgilia, Kristen, Drew, Bruce, Callie, Jerry, Suzanne, Phyllis, Donna, Helen, Ionia, Judy, Marti, Angela, Frannie, and Reuben— but not as they were now. These versions looked older. Wrong. Deteriorated.

Some stared with empty sockets. Others wore vacant, sagging smiles. Their clothing was dirty, outdated, decaying. A few were slumped, unmoving.

This Loretta turned her head sharply toward the camera.

And blinked.

The reel burned white.

For a full three seconds, the screen glowed with pure light, soundless and still, before the projector abruptly shut off with a metallic clunk.

Darkness. A breathless silence followed.

Someone flicked on a flashlight. Dust danced.

The man in the coat was gone. Not a trace of him. No footprints, no scent, no disturbed dust.

The velvet seats behind them were all down now. As if they'd been used.

CHAPTER TWELVE

Loretta pushed aside the urge to laugh. Despite considering herself a skeptic when it came to anything paranormal or supernatural, the strange man and creepy film reel had burrowed under her skin. She was a woman of science and facts, not someone who believed that ghosts were real.

"Someone give that corny, Count Dracula guy an Oscar," Reuben said. "That performance was pure camp. I don't usually like my villains to be that hammy, but he really committed to the role."

"Where the hell did he go?" Virgilia asked, searching the room for trap doors and fake walls.

"You have to hand it to them," Marti said. "That was pretty impressive. I'm definitely unnerved. But that was solid work."

"Where did he go, really?" Bruce said, looking around the room for escape hatches.

"I know I'm going to sound like every idiot in every scary movie ever, but it'll probably be easier if we split up for a bit," Drew said. "It's not going to be easy to navigate every room and floor in a big group."

"I think I might go," said Judy.

"Me, too," Helen said.

"Really?" Virgilia said. "It's Halloween! The one night you're supposed to do scary stuff."

"I think I'd rather be home watching a scary movie rather than living one," Judy said.

"Don't tell me you guys are all superstitious," said Jerry. "This is the fun stuff! The Halloween spooktacular!"

"Hey, why don't we all meet up back at my house later?" Donna said. "I'll make everyone grilled tomato and cheese sandwiches. Cut diagonally, the best way."

"Let's say ninety minutes?" Reuben said.

"I don't know if I can stay awake that long," Callie said.

"This is already way past my bedtime," said Jerry. "I'm usually in bed by nine-thirty."

"We only get Loretta for one night," Donna said. "And you know my place has tons of space. We'll hang out in the den and watch *Beetlejuice* and catch up."

The group agreed. "Helen and I are headed out, but we'll meet you there later," Judy said. "Please don't be late."

"I'm coming with you guys," said Callie. "I need to use my light therapy machine and do a soul cleansing."

"Wait for me!" Phyllis said.

"You guys be safe," Loretta said. "See you in an hour and a half."

"Everybody else, let's take a poll," Kristen said. "Stay or go? Raise your hand if you want to stay."

Everyone except Callie, Helen, Judy, and Phyllis nodded in agreement. The quartet said quick goodbyes and left the room.

"Suzanne and I are going to do a little exploring on our own," said Jerry, fixing his mullet. "We'll meet up with you guys in a bit." He took Suzanne's hand and led her out of the room.

"Well, there are two possible ways we can go from here," Bruce said, pointing to opposite doors on either side of the room. "Who's going this way with me?"

CHAPTER THIRTEEN

Callie, Helen, Judy, and Phyllis moved quickly down the twisting hallways toward the main entrance, their footsteps swallowed by the unnatural silence. The air around them had thickened, growing colder, heavier, like the house itself was breathing against their skin. The flickering overhead lights offered little comfort, casting long, jittery shadows that seemed to stretch and shrink with a life of their own.

They reached a bank of tall windows looking out to the front porch. Through the grimy glass, they could see the woman who had greeted them at the door. Her smile was as wide and frozen as a cracked porcelain doll. Outside, a handful of other visitors milled about the overgrown yard, talking and laughing as if nothing was wrong.

"Look," Helen whispered, pressing her palm against the cool glass. "They're out there, but none of them can see us."

Judy tapped her fingers against the windowpane, eyes wide. "It's like we're invisible. Or ghosts."

The women banged their fists against the windows, yelling to the crowd outside. Nobody even looked their way.

"Why can't they hear us?" said Phyllis.

"What's happening?" Helen said.

Callie's gaze shifted upward. Along the ceiling, a dark shape slithered slowly, its movement fluid and deliberate. Its black eyes were fixated on the women. It stretched across the arches like a thick, oily shadow. Crawling, weaving, always just beyond clear sight.

"Do you see that?" Callie said, voice barely steady.

Helen squinted. The thing clung to the wall now, dragging itself down the far side of the hallway like a writhing mass of tar and limbs. It made no sound but left a faint, burning scent in the air, like scorched leather and decay.

"Keep moving," Phyllis urged, her breath quickening. "Don't look directly at it."

Judy swallowed hard, glancing back nervously. The hallway behind them twisted impossibly long, receding into darkness that seemed to pulse with an unholy hunger.

Callie's flashlight flickered, the beam trembling as her hands shook. The shadow jerked violently toward them, stretching into a thin, spiderlike form with multiple jointed legs, crawling faster than it should have been able to.

"Don't!" Helen gasped, but it was too late.

The flashlight beam caught something. Eyes, wide and unblinking, reflecting a sickly yellow light. The creature recoiled, melting back into the ceiling with a sick, wet suction.

A guttural scream exploded from nowhere.

A man's face appeared inches from theirs, blood smeared across his skin like cracked, fresh wounds. His eyes were wild, desperate, filled with madness and rage. He screamed again, a sound like tearing metal and broken glass.

Callie stumbled back, heart hammering. Her scream mixed with her friends' shrieks.

"Get away!" Helen yelled, grabbing Callie's arm.

The bloody-faced man vanished as suddenly as he had appeared, leaving only the echo of his scream hanging in the stale air.

For a heartbeat, the hallway was silent again. Callie, Helen, Judy, and Phyllis smashed their fists against the windows. Nobody noticed them, turned their heads toward them. The woman was letting people into the house, though the door next to them wasn't opening. At least, not opening to whatever realm they were in.

Judy whispered, "We're not getting out of here."

CHAPTER FOURTEEN

The office felt like it had been sealed for decades.

A massive oak desk squatted in the center; its surface blotched with ink stains that had seeped deep into the grain. The leather of the chair behind it was cracked into spiderwebs, the color of dried blood. Filing cabinets stood against one wall like silent sentinels, their brass handles dull with fingerprints that would never wipe away. Along the shelves, thick law books leaned together as if whispering, their spines faded to the color of weak tea. The wallpaper, striped in muted browns, was peeling in long strips at the corners, exposing plaster underneath. A yellowed calendar from a year long past still hung behind the desk, the days marked with small, precise handwriting.

Suzanne stood near the desk, her gaze moving over the clutter. An empty inkwell, a fountain pen with a bent nib, an old clock that ticked unevenly. Jerry was by the shelves, studying a crooked row of framed photographs, all the subjects staring directly into the camera with unsmiling eyes. The lamplight hummed faintly, casting warm, steady illumination.

At first, the movement on the floor didn't register. It was subtle, just a thickening of darkness in the far corner, as though the light were being drained away. It grew, spreading like spilled ink, its edges alive with minute shivers.

Suzanne's eyes caught on the shifting shapes. Within them, deep inside, something moved. Not the flat, formless flutter of shadows, but weight, dimension. Limbs. Heads. The suggestion of human torsos pressing against the surface of the dark as though submerged just below it. Their outlines bulged and flattened with slow, unnatural rhythms, like figures turning over in deep water.

"Jerry," Suzanne said quietly. "What is that?"

Jerry turned to look, his expression tightening. The darkness slid toward them, splitting into separate veins that crept along the floorboards, wrapping around the legs of the desk, climbing the walls in slow, deliberate ascents. One tendril dragged itself up toward the clock, smearing along the wallpaper until the numbers on the face seemed to distort beneath its weight.

A shape inside the shadow nearest Jerry's feet seemed to rotate toward him. It had the form of a human head, elongated, jaw slack. Its mouth opened in silence. As it passed along the wall, another form pressed out from the darkness, its hand-shaped bulge leaving deep impressions in the wallpaper before sinking back in.

Jerry stumbled backward, his gaze flicking between the shifting walls and the spreading floor. His shoulders struck the wall, and his palm flattened against the striped wallpaper, then didn't come away.

The shadows surged toward him, the human shapes inside writhing closer, their faces flattening against the wall behind him. Pale hands burst through the plaster. Not from cracks or seams, but from nowhere. Dozens of them. Their fingers were long, joints bending wrong as they gripped his arms, his chest, his face. The skin was ice-cold, clammy with something slick that smeared across his clothing.

"Jerry!" Suzanne screamed, rushing toward her husband. It was too late.

The wallpaper seemed to swell and undulate behind him, the human shapes within it pressing forward as if desperate to trade places with him. Their eyeless faces rippled beneath the surface like trapped things trying to force their way out.

"Suzanne! Help me!" Jerry's voice broke as the wall accepted more of him, his spine vanishing into it as if the plaster were liquid. He thrashed, his nails tearing strips from the wallpaper, revealing damp, grey material beneath. The shadows on the floor quivered, their submerged shapes reaching upward like swimmers breaking the surface, mouths open in silent screams.

Suzanne moved toward him, but the shadows swelled between them, one rising like a wave and showing the silhouette of a hunched figure inside, its head lolling. A pale hand slapped against the inside of the shadow's surface from within, and then the figure dissolved back into the darkness.

Jerry's face was the last part of him visible, his features twisted in terror. More hands shot out of the wall, gripping his head, pushing it backward. His eyes locked on hers, then rolled upward as the surface behind him peeled open.

For a single, impossible moment, Suzanne saw inside.

The plaster yawned like an open wound, revealing a black, endless space crawling with motion. Jerry was there, flailing soundlessly, surrounded by other figures—dozens, maybe hundreds—twisting, writhing, their bodies tangled, their faces pale blurs in the void. Some clawed toward her as though they could see her, their mouths wide in noiseless screams; others floated limp, drifting away into the deeper dark. And farther back, something vast shifted, its outline impossible to fully take in, but its attention fixed entirely on her.

The wall slammed shut. The wallpaper lay smooth, only the faintest ripple remaining. The uneven ticking of the clock filled the silence.

Suzanne stood frozen, staring at the place where Jerry had vanished. Behind her, the shadows on the floor were shifting again. Thicker, closer, their shapes more defined now, as if whatever lived inside them had decided she was next.

She turned to run. Between her and the door stood a towering, black figure, cloaked in dark rags and shrouds. Impossibly tall. The white of its eyes barely visible beneath the veil-like cloth over its head.

Suzanne thought of her beloved children and the wonderful life she'd had with Jerry. The happy memories that had made her heart full.

Those were her last thoughts as the cloaked figure opened its arms and drew her, against her will, into it. She fought and clawed at the walls, but it was no use.

The cloaked figure enveloped her whole.

CHAPTER FIFTEEN

The door groaned open, revealing a dim, claustrophobic room. Bruce entered first, followed by Angela, Donna, Drew, Kristen, and Loretta.

The walls were plastered from floor to ceiling with photographs. Old, yellowed prints of people long gone. These weren't ordinary portraits.

Kristen leaned close to Loretta's ear and whispered, "Spirit photography. It's from the early 1900s. People believed they could capture ghosts or spirits lingering near the living in these photos. Usually faint, blurry shapes or faces hovering just behind the subjects."

Loretta's eyes scanned the walls. Some images were almost normal, like a family smiling stiffly at the camera. But others were unsettling. A man stood beside a little girl, his face blurred into a smoky haze that seemed to stretch and twist. A woman's faint silhouette hovered just above her own shoulder, her eyes black voids staring straight out from the photograph. Another showed a group of soldiers, but behind them, an indistinct figure with hollow eyes leaned in close, like a watcher from another world.

"God," Donna said. "Some of these look like nightmares caught in glass."

They moved cautiously toward the far end of the room, where two men stood chatting.

"Loretta?" one of the men said.

It was Keith Nemser and Mitch Pechukas, though time had aged them both.

"Keith?" Loretta replied.

Keith's eyes lit up with recognition. "Loretta! Wow, I never thought I'd see you here. What a trip."

Kristen smiled, elbowing Loretta. "Keith Nemser. He used to have the biggest crush on you. Remember how he'd always ask you to go to Herbie's Hamburger Place with him?"

Keith walked over. "It's great to see you again." He gave her a warm, genuine smile. "This place is something else, huh?"

Keith and Mitch greeted the rest of the group warmly.

"Wow," Keith said. "Loretta. You look great."

"Thanks."

"You look really great."

IT'S ALWAYS HALLOWEEN HERE

"Move it along, Keith," said Kristen. "She's a doctor. She's brains and beauty."

"A doctor? Really? That's amazing." Keith said. "How many years has it been?"

"How many years since I've seen you or since I became a doctor? Probably around the same. I don't get back here much."

"We're working on fixing that," said Kristen.

"How long are you in town for?" Keith said.

"Only a few days," said Loretta. "Just for my cousin Tiffani-Amber's wedding. Then back to Boston."

"What are you guys up to?" Kristen said. "Is your wife here?"

Loretta threw a side glance at Kristen. She knew what Kristen was up to.

"Oh, uh, no wife," Keith said. "We're divorced. My kids are at home eating candy, playing video games, and watching *Hocus Pocus*. I have to get back to them soon. Make sure they haven't burned the house down. Things I never thought I'd say, until I became a parent."

"So, you're single?" said Kristen.

Keith laughed. "Yes, I am."

"That's funny," Kristen said. "Loretta is single, too. She has such a busy schedule. I always tell her to find the time to meet a suitable partner."

"Subtle as a jackhammer," Loretta said under her breath.

Donna sidled up beside Loretta. "We're coming back to my place later, if you guys want to join. You and Loretta can catch up properly. I'll give you my number."

Loretta gave Donna the side eye. This was not the time for matchmaking.

"I'd love to know what you've been up to for the past twenty years," said Keith. "I don't know if my life is as exciting as yours in Boston."

"I had to remove a fire poker stuck inside a man's rectum last week. It's all glamour and rainbows."

"Loretta Ward," Keith said, unable to stop smiling. "I remember how you used to help everyone with their homework. I always knew you were destined for big things. You really do look great." He clocked Kristen and Donna's look. "I mean, your brain looks great. Your brain is great."

"Okay," Loretta said. "It was nice to see you, Keith. I'm glad you're well."

"Hey, we should get going," Mitch said to Keith. He nodded, smiling

49

again at Loretta as they headed for the door.

Kristen and Donna turned to Loretta. "Keith Nemser!" Kristen said. "It's like a Hallmark movie. Big city girl goes back to her hometown and finds love with a blue-collar stud."

"No Hallmark movie for me, but thanks," Loretta laughed. "I love you guys for wanting to marry me off, but I'm doing just fine."

"Okay, so no marriage, but how about a fling?" Kristen said. Loretta shook her head.

"A fire poker?" said Donna. "Did he put it there intentionally or did he fall awkwardly on it?"

"You'd be surprised what people put up their butts," said Loretta.

"Do you think Keith puts fire pokers in his butt?" Donna said.

"What? I don't—what? Can we move this along?" Loretta said.

Bruce and Drew beckoned to the women, wanting to show them something. Loretta found herself alone by one photograph. A blurred image of a man and woman posed stiffly, their eyes unnaturally bright and staring. Behind the woman, a dark, twisted shadow curled upward, almost like a tendril reaching out.

As she stared, a sudden, cold brush grazed her skin, like dozens of icy fingertips running lightly across her arms and shoulders. The feeling of multiple sets of hands grasping at her, pressing against her. She felt them, though she didn't see them.

She gasped, spinning around. No one was there. The room was suddenly empty and silent. Her friends had forged ahead, leaving her alone in the gallery. The photographs seemed to watch her, their ghostly eyes unblinking.

Loretta felt the cold wash over her body. She touched her arm, feeling the chill linger, though nothing remained.

"Hello?" Her voice was a fragile whisper, swallowed by the thick stillness.

Only the faint rustle of fabric and the heavy, unseen gaze of those ghostly faces answered back.

In an instant, Loretta snapped out of her haze. She hurried forward to rejoin the group.

CHAPTER SIXTEEN

Reuben, Ionia, Frannie, Marti, and Virgilia stepped cautiously into the room, the heavy wooden door wailing on its hinges as it swung closed behind them with a slow, mournful creak. Soft shadows pooled thick and suffocating in every corner, swallowing the dim glow cast by a solitary oil lamp perched on a side table. The flickering flame sputtered, casting elongated, jittery shapes that danced on the peeling wallpaper like restless spirits.

The room was frozen in time. A perfect, unsettling snapshot of a salon from the early 1900s, painstakingly preserved but tinged with a deep, unnatural stillness. Fragile and ornate antiques cluttered the space like relics waiting for some long-forgotten ritual.

Delicate china teacups, their rims chipped and stained with age, balanced precariously atop lace-covered tables that had yellowed with decades of neglect. Porcelain figurines lined the shelves, once delicate and pretty, now stood cracked and grotesque in the dim light, their painted eyes seeming to glint with a secret awareness. Ornate, dark wooden furniture loomed in the shadows.

High-backed chairs carved with twisting vines, a fainting couch draped in moth-eaten fabric, and a heavy writing desk polished to a sinister gleam. Every piece looked unique, handcrafted with obsessive care, yet the atmosphere was one of brittle fragility, as if the slightest touch would unleash shattering chaos.

"Feels like stepping into a museum," Ionia whispered, her breath visible in the chill air as her fingers trembled, hovering nervously over the rim of a tarnished silver tray that caught the lamp's flicker.

Marti nodded, eyes darting around. "Yeah. I'm waiting for something terrible to happen."

"Or for one of us to break something," Frannie chuckled.

Reuben ran a hand over his face, the faint light catching the lines of worry etched deeply there. "Yeah. It's way too quiet. This room. Like it's not just waiting. It's watching us."

"Let's stop being so dramatic," said Virgilia. "You're freaking me out."

"I'm just having some fun," Reuben said.

Virgilia's gaze swept over the room with a hunter's sharpness, taking in the thick, heavy curtains that sagged like dead wings, the yellowed wallpaper peeling in ragged strips, and the portraits looming above. Faces frozen in stern judgment, their eyes dark and accusing.

Without any warning, the air shifted. The room exhaled in a long, slow, unnatural sigh. The creaking floorboards groaned like old bones, and a chill rippled through the space, sinking deep into their skin. The oil lamp flickered violently, casting grotesque shadows that writhed and snapped like living things.

And then everything reversed.

The delicate teacups spun on their rims with a soft, eerie clinking, righting themselves but now facing the opposite direction, their pale surfaces catching the flicker of flame like ghostly faces. Saucers slid and clattered softly, pictures on the walls rotated with slow, deliberate creaks, their backs turned to reveal aged, cracking frames. The high-backed chairs, the fainting couch, even the heavy writing desk. All shifted imperceptibly, turning precisely 180 degrees, as though some unseen hand had reached in to rearrange the entire room.

Marti rubbed her eyes. "Did...did you see that?"

"Holy—" Virgilia gasped.

Reuben took a cautious step forward, eyes narrowing into slits. His voice dropped to a whisper thick with disbelief. "What the hell just happened?"

Ionia linked her arm in Frannie's. "Hold me closer, Tony Danza."

They scanned the room for pulleys and wires, trying to locate the source of the magic trick.

"They really go all out at The Faulkner House," said Marti.

Ionia's gaze snapped to a shadowed corner they hadn't noticed before, a place where the flickering light seemed to shudder uneasily.

There, slumped and almost blending into the darkness, sat a figure.

He wore threadbare, dirt-streaked work clothes that looked decades out of place. Pants held up by worn suspenders and a shirt faded to sickly yellow, its cuffs frayed and stained. What made the figure truly unsettling was his head, covered by a burlap sack, crudely cut with two eyeholes. The edges of the sack were ragged and torn, frayed and rough. The rough fabric clung to a skull beneath, shifting with subtle, almost imperceptible movements, as if the man was alive and breathing, silently watching them.

"Hey," Virgilia called out, voice trembling with a mix of fear and disbelief. "What's going on here? Who are you?"

"Okay, time to go," Frannie said.

The figure didn't move a muscle. No response. No sound. Then, with a slow, deliberate motion that made the air seem heavier, he lifted one stiff, jerky arm. The motion was unnervingly mechanical, like a puppet tugged by invisible strings. His fingers, gnarled and pale, pointed toward an exit on the opposite side of the room.

The silence pressed down on them, thick and suffocating. The lamp's flame sputtered again, casting the room into a brief, suffocating darkness before flickering back.

Marti swallowed hard, voice barely audible. "Is he telling us to leave?"

"Or warning us not to," said Reuben.

The sack rustled faintly, as if the man beneath it shifted slightly. Eyes, or the holes where eyes should be, glinting like wet stones in the shadow.

The feeling was unmistakable. They weren't alone.

"What is he pointing at?" Ionia said. They followed the trajectory of his finger to a small, almost hidden, doorway.

"What do you think?" Virgilia said, almost excitedly.

"Are you having fun right now?" said Frannie incredulously.

"After you," Marti said.

CHAPTER SEVENTEEN

The quintet stepped into a new chamber. Darkness swallowed the space whole, save for a single pool of flickering light spilling from an old oil lamp perched atop a battered wooden table at the center of the room. The air was thick with the scent of melted wax, incense, and something faintly metallic, like blood long dried.

Around the table sat six figures, their faces pale and drawn, lit by the wavering glow. Each was absorbed in a silent ritual, hands clasped tightly, eyes closed or flickering with nervous anticipation.

They did not acknowledge Frannie, Ionia, Marti, Reuben, and Virgilia.

One was a gaunt man with hollow cheeks and thinning silver hair slicked back; another, a woman with sharp cheekbones and wide, frightened eyes that darted constantly to the shadowed corners. There was a younger man whose knuckles gleamed white from his grip on the table edge, a woman in a faded floral dress clutching a tarnished locket, and two others whose expressions were unreadable in the dim light; one seeming to tremble, the other unnervingly still, like a carved statue.

A low chant began, a whispered litany curling and twisting through the silence.

"Spirits lost and wandering. Hear us! We call you from the darkness! Cross the veil and speak! Come forth from the shadows. Answer our pleas! We beckon you! We summon you! Reveal yourself!"

The words slithered out like smoke, thick and choking, curling around the five friends standing in the shadows, unnoticed, unacknowledged, as if they were ghosts themselves. The séance participants' eyes never flickered toward them, never paused in their communion.

Reuben stifled a laugh. "So cheesy," he whispered to Frannie. "Didn't the theater guy say there was no séance? False advertising."

Then came the response.

A sudden *knock*, sharp and deliberate, sounded from beneath the table. Marti jumped, grabbing Virgilia's arm.

Another *knock*, louder this time, rapped rhythmically, echoing unnaturally against the stone walls like fingernails scratching on a coffin lid.

The air thickened, pressing against their lungs like a heavy fog of rot and decay. The lamp's flame shuddered wildly, casting monstrous,

IT'S ALWAYS HALLOWEEN HERE

writhing shadows that clawed along the cracked plaster walls. Shapes that seemed to stretch impossibly long, twisting into grotesque figures just beyond the edge of sight.

The table itself trembled subtly, an almost imperceptible shaking that grew steadily until the teacups and a candleholder rattled and slid precariously, threatening to crash to the floor with a shatter that would split the night.

The youngest man gasped, his body seizing as though invisible hands squeezed his throat, eyes rolling back in a silent scream.

The woman clutching the locket let out a strangled cry, her head whipping toward the ceiling as her fingers beat frantic, pounding knocks against the wood, faster and more urgent, like a warning or command.

The entire room seemed to pulse with unseen energy. A deep, guttural moan rising from the shadows, swelling to a spine-shaking crescendo as the lamp flickered violently, threatening to plunge them into utter blackness.

The scent of something foul, like burnt hair and sulfur, seeped into the air, causing the hairs on the back of their necks to prickle with icy dread.

Then silence. Absolute, suffocating silence.

The candlelight steadied, flickering softly once more, but now the figures around the table slowly opened their eyes. And, in unison, their gazes lifted, turning with unnatural synchronization toward the intruders.

Frannie, Ionia, Marti, Reuben, and Virgilia froze beneath the weight of those six identical, unblinking stares. Eyes wide, pale, and void of any recognition, but full of something far more terrible.

They were seen.

The friends stood rooted in place, their hearts pounding in their ears as the six seated figures continued to stare at them in unnatural silence. The candlelight flickered slowly, and in that wavering glow, the air above the table began to ripple.

"What the—" Ionia said quietly. "Is this part of it?"

From beneath the battered wooden tabletop, a shape stirred. A dark outline at first, barely perceptible beneath the extinguished shadows.

A red glow bloomed at the center, diffuse and unnatural, pulsing with a heartbeat all its own. A translucent red shroud began to rise, lifting like a heavy fog that might suffocate.

The shroud grew upward, materializing into a humanoid form cloaked in scalloped folds of gauzy red fabric. It was diaphanous yet somehow solid enough to cast a long, trembling shadow on the floor

55

beyond the table's legs. Blood-red veins pulsed within the translucent folds, as though the shroud was not cloth, but skin. Or something alive.

The flame trembled once again, causing the figure's outline to warp and flicker like a living nightmare.

The cloaked being stretched upward slowly, revealing only hints of shape beneath. Suggestions of limbs and shoulders, ghostly blurred by the shimmering veneer of the red cloth. The edges of the shroud gave the impression of movement, as if the entire thing was breathing.

With each second that passed, the entity grew taller, its surface rippling with an internal light that glowed bright and sickly, like embers beneath a corpse's flesh.

The friends exchanged bewildered looks, their silence communicated between them. *Is this real? Do we stay and watch the show? Should we leave?*

The chanting, faint in the background, resumed, but no longer from the seated figures. It came from within the emerging figure itself: a low, echoing murmur that seemed to reverberate through the table, through the air.

"Come forth! We are here! We are here!"

Marti's skin prickled. "That...that thing."

Before she could finish, the creature extended a pale arm from within the shroud. Its hand emerged. Semi-transparent, bone-white, knuckled and slender, fingers tapering into faintly luminous tips. It hovered just above the table's surface, trembling as though eager to touch something. Or someone.

Marti pressed her hands over her ears. Virgilia's eyes widened in stark horror. Ionia stared, rooted in disbelief. Reuben moved to hide behind Frannie. The entity's attention felt like an avalanche bearing down.

With horrifying grace, the red figure leaned forward. The shroud parted slightly, revealing a face beneath. Sharp-cheeked, hollow-eyed, and ringed in blood-red tears that ran down pale skin. Its mouth opened, yawning with teeth like broken glass.

The lamp flickered out. Darkness swallowed the room. A weightless stillness shattered across the five intruders' senses.

The shroud slammed downward, fists banged against the underside of the table like living thunder, and the floor beneath them seemed to twist as though the room itself recoiled in shock.

But then nothing.

The oil lamp reignited itself, sputtering back to life with a soft pop. The red shroud collapsed into nothingness. The smoky residue of fear lingered in the air, thick and coppery.

The six people seated remained motionless, eyes fixed coldly on Virgilia, Ionia, Marti, Frannie, and Reuben, their gazes unreadably still.

The hovering figure was gone. As if it had never been there.

Everyone in the room was looking at them, as if they'd become part of the ritual, part of something far more sinister than anyone intended.

"That's enough of that for me. Time to go," Ionia said. Her friends nodded in agreement.

CHAPTER EIGHTEEN

Callie, Helen, Judy, and Phyllis stumbled through another dim hallway. walls with cracked wallpaper illuminated only by their feeble flashlights. The air felt thick, humid, and stale, as though the house itself absorbed breath. Their voices echoed hollowly, swallowed by the darkness.

They entered a small room lined with dusty, heavy curtains. In the dim light, a single tall window stood, its glass grimy but intact. Callie raised her fist and pounded on it, then grabbed a nearby chair to smash it.

No matter how hard they struck, the window did not budge. The glass held firm. It neither cracked nor shattered.

Helen's hands were shaking. "What is happening? It's like the house won't let us out."

Phyllis pressed her palm against the window, eyes misting. "I can see outside. I can see people. But they can't see that we're in here."

They stared out the windows. As they did, someone passed by in front of them on the wraparound porch. Marching past each window then turning on his heel to march back. Back and forth, rinse and repeat. Like a soldier standing guard. He did not acknowledge their presence, despite the women calling out to him.

"Back up!" Helen said, picking up a chair. She swung it at the window. Once, twice. No effect. The window didn't crack.

The women turned and saw an older couple, ones they recognized from the walk up to the house, standing on the other side of the room. Admiring the décor and talking among themselves.

"Hey!" Judy said. "Can you help us?"

The couple ignored them, simply exiting the room.

Tap! Tap! Tap!

The sound was coming from one of the windows. Helen, Judy, Phyllis, and Callie slowly turned their heads toward the tapping.

A face, made from nightmares, stared directly at them from the porch. A hideous, elongated, red-lipped grin on a skeletal, ghostly-white visage.

The room filled with screams, wails, and moans. The decibel level was overwhelming, like a dozen planes taking off at the same time. The women covered their ears. The man on the porch laughed at them.

They rushed to the door, stepping inside the previous room. The furniture was mirrored, the walls reconfigured, doorways turned into dead-ends, staircases twisted back on themselves. These rooms weren't the same ones they'd passed through. They'd changed.

Panic edged into their voices.

"We need to keep moving!" Callie hissed. "If we stay here, we'll just go insane."

Judy nodded, trying to stay calm. "Okay. We're going left. And if that's wrong, we'll try right. Keep trying."

Only their flashlights cut through the dark. Each room they entered twisted reality. Walls bowed inward. Ceilings lurched. A horrifying sense that the house was reshaping around them grew stronger.

They heard it. Whispering. Soft, slithering voices echoing through hidden vents, beneath floorboards, behind walls. Words were indistinct at first: distant murmurs, syllables too faint to parse. But they found them:

"Lost…unwanted…scared…"

The whispers began to circle. Behind them. In front. Above. Beneath.

"Why are you here? You don't belong."

The voices grew louder and sharper, taunting.

"Find the door. You can't."

"Getting close, but you never leave."

Judy pressed her fingers to her ears as the whispering crescendoed, harsh buzzing in her skull.

Callie's eyes darted around frantically. "Where are the exits? Anything that looks like the door we came in. It has to be here."

They broke into brief conspiratorial whispers, searching for landmarks in this impossible labyrinth.

Phyllis glanced back at a wall that had shifted only seconds before. "That archway wasn't there," she said. "And it's gone now."

Callie's flashlight caught movement. The shadows seemed to pulse, the hall elongating, corridors spiraling outward.

The whispering turned into a chorus. Words piling atop words, taunting, laughing.

"Stay."

"Forever."

"Party's over."

They kept pushing forward. Kicking at warped doors, yanking handles, smashing frames, prying boards. Helen thrust a chair at a stuck door. It didn't move.

Judy raked her nails across a rotted windowpane, only to find another mirrored glass behind it, untouched. Their panic mounted, but so did their resolve. They screamed defiance into the darkness.

"We are leaving!"

"We're not afraid!"

The whispering paused, then intensified in frustration.

"Run..."

"Run..."

As they sprinted from the room into the hallway, the whispers chased them, low and fierce behind their heels.

They turned a corner into a long corridor, then halted. The hallway was empty, silent. No sign of whispering. No sign of friends. Just oppressive quiet.

Judy's chest heaved. "Keep going. We don't stop."

Phyllis, Judy, and Helen hugged close, flashlights crossing beams, scanning every door and shadow.

"Where's Callie?" said Phyllis. They anxiously searched the darkness for her.

The door to the next room opened slightly. Only an inch or so. In the darkness, Helen and Judy saw Callie's face.

The door swung open, wider this time, revealing more of Callie. Standing still, as if frozen in place, unable to move or scream.

"Callie!" Judy screamed.

The door swung open again, even wider, knocking Judy back. Callie had rivulets of blood trickling down her face.

Each time the door opened, then closed, Callie was bloodier. Each swing of the door revealed her features becoming more like a doll's. Expressionless, motionless, soaked in crimson.

The door swung open and shut once more. Callie was gone. Faded into the mouth of the darkness. Taken by the house.

Judy, Phyllis, and Helen rushed to open the door. It wouldn't budge.

CHAPTER NINETEEN

Bruce had decided that they should explore other floors, so he led the charge, followed by Loretta, Kristen, Donna, Angela, and Drew.

"I don't see a staircase here," he said.

"Maybe we should find Keith and ask him," Kristen said. Loretta shook her head.

"Okay," said Angela. "This is creepy."

The hallway stretched before them like a tunnel into a nightmare. Narrow, dimly lit by a flickering overhead bulb. Lining both walls were mannequins. Dozens of them. Maybe hundreds.

They stood stiffly, shoulder to shoulder, forming an eerie gauntlet. All were life-sized, dressed in elaborate Halloween costumes. A clown in a blood-specked ruffled collar and cracked porcelain mask. A Victorian doll with glass eyes and a stitched mouth. A towering skeleton in a priest's cassock. A werewolf whose snout was inhumanly long, teeth yellowed and glistening. A scarecrow with a bloated crow impaled on one outstretched arm. A witch in a rotting velvet gown, fingers curled like dry roots. A ballerina in a red tutu, her arms bound with wire behind her back.

Some wore masks. Others didn't. Some looked human. Others like weird replicas of humans.

Kristen took a slow step forward, her voice barely a whisper. "Why would anyone make this many? It's excessive."

"They're probably props from an old haunted house," Bruce offered, though unease crawled up his throat like ivy. "Movie leftovers. Or someone's really twisted collection."

Drew kept close to Loretta, eyeing each figure with suspicion. "They feel wrong. Not just creepy. Just wrong. Like they're real."

Loretta nodded silently. Her flashlight beam passed across a mannequin in a rabbit costume. Its pink ears torn, one eye missing, mouth painted in a wide, deranged grin. The beam caught something in its fur. Dust, maybe. Or hair.

A soft metallic creak echoed from somewhere down the hall. All six of them froze.

"I heard that," Donna whispered. "Something moved."

Ahead of them, maybe twenty feet away, a figure in a plague doctor costume—tall, draped in black, with a long, curved beak—tipped ever so slightly.

Not a fall. Not a wobble. A tilt. Toward them.

"Okay," Kristen said, forcing a smile. "Still probably animatronics. Creepy, but it's a show, right?"

No one answered. The hallway continued ahead, the mannequins forming a suffocating corridor of silent onlookers. At the far end, a dull red exit sign buzzed weakly. It cast the end of the hall in a surreal glow.

"Should we blow this popsicle stand?" Loretta said.

"I think I've had enough fun for one night," said Drew, avoiding any eye contact with the mannequins.

"Grilled cheese and *Beetlejuice*?" Donna said.

They moved in a tight line, flashlights shaking slightly as they passed the staring figures. The smell in the hallway was strange. Something between wax and formaldehyde, tinged with copper. The mannequins loomed in their periphery. Tall, silent, and inexplicably present. Some had cobwebs on their shoulders. Others were clean, as though they'd just been placed there.

About halfway down the corridor, Drew's flashlight flickered. Something darted across the hall ahead of them.

It was a flash. Quick as a blink. A figure in a tattered bridal gown, hunched, barefoot, hair hanging over its face. It moved with impossible speed and vanished into the figures on the other side of the hallway.

They all screamed.

"What the hell was that?" Donna said, grabbing Loretta's arm.

"Not fake," Loretta said. "That wasn't fake. No actor moves like that."

Drew turned, her voice hard with panic. "We have to move. We have to keep going."

Kristen was shaking her head. "None of this makes sense. If this is all staged, why hasn't anyone broken character? Why haven't we seen a staff member? Or the other people who were with us on the path?"

No one answered.

As they walked faster, more of the mannequins seemed to shift. Only slightly. Just enough to make them question what they'd seen. A clown's head turned imperceptibly. A ballerina's hand twitched at her side. A knight in armor leaned, ever so slightly, inward.

"Don't look at them," said Angela. "Just look at the exit."

The exit felt farther now. The hallway seemed to stretch, subtly, but certainly. The walls closing in. The exit shimmering.

IT'S ALWAYS HALLOWEEN HERE

"I think it's real," Donna said. "All of it. I don't think this is an attraction anymore."

Kristen's voice was barely audible. "What does that mean? What's the alternative?"

Drew spoke, hollowly. "It means we're trapped in something we don't understand."

The mannequins behind them began to creak softly. The ones ahead started to breathe. Not loudly. But enough. Enough to know. Something was inside them. And it was waking up.

They ran the last stretch of the hallway, hearts hammering, flashlights jerking wildly across mannequins that now seemed unmistakably alive. Limbs shifted. Heads swiveled just out of sync with their footfalls. The exit sign above the door buzzed louder as they approached, casting a harsh red glow onto the handle below.

Kristen reached out first, shoved the bar. The door opened, but not to the outside.

Instead, it led into a small vestibule with cracked tile underfoot and pale gray walls. The air inside was still, like a dead lung holding one last, dry breath. No night sky. No cool wind. No driveway. Just more inside.

"We're still in the house," Donna said.

"I don't understand," Kristen whispered. "That was the exit. We all saw it."

Loretta turned quickly. "Drew?"

She spun. The hallway behind them was empty.

"Drew?" Her voice rose.

Bruce clicked his flashlight back toward the corridor. Nothing. Just the line of mannequins. The door hadn't closed. Hadn't even creaked. But Drew was gone.

"Drew!" Kristen shouted, rushing back two steps before Loretta grabbed her arm.

"He was right here," Donna said. "He was with us."

Loretta's voice dropped. "Maybe he went through first?"

"No," Kristen said. "No way. I would've seen him. I was first."

"Drew!" Bruce yelled into the mannequin-lined tunnel.

The silence that came back was thick and unnerving. Something about it felt deliberate. Like the house was playing games with them.

Somewhere deep in the corridor, one of the mannequins fell. The friends didn't go back. They moved forward, through the vestibule, into the next room.

The new space made them stop dead in their tracks. It was a single, large chamber. Perfectly split down the middle. A bold line painted floor to ceiling marked the divide.

One side was bright red; garish, glossy, almost wet-looking, like a fresh coat of lacquer over old meat. Every object—chairs, wallpaper, books, lamps—was bathed in that aggressive, eye-watering hue. The air on that side felt warmer somehow, and close.

The other side was deep crimson, verging on black. The texture of the paint was matte and velvety, like dried blood on wool. This side felt cold. Oppressive. The shadows here were darker, almost liquid. The furniture looked older, too. More Victorian, decayed, like it had sat abandoned for years.

Even the lighting was split. On the bright red side, a sterile overhead bulb hummed dully. On the dark red side, a single flickering candelabra cast dancing shadows that didn't quite match the shapes of the things around them.

"Where is Drew?" Loretta said.

"Is he playing a joke on us?" said Donna. "Drew! Not funny!"

They half-expected Drew to emerge from the mannequin line, laughing at them. Their attention momentarily shifted to the strange room.

Bruce squinted. "Is this supposed to be art?"

Angela stepped closer to the dividing line. "It's like two worlds stitched together."

Donna whispered, "I don't like how the shadows move. They're off. Like they're not connected to what's casting them."

Loretta walked the line cautiously, not stepping across. "It's monochrome, but not flat. Look." She pointed toward a painting hung on the bright red side. It showed a woman screaming. Every color, every stroke, was red. Only red. Somehow, even the whites of her eyes were a paler scarlet, her pallor glistening like pinked ivory.

Opposite it, on the dark red side, was a mirror. At least, it seemed like a mirror. But their reflections weren't quite right.

They didn't move in sync. But there were six again. Drew. He was here, or there. Just standing silently in the background of the reflection, unmoving, staring directly into the camera of the room.

"Do you see that?" Loretta said, her voice barely audible.

Kristen nodded slowly. "He's in the mirror."

"But not with us."

"That's not possible," Angela said.

An air of collective realization washed over the group. As if their frightened, panicked thoughts had formed a cloud over them at the same time.

"Drew!" Kristen said. "Drew!"

"Is this some kind of magic trick?" Bruce said. He banged on the mirrors, as if he would uncover the secret and Drew would jump out, laughing at scaring them.

Behind them, a soft shuffle. A mannequin, dressed as a plague nurse in a long red cloak, was now just inside the vestibule, half-in shadow. Still. Watching.

More movement. Another stepped just past the doorway. Then another.

"They're following us," Bruce whispered.

"Or herding us," Donna said.

Kristen stepped one foot over the dividing line into the bright red side. The floor beneath her boot creaked, and the light above flickered sharply.

All of them froze. The mirror cracked. A thin line down the middle. Slowly. Like a split forming in old skin.

Behind the mirror, or within it, Drew smiled. But it wasn't Drew's smile. Not really.

For the first time that night, Loretta realized. What was happening wasn't illusions.

It was real.

CHAPTER TWENTY

Virgilia, Reuben, Marti, Ionia, and Frannie entered through grand, open double doors, revealing a cavernous room that should have been a garage, or maybe a storage space. Inside, logic unraveled into nightmare. The room vibrated with a sickly sweetness, a rotting scent tangled with fresh earth and something darker, something alive and watching.

"What the actual fuck?" Virgilia said. Everyone else was wide-eyed and speechless. Their eyes belied the terror they felt.

Before them sprawled a tangled pumpkin patch, impossibly vast and sprawling, vines twisting like serpents across the cracked concrete floor, snaking up the walls, clutching the rusted pipes and disappearing into a ceiling swallowed by unnatural dusk. The pumpkins themselves bulged grotesquely. Some small and cracked open, others bloated and slick, their orange skins mottled with bruises, oozing dark, viscous sap that gleamed wetly under the flickering light.

Bodies lay half-swallowed by the thick vines, skin pale and clammy, eyes flickering between fractured consciousness and a haze of broken dreams. A woman moaned low and broken, lips cracked and trembling, as a pumpkin's rough rind pressed against her throat, tendrils curling like hungry fingers burrowing into her flesh. Her hands clawed at the vine, but the grip tightened with cruel inevitability, sucking slowly. Wet, muffled sounds leaking where fruit met skin, a grotesque feeding twisting flesh and bone beneath the pulsing rind.

Along the wall was a shelf filled with carving knives, rusted tools, and various sharp instruments.

"How can this exist?" said Frannie, searching for somewhere to stand, away from the horror surrounding them. "This can't be real." The room, like the house itself, defied all sense.

Reuben's stomach twisted violently, bile rising as the vines writhed closer, glistening with slime and veins pulsing beneath bark-like skin. Leaves brushed against their arms like cold tongues, sending shivers of dread racing down their spines. Frannie gasped, her eyes wide and unblinking as a vine brushed against her ankle, curling with serpentine grace to grasp.

"Ionia, move!" Virgilia shouted. She grabbed a rusty hammer from the shelf and raised it like a weapon against the creeping horror. She swung down, crashing with a sickening *crack* on a thick vine. The vine recoiled with a wet, rasping hiss, spraying sticky sap that clung to her gloves like

IT'S ALWAYS HALLOWEEN HERE

blood. The scent was overpowering. Earthy, sour, and metallic. A nauseating reminder of decay and death.

The pumpkin patch pulsed with life, malevolent and sentient. One massive fruit bulged suddenly, splitting open with a sick *crack* to reveal a dark maw lined with jagged, serrated seeds that gleamed. It sucked greedily on a man's arm, the ragged moans that escaped him broken and desperate, twisted into a death rattle beneath the gruesome sucking sound.

Marti seized a rotting plank of wood, swinging wildly at the reaching tendrils. The vines hissed and snapped back with frightening speed, but more coiled in response, wrapping around her legs like iron bands tightening slowly, crushing. Her scream broke free, raw and ragged, before the vines pulled her toward the grotesque feast, her wide eyes reflecting pure terror.

Reuben dropped to his knees, yanking desperately at a vine that clutched Frannie's wrist, his nails scraping against bark-like tendrils. The rough surface bit into his skin, drawing blood as the pumpkin patch pulsed ominously, throbbing with a sinister rhythm that echoed in his ears. The wet crackling of flesh torn beneath hungry vines.

The moans rose into a cacophony of half-human, half-monster, wailing in agony and surrender. The chorus clawed at their minds, filling the space with hopelessness and dread. The vines writhed with terrible purpose, stretching and coiling to ensnare, to suffocate, to devour until nothing remained but empty husks.

Ionia grabbed a carving knife and plunged it deep into a twisting stem, the blade sinking into fibrous flesh that shuddered and pulsed. The vine quivered and hissed, recoiling briefly, but dozens more reached out, writhing and testing, seeking weaknesses.

"We have to break through!" Virgilia growled, hammer swinging with brutal force, smashing tendrils and shattering rotten wood. The vines screamed, a wet, rasping sound filled with rage and hunger, but the patch fought back with relentless fury.

Frannie yanked free from a vine curling around her waist, tears streaming as the plant's grip burned like acid on her skin. Blood mixed with sap as she struck out blindly, nails tearing at the pulsing flesh.

The room spun in dizzying chaos. The scent of rot and earth overwhelming, the moans of the half-devoured echoing in their ears. The pumpkin patch was alive, an ancient, twisted hunger rooted deep beneath the house, feeding, growing, waiting.

With a desperate surge of adrenaline, they fought their way forward. Arms scratched raw, bodies slick with sap and blood, lungs burning with ragged gasps. Behind them, the screams and sucking noises faded slowly, swallowed by the dark, endless hunger of the living pumpkin patch.

When they finally burst through the far door, the bitter scent clung to them. An unshakable reminder that the house's roots were deeper and darker than any had dared imagine.

CHAPTER TWENTY-ONE

Keith and Mitch made their way toward the exit, their footsteps echoing across the warped wooden floor. The door creaked open. Not to the hallway they expected, but to a dim, unfamiliar chamber heavy with the scent of dust, candle wax, and something fouler beneath.

A single oil lamp flickered on a crate in the corner, casting long, twitching shadows across the room. At its center stood a crooked altar fashioned from cracked floorboards and rusted hinges. Wax figures lined its top. Handmade, deformed, their features warped like they'd been sculpted in a frenzy. Animal bones were arranged in a strange spiral around a blackened chalice, and old, torn, and water-damaged photographs had been nailed into the wall behind it. Every face in every photo had been scratched out with something sharp.

The makeshift altar was a grotesque collage of objects that felt both ancient and disturbingly out of place. At its center sat a cracked porcelain doll, missing an eye, its remaining glass orb dull and lifeless, tilted slightly as if listening. Around it, brittle, yellowed pages from a forgotten prayer book were pinned down by rusted, twisted keys. Each key was different, ornate but corroded, their teeth worn smooth by unknown hands.

Clusters of brittle, blackened feathers lay strewn like fallen wings, brittle as dry leaves, their shadows stretching long and flickering unnaturally in the dim light. Thin strands of spider silk clung to them, glistening with an oily sheen.

Nearby, a collection of tarnished silver rings—some engraved with strange symbols, others blank—were threaded through a gnarled, dried root that resembled a hand reaching upward. The root pulsed faintly with an unseen rhythm, as if it still held breath.

In one corner, a small glass vial half-filled with a dark, viscous liquid sat balanced precariously on a stack of brittle bones, though no one could tell if they belonged to animal or human. The vial's surface was fogged from the inside, the liquid swirling slowly, almost sentient.

Tiny carved figurines, misshapen and crude, surrounded the altar like sentinels. Each depicting a different creature, neither fully animal nor human, their eyes seeming to glimmer with quiet malevolence.

The entire altar was draped with a threadbare black cloth embroidered with a tangled pattern of twisting vines and unfamiliar sigils that seemed to shift when viewed from the corner of the eye.

The air hung thick with a faint scent. Part decay, part incense, and something else, something metallic and cold, like the breath of a grave.

A man knelt before the altar, whispering in a tongue neither Keith nor Mitch recognized. His back was to them, his posture rigid. He wore outdated workman's clothes. Suspenders, mud-caked boots, and a shirt soaked at the back with something that shimmered darkly in the flickering light.

Keith froze. "Do you see him?"

Mitch nodded slowly, his voice low. "What the hell is he doing?"

They stepped forward. The man's shoulders heaved with slow, breathy mutterings. His hands were clasped before him, unmoving. His head tilted slightly, as though listening to something none of them could hear.

"Is it a ghost?" Mitch whispered, more to himself than Keith.

Keith took one cautious step closer, drawn in by the eerie stillness, by the magnetic wrongness of the altar and its kneeling worshipper. His hand rose slowly, almost against his will.

"Wait," Mitch said. "Don't—"

But Keith reached out, fingers trembling, and lightly touched the man's shoulder.

The man vanished. Not in a puff of smoke or a shimmer of light. He simply wasn't there anymore. In that same instant, the lamp flared unnaturally bright, casting the room in a red glow that pulsed like a heartbeat.

Keith stumbled back, gasping, and gripped his arm. His skin had gone pale, waxy, as though drained of all warmth. His breath came fast and shallow.

"What just happened?" he whispered, staring down at his hands. His skin glistened with a slick sheen of sweat. Or something thicker.

Mitch turned to him, eyes wide, mouth moving with no sound. Behind them, the scratched photos on the wall began to peel away on their own, lifting as if caught in an invisible breeze.

The altar groaned. Wood splintering, wax figures tipping, the air buzzing with static and voices just below hearing. The floor creaked behind them. They turned.

A figure now stood in the doorway they had come through. It was not the man. Or at least not as he had been.

He wore the same clothes. But his face was wrapped in gauze, stained and twitching, as though something writhed beneath. His hands were empty but curled into fists that bled through the bandages. The gauze around his mouth began to dampen.

"Run," Keith said hoarsely.

The doorway behind them had vanished.

Keith let out a pained scream. One of deep anguish and horror. His skin began to sizzle. Slowly at first, then more rapidly. His skin was melting off of his body, falling to the floor in goopy, meat-filled chunks. His blood and bodily fluids spraying from the spontaneous open wounds on his body.

Mitch backed away, horrified. There was nothing he could do to help his friend. Keith's eyes were wide and filled with terror. Until his eyes, too, melted and disintegrated.

Mitch backed away, terror seizing his entire body. He backed closer to the wall…closer…

Right into the man from the altar, who was cloaked in darkness. Waiting.

The man grabbed Mitch. Mitch struggled but he was no match for the man's unholy strength. The man took Mitch's head in his hands and pressed. Hard.

Mitch screamed, his vision blurring. He had always wondered if it was true that people saw their life flash before their eyes before they died. His mind raced with thoughts of escape, but he was powerless against the absolute force of the man's grasp.

Mitch thought of his wife and children. His parents. His days as an Eagle Scout. His wild nights in college. Happy memories of days gone by.

As if his head was caught in the unforgiving grip of a vice, the man crushed Mitch's skull in between his hands. With a sickening crunch, as brain matter and viscous fluids splattered everywhere, Mitch's entire head caved in on itself.

CHAPTER TWENTY-TWO

Donna, Loretta, Kristen, Angela, and Bruce stood in the strange red room, the oppressive silence pressing in on them like a living thing. The absence of Drew was a gnawing weight. They had called for him again and again, but the room swallowed their voices, offering only a hollow, unanswered echo in return.

"Do we stay and wait for him?" Kristen said.

"I don't think he's playing a joke here," said Loretta. "I think the house has him. I know that sounds insane."

"We saw him in the mirror," said Angela.

No windows pierced the walls, which bled the color red in two stark halves. One side a bright, almost garish crimson that seemed to pulse faintly in the dim light, the other a dark, bruised maroon that drank in shadows and swallowed sound. The air was thick, stale, and unnervingly still, smelling faintly of old blood and burnt fabric.

"Where did Drew go?" Kristen said.

"This isn't part of the tour," Bruce said. "Something is really wrong here."

Loretta's head was spinning with worst-case scenarios. A cult? A portal through time and space? Serial killers and mass murderers? Ghosts, spirits, and apparitions? Demons from the netherworld?

"Okay, okay, we can't lose our heads," said Donna. "Let's acknowledge that yes, this is incredibly weird and freaky. But our feet are on the ground, and it's not possible that this house is alive. We can't jump to the wildest conclusion."

"No one is ever here," Angela said. "That's why. The house. It swallows people."

"What is that?" said Kristen, staring at the wall.

Kristen hesitated, then reached toward the peeling edge of the wallpaper, tugging gently. The paper came away with an unsettling ease, curling back like dry skin. Beneath, scrawled in hurried, uneven handwriting, was the word "Greeter."

Not just once, but repeated obsessively, sprawling across the wall like a manic chant. Surrounding the word were dozens of dates and times, some written in looping, elegant 19th-century script, others scrawled more recently in frantic strokes. The earliest entries dated back to the mid-1800s,

IT'S ALWAYS HALLOWEEN HERE

etched with a certainty that suggested ritual or warning, while the latest were blotchy, rushed, as if penned by trembling hands.

Donna's fingers trembled as she peeled away more wallpaper, revealing layer after layer of haunting, faded photographs plastered beneath. The portraits were individual, unframed snapshots that chronicled a strange, endless lineage: faces lined with time and hardship, eyes hollow and glassy, gazing past the surface as if trying to reach someone on the other side. Some smiled faintly—forced, tight-lipped—while others wore expressions of cold resignation or quiet terror.

"Look at this one," Loretta whispered, pointing to a photo nearly one hundred and fifty years old. The man's eyes seemed to follow them, dark and unreadable beneath a tattered hat. "He looks like he's been trapped here forever."

Kristen's eyes widened as she traced the dates along the bottom of the photographs, moving steadily toward the present day. The faces became sharper, the photographs crisper, but the eyes remained empty, haunted.

The most recent photograph caught their attention. A color image, slightly glossy, worn at the edges. It was the woman they had seen standing at the front door, the greeter. Her smile was the same unnerving, unwavering expression. Her eyes were wide and fixed, like she was an alien pretending to be human.

"It's like the room's been keeping track," Loretta murmured, her voice low and uncertain. "All the greeters. For hundreds of years."

Bruce frowned, rubbing his jaw. "But why? And what does this have to do with Drew disappearing? Why isn't he here?"

Kristen swallowed hard, lingering on the images, feeling the weight of a thousand eyes watching. "Maybe the greeter isn't just a person. Maybe it's a role. Or a curse. Like a chain that binds them to this place, one after another."

"Let's not stay to find out," Loretta said. Something about the word "greeter." What was the implication of that job? What did that unholy honor bestowed upon unwilling candidates entail?

The red walls seemed to close in around them, the flickering overhead light casting long, trembling shadows that stretched and twisted like reaching fingers. It was as if the faces from the photographs themselves were alive, silently observing, their gazes full of dread and warning.

"Drew's here somewhere," Donna said, her voice tight with urgency. "We just have to find him."

Loretta nodded slowly, but as her fingers brushed against another photograph. It was cracked and peeling, the figure almost melting into the paper. She felt a shiver crawl up her spine. The room was alive, breathing beneath the paint and paper, holding secrets in its deep, scarlet heart.

"We have to get the rest of our friends and get the fuck out of here," Loretta said.

CHAPTER TWENTY-THREE

Reuben, Marti, Frannie, Virgilia, and Ionia stepped cautiously into a vast ballroom, their footsteps swallowed by the cavernous space. They hadn't had a moment to catch their breath or discuss what they had witnessed in the pumpkin patch. They had simply run.

"What's happening?" Frannie said.

"I just want to go home," said Reuben.

"We're leaving," Virgilia said. "Keep moving." Her thoughts drifted to her kids, who made fun of her jacket before she'd left. What she would have given to be with them now, to hear them tease her.

"Let's all go to The Faulkner House," Reuben said mockingly. "It'll be fun. We definitely won't die there."

The ballroom was vast and majestic, a grand expanse of opulence that exuded timeless elegance. Its high, vaulted ceilings stretched above like a painted sky, adorned with intricate frescoes depicting classical scenes of myth and celebration. Crystal chandeliers, each the size of a carriage, hung in shimmering rows, scattering golden light across the polished marble floor that reflected every flicker and footstep like a mirror.

Along the perimeter, tall arched windows rose from floor to ceiling, draped in heavy velvet curtains of deep burgundy and gold trim. Between each window stood carved columns of alabaster, spiraled and inlaid with gilded filigree, supporting balconies with wrought iron balustrades that overlooked the dance floor below.

The walls were paneled in dark wood and embellished with gilded moldings, while alcoves held statues of muses and cherubs in elegant poses. A raised dais at one end housed a grand piano and space for an orchestra, with acoustics so perfect that even a whisper of strings could be heard at the far end of the room.

Every detail, from the mosaic borders along the floor to the elaborate cornices, spoke of craftsmanship and grandeur. This was not merely a room, but a stage for splendor, built to echo with music, laughter, and the sweep of swirling gowns.

The air was thick with dust and the faint scent of aged wood and fading grandeur. At the center, beneath a towering crystal chandelier that flickered weakly with a ghostly glow, stood a solitary figure. A man dressed in the finery of an old-time aristocrat, his tailored waistcoat and frock coat impeccably preserved, his silver hair swept back with aristocratic grace. His eyes gleamed with unsettling calm as he gestured toward a semicircle of ornate chairs awaiting them.

"Who are you?" said Ionia.

The man didn't answer.

"What's going on?" Marti said.

"Please, remain calm," the man said. "All will be explained in due time."

"Is this part of the show?" Reuben said. "We've had enough bullshit for one night."

"Please, take your seats," he intoned smoothly, his voice echoing softly against the marble floors.

"No, man," said Virgilia. "We're out of here. We're going home."

"You are home, Virgilia," the man said.

As if they had no control over their own bodies, the five friends complied, forced into the plush velvet chairs. They fought against their own bodies' actions, but they were under the man's control.

With a subtle motion of the man's hand, the ballroom was transformed. High above them were small stages. One by one, they lit up, revealing posed mannequins, staged for reenactment. The first section of the high stage surrounding the ballroom was illuminated against the darkness.

Beneath each stage was a plaque, with the scene name and setting carved into the shiny gold plate. Under the first scene, it read:

Scene One: The Faulkner Family, Mid-1800s.

A soft golden light bathed a cluster of wax figures arranged around an ornate Victorian parlor. Each figure was immaculately dressed in fine fabrics that seemed to shimmer faintly under the light—silks, velvets, and delicate lace.

The patriarch stood tall, his frock coat tailored to perfection, a silver pocket watch chain glinting at his waist. His expression was a rigid mask of pride, eyes fixed on some distant point. Beside him, his wife's satin gown pooled elegantly around her feet; her gloved hands clasped a delicate fan, fingers unnaturally still.

Their children hovered nearby. Two girls in starched pinafores, clutching faded dolls with glassy eyes. A boy with a solemn face, holding a worn book. The wallpaper behind them was heavy damask, faded to a dusty rose, and the grand fireplace seemed to flicker with a fire that never quite warmed the room.

The man's voice narrated, "The Faulkner family, pillars of society in

IT'S ALWAYS HALLOWEEN HERE

the mid-1800s, wealthy and respected. Their wealth was immense, their influence unquestioned."

The light clicked off for the first section, as the second section lit up.

Scene Two: The Dark Arts.

The light dimmed and shifted. Shadows pooled in the corners of a secret chamber, lined floor to ceiling with cracked leather-bound tomes and shelves sagging under the weight of forbidden knowledge. The wax figures here were draped in heavy, dark robes embroidered with twisted arcane symbols that shimmered faintly as if alive.

One figure knelt at an ancient altar, its surface cluttered with grotesque relics. A tarnished silver dagger whose blade seemed stained with dried blood; a cracked obsidian mirror reflecting not the room, but swirling shadows; a faded leather grimoire splayed open with illegible, arcane script scrawled across yellowed pages. A circle of withered candles, their flames flickering weakly, surrounded the altar, casting long, flickering shadows that writhed on the cracked stone floor.

"However, beneath their refined surface, the Faulkners became obsessed with the dark arts, black magic, and occult rituals," the man intoned. "Fascinated by forbidden knowledge, they dabbled in rites that twisted reality itself."

The second section went dark, as the third lit up. Repeated for each scene.

Scene Three: Terrifying Tales.

The ballroom darkened further as a chilling tableau emerged. Wax figures appeared as twisted phantoms. Faces contorted in silent, eternal screams, their mouths frozen mid-cry. Some pressed ghostly hands against invisible windows, fingers splayed wide as if trying to escape. Their eyes, sunken and hollow, seemed to bore into the visitors.

The air around them shimmered faintly, as if their anguished spirits were just beneath the surface, barely held at bay. Faint, barely audible whispers seemed to drift through the room, a chorus of unseen voices telling tales of despair.

"The house became a locus of terror," the man continued, "where strange disappearances and chilling cries echoed through the halls. The stories spread, whispered in fear by townsfolk and visitors alike."

Scene Four: The Procession of the Lost.

A long, somber line wax figures appeared, each posed as if caught in a moment of tragic fate. A young woman clutched a tarnished silver locket, her head bowed, eyes cast downward in sorrow. A man with torn clothing staggered forward, mouth open in a silent scream, a ragged coat fluttering as if caught in an invisible wind. A child grasped a ragged doll tightly, eyes wide and haunted, standing rigid as if frozen in time.

The figures were lifelike to an eerie degree. Faint smudges of dirt on their skin, strands of real hair, and even the slight shimmer of tears on some cheeks. Their eyes, glossy and unblinking, seemed to follow the four visitors with a desperate plea.

"One by one, souls were claimed," the man said softly, "drawn into the web of the Faulkner House's insatiable hunger."

Scene Five: The Call to Join.

The lighting softened to an eerie, inviting glow as wax figures turned outward, their arms extended in silent beckoning. Their faces, once serene, now bore unnerving, unnatural smiles, wide and sharp, stretching in a way that felt almost alive. Some had eyes that shimmered with a faint red glow. Their poses were intimate, leaning forward slightly, as if urging the visitors to step closer, to join the eternal dance.

"The house sends out its call," the narrator explained, "inviting those who enter to become part of its eternal story."

Scene Six: The House's Need for Souls.

A massive, skeletal tree of souls rose from the floor, its gnarled branches twisting upward toward the ceiling like clawed hands. Hanging from the branches were hundreds of glowing orbs. Souls trapped in eternal limbo, flickering softly with an otherworldly light. The orbs pulsed gently, casting eerie reflections on the polished marble. Shadows danced as the light shifted, and the hushed sound of distant whispers swirled in the air like a mournful breeze.

"The house needs souls," the man said gravely. "Guardians to watch over it, to keep its power alive."

Scene Seven: No Escape.

The lights dimmed to near darkness, save for a faint red glow illuminating a final, forbidding scene. A labyrinth of endless doors, each one closing slowly behind shadowy figures. Their forms blurred, melting into the walls as if swallowed by the very architecture. The air grew heavy, the silence oppressive and final.

"There is no escape," the man whispered, voice low and final. "Once you are part of the Faulkner House, you are bound forever."

As the last scene faded, the five friends sat frozen, the weight of the story pressing down on them like the heavy air of the room itself. The man's gaze lingered on them, calm but unreadable.

"Now," he said softly, "you understand."

CHAPTER TWENTY-FOUR

The house was making noises again. Not the usual groans of settling wood or the distant rattle of old pipes. Low, deliberate sounds that echoed faintly through the walls, like someone dragging their fingernails across the inside of the structure. A soft, rhythmic thudding from above, as if something was walking slowly in the attic, back and forth, back and forth. Beneath it all, a barely perceptible murmur, like someone whispering just beneath the threshold of hearing. It wasn't constant. It pulsed, in and out. Breathing.

"I still don't see where Drew went," Kristen said, spinning in place, her voice pinched and high. "He was right behind us. I saw him."

"He was in the mirror," said Donna.

"How?" Loretta said. "How is that possible? None of this makes any sense."

"He didn't just disappear," Bruce said, though the doubt in his voice was impossible to miss. He glanced behind them, then down at the floor, as if Drew might have fallen through a crack they missed.

Loretta's eyes swept across the strange room again. The painted walls, the unnerving color shift, the stillness that didn't feel like quiet so much as anticipation. The air felt thick, syrupy, as if the room was filled with invisible fog. A low hum pressed at the base of her skull, like static behind her thoughts.

"This isn't a set," she said slowly, firmly. "This isn't trick doors and hidden wires. This place. It's warping around us."

Donna stepped to one of the red walls and ran her fingers down it. The paint didn't feel dry. It had a tacky, almost rubbery texture, like skin stretched too tight. "I've been to every fake haunted house in three counties. None of them pull this kind of psychological crap. This place feels aware. Like it's alive."

Loretta nodded grimly. "It's not just the rooms. It's the rules. They don't make sense. Time doesn't feel right. Space folds in on itself. We're in some kind of—" She hesitated, choosing her words. "Spatial and temporal loop? A structure that defies physical law?"

"A haunted house that defies physics," Bruce said dryly. "Great."

Loretta ignored him. "Whatever this is, it's not a prank. It's not a haunted tour. It's real."

Kristen folded her arms tightly, glancing toward the door. "So, what do we do?"

"Find weapons," Donna said immediately. "Find something, anything, we can use to protect ourselves. I don't care if it's a candlestick or a busted chair leg. I'm not going down without swinging."

"I agree," Loretta said. "And while we're at it, we need to learn everything we can about those greeters."

"You mean the woman at the front?" Kristen asked. "The one we saw through the window?"

"There are more than one," Loretta said. "We saw the names under the wallpaper. Generations of them. Same name. Same role. The Greeter." She swallowed hard. "They're not just actors. They're sentinels. Watchers."

"Watching for what?" Donna asked, her voice suddenly smaller, the red shadows around her face making her look drawn and haunted.

"I don't know," Loretta whispered. "But I think they're the link. Between whatever this house really is, and whoever, or whatever, it belongs to."

Bruce paced a few feet away, rubbing his arms as if cold, though the air was stifling. "So, what are they? Ghosts? People trapped here? Something else?"

"Maybe none of the above," Loretta said. "Maybe they're echoes. Or constructs. Or parts of the house itself."

"Maybe this house holds everything dark," said Donna. "Maybe everything evil, everything malicious and vile, has a home here. The deranged, the demented, the monsters under our beds."

Angela looked at her, voice trembling. "Do you think we're dead?"

"No," Donna said, unwilling to even consider the thought. "No, don't say that."

Loretta shook her head slowly. "I don't feel dead. But I also don't think this place plays by the same rules. It could be a trap. A loop. A feeding ground. A kind of purgatory. Or worse."

"Hell," Bruce said quietly. "You think this is Hell?"

No one answered right away. The silence grew like mold between them, clinging to the corners of the room, thick and pressing. The line dividing the room's red tones almost seemed to breathe.

Kristen whispered, "If it is, it's not our Hell. It's someone else's."

"And we're the guests," Donna said darkly. "Or the offering."

"I didn't mean for any of this to happen," Kristen said, holding back tears.

Loretta put her arm around her. "Of course not. We're going to get out of here, okay?"

"This is the worst escape room ever," Bruce said. Loretta elbowed him.

They stood still for a long moment, the deep reds of the room soaking into their skin like heat. Somewhere behind the walls, something creaked, like wood under strain.

"We find something to defend ourselves. And we find Drew. We don't split up again," Loretta said.

Bruce stepped toward the hallway, his shadow stretching long and jagged across the maroon-painted floor.

"I don't care if this house twists sideways," Donna said. "We're getting out. Or we're burning it down."

Loretta stepped last toward the door, her eyes trailing one last time over the painted division in the wall.

A sound. Faint at first. They thought it was just the building settling again. A soft scrape. Then another. Like fingernails gently dragging across the underside of the floorboards.

Kristen turned her head slowly. "Did you hear that?"

"Yes," Donna said. "And it's not rats. That's closer."

The air in the red room shifted. Barely perceptible, but pressing. The atmosphere grew denser, heavier, as if it had thickened with something unseen. Something present.

A faint vibration crept up through the soles of their shoes. Not enough to knock them off balance. Just enough to be felt, like a hum deep in the bones. The oil lamp in the corner flickered, though there was no draft.

Then came the breathing. It wasn't theirs.

It circled them. Slow. Wet. Labored. It seemed to move from one end of the room to the other, but when they turned to look, there was nothing there.

Kristen backed against the wall, eyes darting. "Where is it?"

"Shhh," Loretta whispered. She held up a hand, listening, watching the dim glow of the lamp stretch their shadows like grotesque reflections against the warped red walls.

Angela hissed and slapped her arm. "Something touched me."

"I felt it, too," Bruce said, his voice cracking. "Cold. Right across my neck."

The air rippled, visibly this time, as if heatwaves were undulating through the room. However, the temperature dropped. The wallpaper began to curl.

Right where they'd torn it earlier, a strip began to peel outward on its own, lifting with a soft, papery hiss. Letters bled through beneath the layers. Dozens of instances of the word Greeter, as though ink had soaked up from inside the wall. More dates. Names. All moving. Shifting.

The photos underneath pulsed faintly, as if lit from behind. In one, the woman who'd greeted them at the entrance now appeared closer in the frame than before. Her face was still smiling. Her eyes had shifted, just barely, toward the camera. Toward them.

A low growl, not animal, not human, vibrated from the baseboards.

Bruce swore under his breath. "This thing's in the room with us."

Loretta took a step toward the center, slowly turning in place. Her voice was tight. "It's not showing itself because it doesn't have to."

The growl became a snarl. A layered, guttural noise that came from every corner at once. And then silence.

The lamp went out. Total darkness. A breath, not theirs, exhaled inches from Kristen's ear. She screamed.

In the dark, something small and sharp ran across Loretta's calf. Bruce swung wildly with a broken chair leg he'd picked up earlier, hitting nothing but air.

From behind them, or maybe above them, a sound. A voice. A whisper, like a taunt.

"Choose."

The room seemed to pulse again, the reds on the walls glowing faintly from beneath the paint, as if blood vessels had begun to light up inside the plaster.

Footsteps. Heavy. Determined. Moving toward them but leaving no trace. The voice came again, a hiss from everywhere and nowhere:

"No one gets out."

They couldn't see it.

But it could see them.

IT'S ALWAYS HALLOWEEN HERE

CHAPTER TWENTY-FIVE

Helen was the first to see him. Halfway down a corridor lined with flickering wall sconces and distorted reflections in dusty glass frames. Drew stood at the end, hands raised in greeting, his expression bright and oddly relieved.

"Hey! I've been looking all over for you guys," he called out, his voice weirdly chipper, bouncing unnaturally off the cracked wallpaper and warped wood.

Judy gasped. "Drew! Thank God."

Helen stepped forward, gripping her arms. "We are so glad to see you! Something really weird is going on."

"Come this way," Drew said quickly, already motioning them forward. "This place is nuts. But I think I found a way out."

They hurried to him, grateful faces and shaking limbs, and for a moment, it felt like the tide had turned. The air buzzed faintly around them, the overhead bulbs dimming with each step.

"Where are the others?" Phyllis asked, her voice tight.

"Scattered. We got separated. But I found a room. One that looks different from the others. It's got an old service passage, or maybe a root cellar, but I think it leads out. Come on."

He started walking before they could respond, his steps confident, almost rehearsed. Judy, Phyllis, and Helen exchanged uncertain glances, but the glimmer of hope was too bright to ignore. They followed.

The hallway twisted strangely, narrower than before, the walls pressed closely, smelling of damp plaster, old smoke, and something more pungent, like wax, mildew, and spoiled incense. A low hum seemed to pulse from the floorboards, as though something massive turned slowly beneath them. Drew moved ahead steadily, his frame casting long shadows that warped and stretched, occasionally twitching in the corners of their eyes.

He stopped at a set of double doors. Heavy, wooden, carved with religious symbols that had been crudely defaced. Crucifixes scored through with black tar, angels whose faces had been scraped off, rosaries melted into the grain like veins. The scent here was thicker. Coppery. Rotten flowers in a sealed box.

"Through here," he said. The doors opened with an echo.

The room beyond was colder. The floor was made of uneven flagstone, slick with condensation. Religious artifacts lined the walls. Icons and relics, crucifixes, weeping statues, prayer beads tangled in brittle ceramic fingers. But they were all off.

The saints' faces were gouged out, lips sealed with wax. A statue of Mary wept what looked like ink, black and slow. A chalice in the corner overflowed with something between oil and blood, thick and glistening. The walls pulsed slightly, as if breathing.

In the center of the room were several coffins, plain and wooden, nailed shut. Each bore a single red fingerprint at the head.

Phyllis stopped in the doorway. "Drew, what is this?"

"Sanctuary," he said smoothly. "The only safe room left."

Judy took a step back. "This doesn't feel safe."

Drew turned. His smile was frozen. "You're tired. You need to rest. We all do."

Judy's brow furrowed. "You're acting weird."

His eyes twitched. "We're almost done. You'll see. The house just needs to accept you."

"What do you mean, accept?" Helen asked, her voice barely a whisper now.

Drew tilted his head. "Every soul has its place. You came here willingly. That matters. The house appreciates obedience."

"What are you talking about?" Judy's voice sharpened. "You're scaring me."

Drew stepped closer, and something in his face seemed to ripple. Not visibly, not entirely, but enough to suggest a change beneath the skin. His pupils had grown, swallowing the color in his eyes. His voice deepened slightly, catching in his throat.

"You won't be alone. Not really. The house will keep you. Just like it kept me."

Judy backed up into a display case, a statue clattering behind her, its face shattering against the floor. "Drew?"

He blinked slowly. When his eyes opened again, they were red-rimmed and bulging, as though something was pushing its way forward behind them.

"I watched the door too long," he said softly. "I listened to what's on the other side. And now it's my turn to guide others in."

A scraping sound echoed from the far side of the room, like metal on glass. They turned to the stained window across the room, the light behind it flickering in sick, jerky pulses. Something long and angular pressed against the panes from the outside.

A boneless, pale hand with an abnormal number of fingers splayed against the glass like wet paper, squelching faintly.

Helen grabbed a metal candlestick from a nearby altar, its brass sticky with something old and dried. "Drew, get away from us."

He didn't flinch. He smiled wider. "You'll be beautiful guardians. You'll see. It's not pain forever. It's purpose. Some people embrace their fate. Some people fight it. Some of us like it."

With a crunching sound, the window cracked. Long fractures laced across it like spider legs.

The creature pressed harder, its face sliding up behind the fractured glass. Featureless, save for a mouth that stretched and stretched and stretched, wider than a skull should allow.

Helen screamed, covering her ears as a buzzing sound filled the room like a thousand whispering insects. The light in the room surged then burst with a thunderous pop.

The last thing Helen, Judy, and Phyllis saw before the darkness swallowed them was Drew stepping aside, arms open.

Gesturing to the coffins.

Inviting them in.

CHAPTER TWENTY-SIX

Loretta, Angela, Donna, Kristen, and Bruce burst into the next room, yelling for Drew. Calling out for their other friends. Frantic to find a way out.

Every wall was a seamless screen. The air smelled faintly of fresh linen and projector heat. A subtle buzz of electricity tickled the skin like goosebumps rising. It felt impossibly warm compared to the rest of the house. Underfoot, the floor vibrated ever so slightly with hidden motors pulsing quietly.

A projector displayed images on each wall, like an art exhibit. The shadows and colors of the pictures fell and swooped over their faces and bodies. At first, the projection wrapped them in comfort and calm.

A family laughing at a picnic, sunlight glinting on wind-tossed hair and bright green grass.

Ocean waves rolling softly onto a sandy shore, seafoam rising like whispered applause.

Wildflowers swaying in golden fields, bees drifting from bloom to bloom.

A deer and her fawn drinking from a clear forest stream, dappled sunlight dancing on their coats.

Loretta inhaled deeply. Her breath caught on the scent of summer and dread mingled together. *It's almost healing*, she thought. *A momentary reprieve. We'll get through this.* Determined, she steadied her grip on Donna's hand and scanned the perimeter, looking for exits or clues. The light across her face flickered with resolve.

Slowly, quietly, the tone shifted. A shudder ran through the room as if the screens themselves exhaled.

Waves darkened to swirling blacks and grays, water suddenly churning with oil that sucked in light. Each wave slapped the screen with a dull roar of static. The family smiles lost color and warmth; faces grew vacant and thin. Eyes darkened to hollow pits. Wildflowers wilted on the blade to a sickly green rot. The deer became skeletal, its eyes hollow, the stream muddy and stagnant. Shadows seemed to leak beyond the projection borders.

Shadows lengthened across the screens. Even though on one wall, dark shadows didn't match any projected image, they flickered beyond the scenery. A shape slithered past the edge of the dais. Shapes slid between

IT'S ALWAYS HALLOWEEN HERE

projections. A lean figure slipping behind the tall grass, a hunched silhouette passing through a forest glen, eyes glinting where the light shouldn't reach. Heartbeats synced with flickers of phantom motion.

Loretta's heart pounded. She tasted panic, sharp as iron, but she pushed it down. This was no exhibit. She focused her mind. *I am strong. We're not staying here.* She began scanning frantically, trying to catch movement out of the corner of her eye.

On one wall, a field of sunflowers turned black, mouths opening soundlessly. A sunflower head twisted as though gasping in the wind. On another, ocean waves foamed blood instead of water, and drowned figures drifted beneath the surface. The red tide pulsed, reflecting terror in every droplet. Forest animals became monstrous: rabbits with glowing red eyes, deer with broken antlers dripped black sap, carnivorous birds tearing at invisible flesh. A distant screech echoed as wings beat beyond the projection.

The ambient soundtrack shifted from birdsong to faint whispers, echoing in different tones. Sometimes laughter, sometimes a low keening voice. Donna gasped beside her; her voice cracked like glass. Bruce's flashlight tracked the edges of the room, illuminating floating dust motes too slow to be natural.

"They're hiding in the frames," Loretta whispered, voice tight but low. "Watch the borders, between images." Her fingers brushed Kristen's shoulder. "They can't touch the projection yet."

Kristen nodded, wide-eyed. Fear sharpened by focus.

Across two walls, a flicker. Not a projection, but a ripple of air. Her skin tingled as if someone brushed past. A slender shadow moved diagonally between scenes, slinking from the ruined sunflowers to the ocean blood. It carried the scent of damp earth and rot. Loretta lunged toward the wall, pressing her palm against cool glass that felt too cold to belong in this room.

There were seams, thin lines between each projection panel. Dust collected in these grooves like tiny grave markers. She scanned them, noticing subtle dents, dark figures crouched within those seams. Too wiry to be human, too fast to be static.

"Okay," Loretta said. "We split up. Two by the north wall, two south. Watch the borders. Try to corner them." Her breath steadied, every sense heightened.

Donna picked the north wall; Loretta took the eastern seam. Dread coiled in her gut. Bruce, Angela, and Kristen moved west. They crept along silently, detecting movement along panel joints: a flicker of a limb, a shifting silhouette pulling back where light flickered. Every heartbeat felt like a warning.

As the projections peeled into chaos—flowers rotting, ocean roiling, families dissolving into ash—none of the quartet broke their focus. Their eyes shone with urgency. Loretta's pulse steadied with purpose. Find the exit. Find a weakness. Get Drew. Get out.

At the far corner, near the exit door that glowed faintly in the projection's crimson glow, Loretta saw movement behind the panel. She could smell smoke, fear, and unnatural warmth. She slid forward. Two shapes darted out. Skeletal, elongated bodies, half visible in one projection and vanishing in another.

She switched on her flashlight. *Hold steady*. Hand trembling against metal. *Keep calm*. She pinned frenetic focus to the nearest being and lunged forward, but it vanished behind the seams just as Bruce swung a metal rod at the wall. The crack echoed like a gunshot. The impact cut through the projection light with a dull thud, glass reverberating. Her heart thundered.

All at once, the ambient whispers peaked. Voices merging into one sound, echoing from every projection. "You are home." It vibrated inside her chest.

The projection flickered violently, and for a moment, the entire room went dark. Silence pressed in like water.

The original, peaceful images flickered back. Families laughing, oceans tranquil, wildflowers bright. The calm was suffocating now.

Only it felt colder now, empty. The air felt hollow. The silhouettes were gone. Loretta knew they'd just retreated. The room wasn't done yet.

She looked back at her friends, voice tight. "We keep going. We find the way out of this house." Resolve shone in her gaze.

"This isn't a house," Angela said. "Not a normal one."

"Maybe there's a reason why they never let people inside," said Kristen.

They stood still as the dark projections twisted around her on the walls. Shadows of suffering stitched into the glow of ghostly flowers, of rot curling through peaceful meadows. Blood trickled through old-growth forests. Smiling families now flickered with sunken eyes and gaping mouths. The images bled together, choking the room in a pulsing hush that seemed to press against her skin, thick and suffocating like wet velvet.

But amid the horror, Loretta's thoughts turned inward. *I have to keep it together,* she told herself, a tight knot forming in her chest. *I can't let fear win.* Her heart pounded fiercely, a wild drum beneath her ribs, threatening to burst free.

IT'S ALWAYS HALLOWEEN HERE

She thought of Donna's crooked little laugh that could cut through any tension like sunlight through fog. Of Kristen's steady voice, the calm anchor that held them all when the shadows lengthened. Of Bruce, cracking dumb jokes even when the cold seeped into their bones. And of home. Her mother's kitchen on lazy Sunday mornings, the smell of fresh bread and cinnamon lingering in the air. Her father's old tools hung, just as he left them, heavy with memories. Her dog waiting faithfully by the door, eyes bright with hopeful expectation.

I love them all so much. I just want to go home. Please, just let me go home.

She swallowed the lump lodged deep in her throat, the sharp taste of salt and fear mixing on her tongue and forced herself to breathe. Slow, measured breaths like a mantra. The electricity in the exhibit room thickened around her, heavy and charged, a warmth that felt almost alive, like static brushing the fine hair on her arms. Shadows, too fast and slippery to track, darted just behind the flickering projections, as if the images themselves were alive, hunted by something unseen.

Then she saw it.

A side door tucked into the shadows behind a crumbling pillar, half hidden by the flickering image of a burning field, flames licking the edges like spectral tongues. The door wasn't there before. Or had it been hiding, waiting?

She stepped toward it, each footfall muffled by the oppressive silence, as if the house itself was holding its breath. Her hand reached out, trembling slightly, and the cold metal of the handle bit into her palm, icy and unyielding, a shock against her skin.

She pushed the door open.

The next room was a strange haven of quiet. Soft amber light glowed from sconces on the cracked, peeling walls, flickering like fragile candle flames in a dead wind. The floor was worn wood, creaking faintly beneath her weight, but the room itself was empty. Stark and unwelcoming.

"Donna?"

Only silence answered.

"Kristen? Angela? Bruce?"

Nothing.

Behind her, the oppressive exhibit room, and all the twisted, bleeding images, was gone. So were they.

A cold spike of panic slithered up her spine, tightening her chest until it felt like her lungs might collapse. But she clenched her fists, grounding herself. *Don't scream. Don't panic.*

The quiet there was worse than the noise. It was patient, watchful, waiting. A dark presence that seemed to seep from the walls themselves.

Predatory.

She was utterly, terrifyingly alone.

And the house knew it.

CHAPTER TWENTY-SEVEN

Judy's flashlight flickered as they turned another corner in the endless, suffocating labyrinth of halls. The beam of light jittered across peeling wallpaper and water-damaged portraits whose painted eyes seemed to follow them in the dark.

Helen, Phyllis, and Judy had run away from Drew. Or whatever it was impersonating him.

"I don't think he's following us," Judy said.

"I swear we've been here before," Helen said, her voice hoarse with panic. "We're just going around in circles."

Judy pressed both palms to her temples, pacing. "There has to be an exit somewhere. A fire escape, a window, something. This place can't just move around us."

Judy shook her head. "It can. It is."

Just ahead, tucked behind a sagging velvet curtain, they found it. A narrow doorway, hidden. A rusted metal handle. She yanked it open, and behind it was a spiraling stairwell, old and made of dark wood that bowed in the middle of each step. It spiraled tightly upward, enclosed by stone walls slick with moisture and the faint scent of ash and mildew.

"This has to lead somewhere," Helen said, already stepping inside. "We go up. We keep going. Maybe there's a rooftop. A window. Anything."

The stairs creaked beneath them like brittle bones. The feeling in the stairwell grew colder with each floor, tighter, heavier. The walls seemed to close in the higher they climbed. The dim light from Judy's flashlight swayed over rust-colored smears on the steps. Too dark to be fresh blood, but too red not to have once been.

"Where do you think the others are?" Phyllis whispered, gripping the rail.

"Hopefully better off than us," Helen said, but it sounded more like a plea than a joke.

They climbed in silence for a moment.

Something crashed below them. Loud. Heavy. Like a door being torn off its hinges and hurled into the wall.

They froze. Helen looked over her shoulder, eyes wide. "What the hell was that?"

Judy turned her flashlight downward, but the beam could only catch the spiraling curve of the stairs below. Nothing visible.

The sound started.

Thud.

Thud.

Footsteps. Heavy ones. Climbing. Fast.

THUD. THUD. THUD.

"Run!" Helen cried.

They surged upward, feet pounding the brittle old stairs, the spiraling walls spinning too fast, too tight. The sound of the thing following them grew louder; inhumanly heavy, as though it had claws instead of feet. Whatever it was, it didn't breathe, didn't speak. It just climbed. And climbed. And climbed.

A horrible scraping sound echoed up the stairwell. Metal on stone, or claws against bone. Something was scratching its way up.

"What if we're just going higher into the house?" Helen cried. "What if there's no way out?"

"There has to be!" Judy shouted. "There has to be. Maybe the roof."

THUD.

A new noise. Louder. Closer. The thing was gaining.

They reached a small landing. An arched wooden door at the next level. Helen flung it open, and they poured inside just as something below let out a low, rattling hiss that froze all three of them in place.

Judy slammed the door shut.

For a moment, only their breathing filled the new space. A narrow corridor filled with tall wardrobes covered in sheets. Pale sheets that looked like they hadn't been touched in decades.

Phyllis backed away from the door. "We can't go back down."

"No," Judy said, chest heaving. "We don't. We go forward. We find the others. We get out."

Behind them, through the thick door, they heard one more sound.

Three slow knocks.

Knock.

Knock.

Knock.

Helen gripped Judy's arm. "It knows where we are."

CHAPTER TWENTY-EIGHT

Loretta felt her way through a darkened hallway to a door. She turned the doorknob, trying to be as quiet and unnoticed as possible.

Inside, there was a strange light. Soft, flickering, and colorless. It bathed the space in a spectral glow, neither day nor night, as though time had been scraped clean. The walls were textured with hundreds, maybe thousands, of pale, lifeless faces. They were half-formed, pressed into the surface like wax melting through canvas. Some were blurred like old daguerreotypes, others sharply defined as if cast from life. But they weren't just images.

They moved.

If she blinked, they changed. Eyes shifting, mouths opening in slow-motion to whisper things just below hearing. Secrets. Pleas. Names. Every time she looked back at a face, it was different. As if the wall itself had a memory and it was slowly forgetting who each person had been.

Loretta took a step forward and nearly stumbled.

The room was full. Dozens of people sat silently in wooden chairs arranged in neat, terrible rows. Their skin was dull, almost gray, their faces slack with exhaustion. Their eyes were open but glazed, like something had passed through them and taken most of what made them human.

They weren't statues. They breathed. Barely. Slow, shallow, like breath wasn't a thing they needed but something they had simply forgotten how to stop doing. Their arms hung at their sides, wrists bound to the arms of the chairs with thick iron chains. The metal had sunk into some of their skin. Black scabbing where the cuffs had rubbed raw.

They didn't look at her. Not fully.

A few heads lifted as she entered, but not with recognition. Just a twitch of life responding to the sound of her presence. Then they dropped again, like marionettes whose strings had frayed.

Loretta couldn't discern whether these people were alive or dead, or something in between.

A sour, metallic smell filled the room. Iron, mildew, dust, and something deeper. Something like rot beneath old bandages.

Loretta's pulse quickened. It wasn't fear anymore. It was dread. Dread rooted in her bones, pressing into her ribs like something trying to push its way out.

A man sat near the far wall, separated from the others by only a few inches but somehow impossibly apart. His skin looked paper-thin, yellowed, stretched across hollow cheeks. His eyes were sunken, barely more than glints of dark water beneath his brows. He turned his head toward her, slowly, like he hadn't moved it in years.

"You're early," he said, voice like leaves dragging across stone. "Not your time."

Loretta stepped back. "What is this place?"

He didn't blink. "Purgatory. The waiting room. They keep us here until it's decided."

"Until what's decided?" she asked, her voice sharper than she meant.

The man tilted his head. "Whether you join the house."

She swallowed. "You mean the greeters?"

A few others stirred at the word. Not with alarm, but with something worse. Acceptance. As if they had all come to understand a truth too big to fight.

"They were like you once," the man rasped. "Walked through the wrong door. Thought they were still alive. Thought they'd get out."

Loretta's stomach turned.

"No one comes here on purpose," he continued. "But once you do, the house starts to remember you."

The chains on his wrists rattled as he shifted, their iron sheen smeared with age and dried blood.

She looked at the others. Still unmoving, still staring at nothing. It felt like being in a church built by forgetting, where memory itself had fossilized.

"I'm not staying here," Loretta said, backing toward the door.

The man's eyes followed her. The others didn't move.

"You already are," he whispered. "You are one of the lost souls now."

"I don't believe in any of this."

"That doesn't matter."

"What are we dealing with here? Ghosts? Demons? The supernatural? Mind fuck? Rips in time and physical space?"

"Yes."

"Stop talking in riddles!" shouted Loretta. "How do I get out of this house? None of this is possible."

"Yet, here you are. Just like us. We've been here a very long time. The house has a different layout, a different story for everyone who enters."

"Great," Loretta said mirthlessly. "We picked the *Choose Your Own Adventure* house."

"Being a greeter is a great honor," the man said. "But it comes at a heavy price."

"People will come looking for us."

"No, they won't. You think you're the first person to disappear inside these walls? No one will ever find your body. No one has ever found any of the bodies. You said goodbye as soon as you entered this house."

Loretta turned to the door, gripping the handle. It wouldn't open. Behind her, she heard the whispering from the walls grow louder. The faces began to shift faster, eyes darting, mouths stretching wide in silent screams.

She yanked harder. Nothing. The whispering turned into scratching from inside the walls.

One of the seated figures, an old woman with stringy white hair and chains embedded in her wrists, slowly raised her head and looked directly at Loretta.

"Don't fight it," she said. "It's inevitable." Her face began to change. Her eyes became darker. Her skin turning a sickly color.

Loretta slammed her shoulder against the door with all her strength. It gave. She fell through into the next hallway, breath heaving, vision swimming. Loretta didn't look back.

She didn't want to see which of them had started standing.

CHAPTER TWENTY-NINE

Loretta stood in the quiet, empty room with her back against the now-locked door.

The light was soft, like the filtered glow of late afternoon sun behind storm clouds. It didn't come from any obvious source. No windows, no bulbs. A low, humming ambiance made her skin crawl. The air smelled like old photo albums and something older. Something rotting but hiding beneath dust.

The room was circular, its walls lined with tall, antique mirrors from floor to ceiling. Ornate frames of dark wood, each one just slightly different. No dust on the glass. No tarnish. Each mirror perfectly clean.

She expected to see herself reflected a hundred times over. She didn't.

Instead, the mirrors showed other versions of her.

In one, she was thirteen, kneeling on the ground, hands red with blood from furiously digging in the dirt. Muffled, pitiful screams from someone buried in the earth.

In another, she was walking away from a car accident. Her friends' bodies were strewn across a deserted road, their limp corpses bloody and crushed. She ran down the darkened street, unscathed, alone.

In another, she was screaming at her mother.

In another, she was in this very house, crying over Kristen's limp body.

Loretta stumbled back, heart hammering.

None of that happened, she told herself. *Some of it did. Some of it didn't. The house lies to you. Creates false memories and emotions to confuse and trick you. Makes you believe things that never happened. Convinces you, deceives you into thinking what you're remembering is real. It gets into your head so you can't tell the difference between real and fake memories.*

The mirrors didn't care about accuracy. They knew fear. They knew regret. They showed the things she tried to forget.

She moved slowly toward the center of the room. A circle of faintly glowing glyphs marked the floor. Delicate symbols like a child's handwriting, drawn in what looked like dried sap or wax. As she stepped inside them, every mirror blinked.

And changed. They showed her friends.

IT'S ALWAYS HALLOWEEN HERE

Suzanne, alone in a corridor, calling her name.

Bruce, injured, dragging one leg behind him as shadows crawled after him.

Donna, pressed against a window, pounding and screaming in total silence.

Judy. Callie. Helen. All separated. All suffering.

Loretta pressed her hands to the sides of her head. "This isn't real."

One mirror in front of her rippled. Instead of reflecting images, it pulsed like water. Like a portal. She stepped closer. Her breath fogged the surface.

Her own reflection reappeared. But it wasn't her. Not exactly. This version of her was smiling.

It stepped forward in the glass, until their noses almost touched.

"I know what you're afraid of," it said in her voice, but not her tone. This one sounded amused. Playful. Almost fond.

Loretta couldn't move.

"You're afraid you'll fail them. Again." A pause. "You're afraid they'll die because you hesitated. Like last time." The mirror's edges darkened. Cracks began to form. Only around her reflection, not her. The smile grew. "You're afraid you'll make the wrong choice."

Loretta clenched her fists. Her mind drifted to a patient she had when she was doing her hospital residency. How she hadn't acted quickly enough. How he had died, in terrible pain, because of her indecision. Her mistake.

The glyphs beneath her feet flared. Every mirror shattered simultaneously, except one.

Behind the last pane was a room. A real room. It showed a hallway she hadn't entered yet. Not memory. Not fantasy. A way forward.

The mirror pulsed. An invitation.

She exhaled and stepped through the glass.

CHAPTER THIRTY

The pink and blue banner in the center of the high school gymnasium read, "Prom Night! May 21, 1994."

The bass was already shaking the floor under Loretta's heels as she stepped back from the dance circle, laughing. Her cheeks were damp with sweat, hair curling slightly from the heat, but she didn't care. She was breathless from joy.

The chandeliers were plastic. Everyone said so, but Loretta still thought they looked lovely, suspended from the rafters with silver fishing line that caught the colored lights just right. They spun slowly, a quiet imitation of class, like the night was trying its best. The students had originally voted for either a *Jurassic Park* or *Dazed and Confused* themed prom, but the faculty vetoed it in favor of a more traditional dance.

The gym had been transformed. Streamers of pale lilac and ice blue strung between basketball hoops, folding chairs hidden under satin covers. A rented fog machine hissed at the far end of the stage where a DJ, whose name no one remembered, spun records and occasionally glanced at a notepad scrawled with requests. "That's the Way Love Goes." "The Sign." "Mr. Jones." "Smells Like Teen Spirit." "End of the Road." "Linger." "Jeremy." "I'll Remember."

Loretta stood in the middle of it all, palms still warm from dancing. Her dress, eggplant velvet with sheer sleeves and a sweetheart neckline, clung a little too tight, but she liked it that way. It made her feel composed. Grown. Around her, friends laughed and yelled over the music, bright-eyed, sweat-slicked, still catching their breath from the last song.

"I love your haircut!" Kristen exclaimed. Loretta had gotten a pixie cut just like Winona Ryder's for the prom.

"Thanks!" Loretta said, still self-conscious about the change. "I love your dress!" Kristen wore a blue babydoll dress that she had purchased from Delia's at the mall.

Angela wore a white halter dress that shimmered when she moved, and Callie had gone full goth in black lace and combat boots, despite the heat. Donna's yellow dress looked like something out of a fairytale, and Frannie's high ponytail bounced when she turned.

Helen, elegant in silver, stood arm-in-arm with Bruce, who'd refused to wear a traditional outfit. Instead, he wore two-tone, matching black-and-white checkered Vans sneakers, suspenders, tie, and porkpie hat with

IT'S ALWAYS HALLOWEEN HERE

his suit.

Ionia's gown had a train that trailed after her like spilled wine. Judy and Marti shared a corsage. Phyllis and Suzanne matched in red sequins.

Virgilia twirled near the bleachers, her champagne dress catching glitter like cobwebs. She felt as beautiful as Sharon Stone, Demi Moore, Julia Roberts, and Meg Ryan combined.

Drew clutched a boxy VHS camcorder, narrating drunkenly as he filmed people mid-dance or stuffing their faces with cake. Reuben and Jerry laughed about something near the punch bowl, both of them red in the face, ties askew. Something about "wheezing the juice." Just for the night, they had traded in their flannel shirts, ripped jeans, and Doc Martens in favor of dark tuxedos and fluffy cummerbunds. Their original plan to dress in powder blue and bright orange tuxedos, like Harry and Lloyd from *Dumb and Dumber*, was shot down by Suzanne, who told her boyfriend Jerry that he would respect their special night or else.

"Finally" by CeCe Peniston thumped through the gymnasium, swallowed occasionally by feedback from the giant speakers. The rented lights blinked in jewel tones of fuchsia, green, and gold. The disco ball spun slowly overhead, casting dozens of broken reflections across the dance floor like glittering fish scales. A faint trail of fog clung to the floor, catching the light, making it all look dreamlike.

Callie ran past, screaming with laughter, dragging Suzanne by the hand. "They're playing our song!" she yelled, even though this was the third time she'd said it tonight.

Frannie and Donna clinked plastic punch cups near the folded bleachers, swaying together, singing every word of the song like they meant it. Frannie had sparkles on her eyelids that caught the light with every blink. Her lavender chiffon dress was slightly stained at the hem, and she didn't care. She looked radiant. Everyone did.

Angela spun in slow circles beneath the disco ball, head tilted back, her white halter dress blooming around her like a lily in motion. Bruce and Drew passed a cherry Tootsie Pop back and forth between them as they sang along with dramatic hand gestures.

"Show Me Love" by Robin S. hit next, and the crowd erupted. Loretta grinned. She knew all the lyrics. She wasn't thinking about tomorrow. She wasn't thinking about anything at all.

Virgilia's handmade champagne-colored gown shimmered with the movement of a thousand tiny beads. She shimmied past Loretta, barefoot already, her cheeks flushed, laughing wildly, eyes shining.

Callie grabbed Loretta's hand. "Dance party! To our future!"

Loretta let herself be pulled in. She threw her arms up. Their group formed a loose circle—Angela, Bruce, Callie, Donna, Drew, Frannie, Helen, Ionia, Jerry, Judy, Kristen, Marti, Phyllis, Reuben, Suzanne, and Virgilia—all of them yelling the chorus. Some had their eyes closed. Some didn't stop moving, not even between songs. The room felt like it would float away.

Loretta's chest swelled with a feeling she couldn't name. Something like joy. Something like love. Something like wanting to stay in this moment forever.

Jerry hugged Suzanne tightly to him. Keith Nemser, standing in the corner with Mitch Pechukas, waved shyly to Loretta.

Then the lights flickered. Just once. Barely noticeable.

The song ended too fast. The next track skipped, hissed, then resolved into "Dreamlover" by Mariah Carey. The crowd cooed in delight.

Loretta's heart had hiccupped. She looked up. The disco ball was turning slower now. The reflections on the walls smeared. Not spinning. Dripping, like light liquefied.

She blinked. The girls around her still danced. Judy was mouthing the words. Ionia was lip-syncing into a pretend microphone. Normal.

The lights flickered again. Longer this time. The colored beams went dull, then too bright, then off completely. The gym was thrown into a dim, washed-out yellow. Like a hallway at night. Like a grocery store before closing.

The music wavered. Mariah's voice deepened, slowed, warped.

"Dream...lover come rescue...meeeeee..."

A sharp, static snap. Silence. No one stopped dancing.

Loretta turned to Callie. Her mouth was still moving. Smiling. Moving. But there was no sound.

None. Not from her. Not from anyone. Like someone had hit mute on the world.

Loretta clutched her chest.

What is this?

The girls in the circle kept moving. Their movements no longer matched any rhythm. Marti's arms twitched at odd angles. Phyllis's neck turned slightly too far when she looked over her shoulder, like it wasn't built to stop at human limits.

Loretta backed away.

The fog on the floor had thickened. It wasn't white anymore. It had gone gray. Then darker. A greasy, thick mist that slithered between ankles.

IT'S ALWAYS HALLOWEEN HERE

She turned toward the punch table. The bowl was shattered. Liquid pooled in the center of the table, black and still, reflecting no light.

She heard something. Not music. Something else.

A *clicking*. From the ceiling.

She looked up. The disco ball had stopped completely.

Now something else was hanging from the ceiling. Long. Pale. Motionless. Limbs. Arms.

A cluster of them, in dozens, gripping the beams with bent fingers. Some were twitching.

She stumbled backward.

The wall behind her felt warm. Not wood. Not painted. Warm. Like flesh under fabric. It shifted beneath her palm, and something moved inside it. Something that pressed back, like an organ reacting to a touch.

She screamed. Or tried to. No sound came out.

The crowd was gone now. The gym was full, but not with her friends. Not anymore.

Their dresses were still there. Their suits. Their corsages. But the bodies were different. Elongated. Hollowed. Faces smooth, skin stitched with faint purple veins like worm trails. Their mouths hung open, but only as suggestion. Empty, shadowed spaces that didn't close.

One of them moved toward her.

Its hands were human. Its wrists still wore Suzanne's friendship bracelet. Loretta turned and ran.

The bleachers had rotted. Collapsed. Something squirmed in the debris. A long, blind thing. Wet and slapping.

She passed the DJ table. The DJ was still there, but no longer standing. Bent backward, legs folded under his torso like an insect. The record spun with no sound. A voice, his voice, came from underneath the table, gargling the chorus of "Stay (I Missed You)" by Lisa Loeb, in a crackled, broken timbre, as if he were drowning.

Loretta sprinted for the double doors. They were sealed shut. No handles. No exit. She turned. The lights strobed once, then failed entirely.

From the dark, a voice she didn't recognize whispered against her ear.

"It's still prom night, Loretta."

"You never left."

"You never will."

"You are home now."

"You won't remember this anymore."

"You're bait."

The music started again. But it wasn't any song she knew. Just low, pulsing static.

And the *clicking* from the ceiling. Growing louder. Closer. As if something had decided to come down. The lights flashed on and off, quick blinks illuminating her surroundings.

She was trapped inside a circle of wooden spikes. They had appeared before her, out of nowhere. On top of each spike were her friends' severed heads.

A bloodied man, pale and sickly, hurled himself at her. From out of nowhere, he appeared. His eyes had been gouged out, only black orbs where they used to be.

"I tore my own eyes out so they won't see me!" he shrieked in her face.

She screamed and closed her eyes, stumbling backward. Something in the air around her changed. Loretta's eyes snapped open. Darkness. Real, total, motionless.

She was lying flat, back pressed to something cold and damp. Her hands trembled before she even tried to lift them. Her mouth was dry. Metallic. The taste of old pennies and dust.

She sat up fast. Her head spun, like she was drunk. Shapes rushed toward her and then vanished. Phantoms of the gym lights, the sequins, the mirrors, all still blinking behind her eyes. The music was still there, but warped and distant. That wasn't real. That was in her head.

That's not real.

Loretta pressed her palms to her face. She could still see Suzanne's bracelet. Still hear the distorted voice singing the lyrics. Still feel the fog creeping up her legs. Still see Callie's mouth moving to a song that wasn't playing.

Something had torn through her mind and left pieces behind.

"Just an illusion," she whispered.

A click echoed in the room. Maybe a pipe, maybe nothing. She recoiled. Her hands felt raw. Scraped. She brought them to her face, and in the dark, smelled something sharp.

Soil?

She wasn't in the gym. She knew that now. Wherever she was, it was now. The present. Not 1994. Not prom night. Not the circle of her friends. They were gone. Or worse.

Loretta closed her eyes again. The music in her head started over, broken and slow:

This is the rhythm of the ni—

...the night...oh yeah...

She covered her ears, but it didn't stop. Loretta stood up, using the wall for leverage. Her knees felt weak.

She wasn't going to let the house fool her. She took a step forward, determined to find a way out.

CHAPTER THIRTY-ONE

The corridor ahead narrowed, suffocating in its symmetry. Dozens of doors and wardrobes.

Each one loomed against the walls like a waiting body bag, draped in linen sheets stained with time and shadows. The fabric sagged with the shape of what lay beneath. Some tall and thin, some squat and wide. All silent. All watching.

Judy's flashlight buzzed faintly, the beam jittering every time she moved her wrist. Beside her, Helen moved with rigid precision. Phyllis trailed behind them, dragging her hand across the wall as if trying to steady herself, though she looked less grounded with each step.

They had left the stairwell behind. But the thudding, distant as a heartbeat, still echoed somewhere below. The house had a pulse now. And it was growing stronger.

Judy stopped at a fork where the corridor split into two rows of wardrobes. "Left or right?" she asked.

Neither direction looked inviting. Both halls shimmered slightly, as though the air were bending under heat or pressure.

Phyllis tilted her head. "Do you hear that?"

Judy froze. A faint melody drifted through the air. Tinny. Sweet. A lullaby played on warped keys. It was coming from behind one of the wardrobes.

Judy raised her flashlight. One wardrobe, taller than the rest, breathed. The linen rose and fell ever so slightly. Rhythmic, as though exhaling sleep.

"No," Helen whispered. "We don't stop. We don't touch anything."

Phyllis stepped forward. Her face had gone pale, blank. Dreamlike. She was staring at the sheet.

"Wait," she murmured. "That's my room."

The wardrobe's door creaked open. The sheet slithered off and pooled onto the floor. Inside was not a closet. It was a perfect reconstruction of Phyllis' childhood bedroom.

Blue walls. Posters from teen magazines. A twin bed with bunny sheets. The corner desk, the stuffed animals on the shelf, even the broken lamp with its melted shade. Every detail was precise. And it was warm in there. Safe.

IT'S ALWAYS HALLOWEEN HERE

Phyllis took a step forward. Judy grabbed her arm.

"It's a trap."

"No, it's real. This is mine. That lamp. My dad broke that lamp when I was ten."

Helen moved forward. "Phyllis, don't."

Phyllis shook them both off and stepped inside. The door didn't close. Not right away. Judy stood at the threshold, frozen.

Inside, Phyllis walked across the room. She touched the blanket. Ran her hand along the desk. Smiled faintly.

"I haven't seen this since…" Her voice trailed off.

On the wall, framed and polished, was a photograph. Phyllis and her younger brother. His face had been blurred out. Literally smeared in the frame. As if scrubbed by fingers. His body remained, but the head was an unnatural whirl of motion and static.

Phyllis stared, her body overcome by panic. "I didn't forget him," she whispered. "I didn't. I—"

From under the bed, something crawled. It moved like a child. Fast. Jittery. Its arms were too long. Abnormally big hands. A soft toy rabbit dragged behind it, scraping against the wood. The thing lifted its head.

Where the face should've been was only a stitched X.

"You left me," it said.

Phyllis stumbled backward, knocking over a chair. The desk flipped. The walls groaned. Blue paint peeled away to reveal raw bone beneath the drywall.

"I tried to save you," she whispered, backing toward the door.

"You swam away."

The thing surged forward, crawling at unnatural angles. It reached for Phyllis with needle-thin fingers, pulling her into the wardrobe with it. Only blackness remained inside the wardrobe.

"Phyllis!" cried Judy. She slammed the wardrobe door shut and turned to Helen. "Help me brace it!"

Helen was staring down the hall. All the other wardrobes had begun to stir. One by one, the sheets slid off. Doors creaked open.

Inside each one, a different memory. Some Helen's. Some Judy's. Some they didn't recognize but felt anyway.

A flooded bathroom filled with floating photo albums.

A darkened trail in the forest with someone whispering, "They will forget you."

A childhood kitchen where the walls were caked in soot, bleeding oil and melted metal.

A funeral with no casket. Just a procession of robed mourners in a circle, like a black mass. Chanting in a language they didn't recognize.

Judy grabbed Helen by the shoulder. "We have to move."

"We have to get Phyllis!" said Helen. Judy nodded.

Behind them, the wardrobe Phyllis had entered slammed open. Phyllis emerged, eyes wild, lips trembling. She didn't speak.

She clutched the ragged stuffed rabbit to her chest, though it hadn't been hers since she was seven. Her knuckles were scratched. Her arms stained.

"I think I left part of myself in there," she said.

Judy and Helen wrapped their arms around Phyllis. They ran. The corridor twisted again. Angled walls. Moving doors. Somewhere behind them, the music box played on.

Every wardrobe they passed whispered their names.

CHAPTER THIRTY-TWO

The narrow crawlspace between the walls—the house's hollow veins, the whispered places no one should enter—pressed in around Loretta like a coffin. The wood was splintered and slick with dampness, the faint scent of mold and rot clinging to her skin. Every step sent a dull creak echoing through the tight space, like the house's slow heartbeat. The shadows pooled thick and heavy, pressing against her like unseen hands.

In the corner, where the darkness thickened to black velvet, a man sat with his back to her. His clothes hung in ragged tatters, stained with age and neglect, as if he'd been trapped here for decades. His hair clung to his scalp in greasy mats, dark and slick. His shoulders trembled with low, bitter sobs beneath the threadbare fabric of his shirt, as if the weight of countless years crushed him. His head never turned, fixed on the peeling wallpaper that bubbled and warped grotesquely, like the skin of something sick and alive.

His voice cracked like dry twigs as he muttered, barely audible at first. "There once was a man who tried to outsmart the house."

Loretta's throat tightened. She forced herself closer, the rough wood scraping her palms, the damp chill seeping into her bones. The walls seemed to listen, their silent breaths pressing in.

"He was clever," the man said, voice trembling with the memory, "but the house knows. It hears the silence, tastes the fear. It folds footsteps into the grain, twists fears like paper, presses them into the wood. His shadow stayed behind, stretching longer each night, whispering secrets no one should hear."

The rasp of his voice dipped into something colder, darker, as though the shadows themselves exhaled with him. "The house eats souls, Loretta. Feeds on them like a starving beast, gnawing away until only hunger remains. It traps them here, between the walls. Where time dissolves, hope withers, and nothing lives but fear."

Loretta's heart pounded, the tightness in her chest blossoming into raw panic. "How do I get out? What can I do?"

The man laughed, brittle and hollow, a sound like bones scraping stone. "The house chooses. It keeps what it wants. And what it doesn't? It erases. Like a cruel eraser wiping you from the world. No trace, no echo. No soul."

He shifted slightly, the scrape of fabric rough in the silence. "There are ways to escape."

Enough with this cryptic ghost shit. Tell me how to get the fuck out of here.

"First," he said, voice low and deliberate, "you must trick the house. A lie so deep, so tangled it believes it's real. You offer it a soul in place of your own. Something broken, hollow, false. The house will feast on that shadow, and you slip away, like a ghost slipping through a crack."

He paused, and the weight of his gaze felt like a blade against her back. "Second," his voice dropped to a whisper soaked in dread. "You surrender what makes you human. Your memories, your fears, your very name. Let the house peel them away, bite by bite, until there's nothing left but an empty shell. Then you belong to it forever. Neither alive nor dead. Just nothing. Lost in the walls. Forgotten."

Loretta's skin prickled. The walls pulsed, tightening, cold fingers of shadow unfurling toward her, eager to claim.

"The house waits," the man said, his voice a ragged breath. "Waits for you to break. And when you do, you never leave."

Tears welled in Loretta's eyes, burning hot and bitter. Despair gnawed at her resolve. Beneath the crushing weight of fear, a spark ignited. A fierce, desperate ember of fight.

She swallowed the lump in her throat, her voice barely a whisper, "How do I lie to it? How do I fool the house?"

The man shifted, then turned his head slightly. Enough for her to glimpse the hollowed, haunted eyes rimmed red and dull.

"You must give it a fragment of yourself," he said. "A piece broken beyond repair. Something so shattered it can never come back whole. The house loves broken things. They're easier to swallow, easier to forget."

He reached into his ragged shirt and pulled out a cracked, yellowed tooth. Small and jagged, as if torn from a mouth long dead.

"Offer it that," he said. "Give the house what it craves. A broken thing, a lie dressed as truth. But beware. If the fragment is too whole, too strong, it will devour you anyway."

I don't want your rotted tooth. She took it anyway. Loretta's hands shook, the cold damp biting through her skin. She realized then the terrifying gamble before her. To save herself and her friends, she had to sacrifice part of her soul. Give the house a lie so real, it might steal more than she intended.

The walls pressed in tighter, darkness closing. The house waited, hungry.

CHAPTER THIRTY-THREE

They didn't speak. Not at first. Not while the ballroom sat in breathless stillness, the chandeliers casting sharp, fractured reflections across their faces. Not while the mannequins in the final scene still loomed in the silence, red-lit and frozen mid-fade, as though just a moment ago, they had moved.

Whatever power or spell the man had controlled them with was lifting. Frannie, Ionia, Marti, Reuben, and Virgilia's faculties were slowly returning. Their senses flaring again, minds unclogged. They had no idea how much time had passed. How long had they been sitting in their seats?

Ionia's heart was thudding in her chest. She hated how loud it sounded. She hated how quiet everything else was.

Reuben was breathing through his nose like he was trying not to cry. He wasn't looking at anyone. His eyes were fixed on the statues in the alcoves along the walls. Had they turned?

"I don't want to die in this stupid costume," he said, peeling off pieces of his Halloween get-up. The others followed suit, as much as they could, stripping themselves of any cumbersome, clunky costuming.

"Why did I think this costume was a good idea?" Ionia huffed.

Marti finally whispered, "Was that real?"

No one answered. She knew if they answered, that meant they were accepting that it was.

"We're stuck here," said Ionia. "This house is a labyrinth."

The man—the host, the narrator, the thing—still stood before them. He hadn't moved an inch since the final scene. His gloved hands rested lightly on the back of one of the empty chairs.

Except the chairs were no longer empty. Marti noticed first. She gasped and stood abruptly, almost knocking hers over.

The seats behind them, eight now, were all occupied. Each one contained mannequins that looked like them.

Not the them of now, but versions of them. Some older. Some worn. Some with cracked porcelain skin and too-wide eyes. One wore Reuben's favorite Toad the Wet Sprocket T-shirt from high school. Another wore Virgilia's old prom dress, now torn and bloodstained.

Each one sat perfectly still, mimicking their posture. Legs crossed, hands folded, heads tilted slightly as if listening.

Virgilia's voice cracked. "Those weren't there before."

Ionia stood slowly. "They look like ghosts of us."

Reuben made a strangled sound in his throat. "No. No. This isn't happening. That was a show. A setup. A projection. We were drugged or hypnotized or, I don't know, part of some government experiment."

"Reuben," Virgilia interrupted gently. "You're bleeding."

He looked down. His knuckles were raw. Torn open. He didn't even remember clenching his fists.

The man stepped forward. He smiled, but there was no kindness in it. Just possession.

"You saw the truth," he said, voice calm and luxurious. "And now you understand what's required."

Ionia backed up toward the double doors. "They didn't open before," she said. "But maybe now."

The chandelier above them shivered. The doors groaned and then opened. Light spilled in. Warm. Real. Freedom.

Reuben didn't wait. He ran. Ionia shouted his name.

He was already halfway across the ballroom. He reached the doors. He touched the threshold and screamed. A squishy, tearing sound filled the room.

His skin peeled away from his back in long ribbons, like a paper doll soaked and torn. His body jerked back into the room as if pulled by a hook, landing with a sickening thud against the cold marble. He twitched once. Then lay still.

The doors shut. The light vanished. Reuben's breath came in shallow, bubbling gasps.

"Reuben!" The four women cried out for their friend. The shock hit them at once. They wanted to rush to him but stopped themselves when they saw.

The mannequins still seated in the chairs began to slowly, subtly, change position. One tilted its head more. Another curled its fingers around the armrest.

"What do we do?" Frannie said, trying to keep from screaming.

The man in the finery turned away. "Your seats are no longer yours," he said, voice like the brush of dry leaves. "They belong to your echoes. And they are quite impatient."

"Why us?" Marti asked. "We didn't do anything."

The man turned his head just slightly. "But you entered." A pause. "And you stayed."

IT'S ALWAYS HALLOWEEN HERE

The ballroom lights flickered. Once, then again. With each flicker, the mannequins' heads turned closer to the group.

Now they were all looking at Marti. She couldn't breathe. "I don't want to be here," she whispered.

"Then leave," the man said softly.

"But I saw what happened to Reuben."

"Ah." His voice turned wistful. "But he ran. He didn't understand."

The lights dimmed again.

Scene One lit up.

The figures were no longer wax.

They were flesh. Living, breathing. Eyes blinking. One of the girls turned to look down at them. Her lips parted, and her mouth moved, but no sound came out.

The plaque below the scene changed, letters shifting like sliding bones.

Scene One: The Visitors Take Their Place.

And suddenly there were more chairs. Dozens. A hundred. Stacked up in neat rows behind them. All empty. Waiting. All facing the center of the ballroom, where the five of them now stood like performers on a stage.

Ionia grabbed Virgilia's hand. "We're not going to let it win," she said fiercely.

Virgilia set her jaw. "Then what do we do?"

The chandelier above groaned again. Hairline cracks spread across the marble beneath their feet.

Marti looked at Reuben's motionless body, then at the doors. "No way out," she murmured.

Ionia took a deep breath. "Then we find a way through."

As she said it, she felt something listening. Observing. The mannequins in the chairs smiled. The ceiling began to lower. Inches at a time. Slow. Quiet. The room shrinking around them.

The performance had begun.

CHAPTER THIRTY-FOUR

Loretta stood in a narrow passage lined with cracked plaster walls, the air dry and metallic. Behind her, the shattered mirror pulsed faintly, like it was trying to repair itself. Ahead, only one direction remained.

Loretta moved forward, flashlight in hand. The beam flickered, but not from battery failure. The shadows were shifting ahead of the light, moving before she arrived, as if anticipating her presence.

A hallway stretched out impossibly long. Doors on either side, all closed. As she passed, she saw flickers of her reflection in the dusty doorknobs, each one slightly distorted. One smiled. One was crying. One held her breath like she'd drowned minutes ago.

A clock ticked above the last door at the end. Large, wooden, old. The kind from a train station. The hands spun backward, then stopped at 3:16 a.m. She didn't know why that time made her stomach drop.

At the exact same moment, Helen, Judy, and Phyllis were on the other side of the same wall where Loretta stood.

"This hallway is wrong," Judy said. "Did we get turned around?"

Helen was already checking her phone. "It's been twenty minutes since we left the stairwell, right?"

"More like five," Phyllis said.

Helen turned her screen to them. 2:23 a.m. Judy blinked. Her own watch said 3:16 a.m. They stared at each other.

"We lost an hour," said Judy.

"No. We didn't lose it." Phyllis' voice was thin. "It skipped."

The hallway around them rippled like heat on pavement. A door nearby stood ajar now, though they were sure it hadn't been before.

Inside, dim blue light flickered. Judy stepped in first.

The room was shaped like a hospital ward. Beds along the walls. But instead of patients, each bed held a TV set, the old boxy kind, glowing faintly.

IT'S ALWAYS HALLOWEEN HERE

One of them showed Loretta, walking down a corridor.

Another showed Kristen, crying in a room full of broken chairs.

A third showed Helen, curled in a fetal position, though Helen was watching from right behind Judy.

"That's me," she whispered. "But I haven't—I haven't done that."

"Not yet," Phyllis said.

A fourth TV flickered to life. It showed Judy, standing in the center of this room, watching the TVs.

"Shut it off," Judy said. "Shut them all off."

Loretta's phone blinked and buzzed. The time flicked back and forth. 12:35 a.m. 4:51 a.m. 3:54 a.m.

The hallway ended at a black door with no handle. Just a brass slot, like an old mail chute. A faded plaque hung above it.

YOU ARE ALREADY INSIDE.

She didn't know what that meant. She didn't want to. She reached forward and the door opened by itself.

Inside was a kitchen. Her family's kitchen. The smell of cinnamon. Bread. Her mother humming. Loretta stepped inside like someone stepping onto thin ice.

There stood her mother. Young, whole, smiling as she stirred something on the stove.

"Mom?" she said, voice cracking.

Her mother turned. Her eyes were blank white. With a sudden jerk, her neck snapped backward, cracking as though strings had pulled it too tight.

"I never left," the body whispered. "You did."

Loretta stumbled backward, hitting the table, which was covered in photographs, each one charred at the edges. One picture floated down and landed picture-side up.

It showed Kristen, standing in the kitchen doorway. Looking at Loretta. Mouth open. Behind Kristen stood a tall, dark figure. Eyeless. Biding its time.

As if hearing Judy's command, the television screens all turned off at once. Silence hit like thunder. Only the sound of clocks ticking echoing through the hall.

Judy turned to leave but the hallway outside was gone. Replaced by a different one. Wood-paneled. Flickering with red exit signs that didn't exist before. In the distance, a motionless figure stood.

Helen whispered, "Loretta?"

"No," Judy said. "That's not Loretta."

The figure stepped back and vanished into the wall, like slipping between pages in a book.

The soft ticking sound filled the room, becoming louder and more invasive. Several clocks ticking off-rhythm, all at the same time.

Helen looked around. "Where's that coming from?"

Judy pointed upward. A train station clock, just like Loretta's, hung from the ceiling. It now read 3:17 a.m.

Helen's voice shook. "That's impossible. Time doesn't move the same for us, does it?"

"No," said Phyllis. "And I don't think we're in the same place anymore."

Loretta stepped out of the kitchen. The hallway was gone. In its place was a circular room with five doors, each marked with a name.

Donna. Kristen. Bruce. Judy. Callie. All locked. Only one door pulsed with faint red light. Loretta stepped toward it. The doorknob felt electric.

She turned it. On the other side, she saw a hallway made of shifting mirrors. One mirror wasn't a reflection.

It showed Judy, staring back at her. They were looking at each other. Both froze. Loretta reached out.

IT'S ALWAYS HALLOWEEN HERE

The mirror shattered. Judy vanished.

Phyllis turned toward a table in the hallway, placing her hands on the wood. Her eyes rolled back in her head, turning off-white. Judy and Helen faced away from her, staring at the clocks.

The hands of the clocks began to spin, rapidly syncing with each other. 3:14 a.m.

"They always scream the same, no matter how different their faces," Phyllis said, her voice hushed. "The house teaches them."

Helen and Judy barely heard their friend. They were still not facing her.

"He kept knocking every night after I buried him." Phyllis' voice was still low, but had taken on a deeper, more distorted sound and cadence. "Louder, every night, like he's learning where the walls are."

"Phyllis?" Helen said.

"If you hear her crying, it's too late. That means she already took your mouth."

"What?" Helen's attention was diverted when Judy's foot hit something. She flinched. Flashlight down. It was a wristwatch, old and cracked, half-sunken into the carpet. Not hers. She picked it up.

The screen blinked, then glowed blue with a soft ping. T-02:00:00. Time Remaining: Unstable.

Behind her, Helen asked, "What is it?"

Judy didn't answer. She couldn't. The watch wasn't showing seconds. Instead, the last digit kept changing symbols. A spiral. A static icon. A crescent moon. Runes she didn't recognize.

It reset. T-01:59:59. Something was counting down. But to what?

The hallway lights above them flickered. Buzzed. Went red. The clocks read 3:55 a.m.

"She smiles just like my mother did," Phyllis whispered. "Only my mother is still rotting in the basement."

Phyllis' bones cracked and popped. Helen and Judy turned to look at Phyllis. Her skin had become discolored, with giant blue veins surging along her body.

Whatever dwelled in the house—the ghosts, spirits, demons, creatures, things—were inside of her, speaking to her in thousands of timbres and tones. Filling her mind with every horrible emotion and memory the house could dredge up.

"Phyllis!" Judy gasped.

"You're out of time," she said. "Your lives have been a waste."

The floor beneath them began to cave. The wood crackled and splintered, opening a hole in the ground. Helen slipped, falling partway into the abyss.

Judy lurched forward to catch her friend. Phyllis took a step toward them, her eyes on fire.

"Come on!" Judy cried, grabbing Helen's arms as tightly as she could.

"Judy! Please, Judy!" Helen sobbed.

Judy yanked Helen as hard as her strength allowed. Helen emerged from the hole.

At least, the top half of Helen did. She had been bisected at the waist. Her innards spilled on the floor. The smell was overpowering. Judy gagged and stumbled back, letting go of her friend's hands. What was left of Helen slumped lifelessly on the ground.

"Judy," Phyllis said.

Before Judy had the chance to run, Phyllis reached her hands up to her own face.

Judy watched, screaming, as Phyllis tore her own skin and muscle from her face. Down to the bone. Gristle, blood, and viscera sprayed forth. What remained was a mess of meaty chunks, fat, and exposed skull.

Judy ran. She kept looking behind her, checking to see if anyone, anything, was following.

A taunting voice rang out. "Run, Judy, run! See Judy run!"

She turned the corner and nearly ran into a wall of antique wardrobes. Huge, Victorian-style, ornate, too many of them crammed into the hallway like a maze. Dozens. More than should physically fit in the space.

Some were open. Some slightly ajar. Some sealed shut with chains. The air around her turned cold, tinged with lavender and mothballs. The smell of her grandmother's house. Judy felt her fingers go numb.

The nearest door swung open. Inside was a passage to a different room. Bright. White. Buzzing with fluorescent light.

Judy crawled inside the wardrobe. The door slammed shut. The clock on the wall ticked 3:16 a.m.

CHAPTER THIRTY-FIVE

The hallway was lined with six wardrobes, all towering, ancient things, heavy with dust and time. The kind of wardrobes that didn't just hold clothes. They held memories. Forgotten ones. Repressed ones.

Frannie hesitated. Ionia, Marti, and Virgilia were behind her.

They'd followed the winding corridor, hoping to get away from the ballroom, but now stood in a narrow hall, the air thick with mildew. Each wardrobe was different. Styles from different eras, carved from dark woods, inlaid with symbols none of them recognized.

Piles of junk, like a collection of people's possessions and belongings, lay scattered in the hallway. Electronic devices, backpacks, books, tools, shoes, clothing, and various items. Some modern, some antiquated.

Ionia paused at a pile between two of the wardrobes. She knew. The miscellaneous items were the remainders and remnants of what the house didn't eat. It took the people who owned them, but left their things.

"We shouldn't be here," Marti said.

"No," said Virgilia. "But we are."

Frannie shivered. "It feels like we stepped into an alternate dimension. Like some glitch in the matrix. I keep telling myself that none of this is right. But every exit isn't an exit."

"And poor Reuben," said Marti. She looked down. "Reuben."

"Please let this all be a nightmare we wake up from, safe in our beds," Ionia said.

"We're not dreaming," Virgilia said. "All we can do now is find the way out."

Ionia reached for the handle of the first wardrobe.

"Don't," Marti whispered.

"I have to know what this house wants us to see," said Ionia. She pulled. The door opened with a moan that echoed through the hallway like something ancient waking up.

At first, there was nothing inside but a long, velvet coat hanging from a crooked iron hook. It looked like it belonged to a child. Faded blue, moth-eaten, short sleeves.

A cold wind poured out. The coat lifted. There was no body inside. The coat twisted, flailing in the air like a puppet on invisible strings. Then it turned its head, if it had a head, and looked at Ionia.

It screamed. Not a child's scream. Not human. The other wardrobe doors rattled violently.

"Close it," Marti shrieked.

The coat launched itself from the wardrobe, knocking Ionia back. It flapped wildly in the air like a bird of prey, dragging icy air with it. She scrambled away, and the coat hit the floor and stood up.

Legs formed. Not bones, not flesh. Just shadow, wrapped in fabric, dragging itself forward.

It took a step. Then another, and another, until it collapsed into a puff of dust and thread.

Marti reached for Ionia. "Are you hurt?"

The second wardrobe opened on its own. This one was taller. Victorian. The inside was pitch black, like a pit that didn't end.

A hand reached out. Old. Wrinkled. Covered in filth. It gripped the doorframe and pulled.

A woman emerged. Bent. Dressed in rags that dragged on the floor, stitched with pieces of her own hair. Her mouth hung open in a silent scream. Her eyes were milky white but leaking black tears.

Marti's mouth dropped open. She whispered, "That's my mother."

"What?" Virgilia gasped.

"She died when I was thirteen. That's her. That's her nightgown. I buried her in it."

The thing tilted its head at Marti and whispered, "Why did you leave me in the tub?"

Marti fell to her knees, sobbing. "No, no, I didn't! I called the ambulance! I tried!"

The thing took a step toward her, dragging something behind it. A length of hose. Dripping, slimy.

The third wardrobe opened. Reuben walked out. Or rather, a version of Reuben. Hollow-eyed. Gray-skinned. Rope burns around his neck.

Virgilia backed away. "He's dead. He died!"

He opened his mouth. Virgilia's own voice came out. "I should have saved him."

The real Virgilia fell against the wall, shaking. "You're not Reuben."

The fake Reuben stepped forward, dragging a rope behind him like a tail.

The hallway lights began to flicker. The remaining wardrobes

IT'S ALWAYS HALLOWEEN HERE

shuddered violently.

"Close them," Ionia cried. "We have to close them!"

She rushed forward, trying to slam the second wardrobe shut, but the woman was blocking it. She was grinning now.

"Marti!" Ionia shouted. "Help me!"

Marti couldn't move. Her "mother" was kneeling in front of her now, stroking her face with cracked fingernails.

"Cold in the tub," she whispered. "So cold."

The fourth wardrobe burst open with a howl. Fire poured out. No heat. Just light, like the flicker of a house on fire. A silhouette stumbled forward, arms flailing, skin charred and blistered.

"Ionia," it rasped. "Save me!"

She stopped cold. It was her younger brother. The one who had died in the fire when they were kids. He reached for her. His skin peeled as he moved.

"You ran. You left me."

"No," she sobbed. "I tried! I got help!"

"You locked the door," he whispered. "You said it would keep me safe."

The fifth wardrobe opened, and all the lights went out. They were in total darkness. Only the sound of breathing. Sobbing. Shuffling feet. Hands touching wood.

"Stay close to me," Frannie said. "Put your hands on me." She felt the warm touch of Ionia, Marti, and Virgilia's hands. And a cold, slimy one, running down her back.

"This isn't real," Ionia said, shaking her head. "None of this is real. None of these things." She looked at Virgilia, an understanding and realization washing over them. A shock of clarity breaking through the façade. As if they'd just woken up.

"These are manufactured memories!" Virgilia said. "These aren't real. The house is putting it inside our heads. The house is using us, feeding off of us. It's prolonging our suffering. It's torturing us to feed off of our fear."

"Virgilia's right," said Frannie. "Marti, that's not your mother. Your mother is alive and well. Ionia, your brother never died in a fire. It's the house."

As if their realization angered the house, a loud crack reverberated through the room. Followed by laughter and voices. Low. Childlike. It didn't belong to any of them.

"It's not nice to tell lies."

"You'll pay for that."

A whisper, just behind Ionia's ear. "Now we're together again." She turned. Something grabbed her ankle. The moment she screamed, the lights jolted back to life.

Virgilia stood before them. Her body frozen. Covered in moss, leaves, twisting vines, and soil from the earth, vibrating and pulsating on her.

"Help me," she whispered weakly.

Her bones began to crack as she screamed out loud. As if invisible hands were ripping her open from the inside out. Her chest burst open, ribs splayed outward. Blood and bone fragments splattered in every direction.

"Virgilia! No!" Her friends cried out. There was nothing they could do.

A humanoid figure emerged from Virgilia's skin. Like it had been wearing her as its disguise. Her body convulsed as the thing writhed and contorted. Her skin slopped to the floor.

The walls sweated. Black moisture slid down from the ceiling beams like the place itself was rotting inside out.

The figure towered before them. Tall, still, head tilted as if listening to a frequency only it could hear. Its face wasn't blank. It was worse. It was a face trying to be one. Crooked features, misplaced and asymmetrical. Ionia stepped back.

It moved faster than it should. Frannie took the hit, thrown clean into the stone wall. She struggled to get back up.

Marti and Ionia frantically searched through the piles for anything they could use to defend themselves. Marti almost cried from relief when she discovered a rusty machete among the heaps. Ionia, beside her, wielded a vintage screwdriver.

She faced the thing, machete raised. It didn't dodge. It let her bury the blade in its shoulder. It grabbed her wrist, and she froze. Not from fear. She was rigid, like it had some sway over her, like her body forgot what muscles were. Her eyes bled. The figure leaned in, opening its mouth like it was about to speak.

Ionia tackled it from behind.

They went down hard. It didn't fight back with hands. It fought with presence. Its skin felt like open wounds and sandpaper. Its hiss was inside her ears, whispering in a voice that wasn't a voice at all.

She jammed the screwdriver into its throat.

It shrieked. Sound tore the room in half. Marti dropped to the floor,

IT'S ALWAYS HALLOWEEN HERE

gasping. The creature flailed, but not randomly. It learned. It mimicked the way Marti moved. Then Frannie.

It began to split. Two sets of limbs, then three. Copies. Imperfect. Fast.

Ionia screamed. "Kill it!"

Frannie saw it first. The root pit. A dusty grate next to one of the wardrobes, leading deeper into the house. She crawled to the grate and heaved it open. Below, a black shaft packed with tangled, clinging roots. Living, twisting in the darkness. Something moved down there. Feeding. Waiting.

Marti got to her knees. "Can we even get it in?"

"Yes," Ionia said. "We make it chase us."

They backed up toward the grate. The figures followed. Limbs scraping walls, heads twitching like diseased birds. The things couldn't resist mimicking motion.

Frannie dropped first, dragging one of the copies with her. It tried to pull back, but it was too late. The roots seized it.

Screams. Not Frannie's. The others turned, all three of them. Confused. Ionia and Marti stood at the mouth of the pit.

One of the remaining two things crawled up the wall and vanished into the wood.

"Marti!" Frannie said, throwing a chain from one of the piles. Marti caught it.

The third and final creature lunged and tripped as Marti looped the chain under its knees. Ionia shoved it forward with everything left in her body.

It fell into the pit. The roots welcomed it. Not like prey. Like kin.

The figure didn't scream again. It just stared as the roots climbed inside it, unmaking it cell by cell. Not eating. Absorbing. It reached toward them one last time, a hundred fingers trying to learn the shape of goodbye.

It was gone. Silence. Roots slithered back into the dark. The pit closed itself. Frannie slammed the grate closed.

No one spoke for a long time.

Marti whispered, "We didn't kill them."

Ionia nodded. "No. We fed them to something hungrier."

CHAPTER THIRTY-SIX

Kristen, Donna, Bruce, and Angela followed a stairwell to the top floor. They hadn't found Loretta, though they had searched. Unwilling to admit to the thought that the house may have taken her, they came to an old, wooden door. Donna pushed it open, revealing the inside.

Her light shone on the blood trail leading from the door to the windows. Windows that were nailed and boarded shut.

"We're at the top of the house," said Donna. "Nowhere else to go but down."

"What were they trying to keep out?" Kristen said, looking over the dozens of locks that lined the door. "Or in."

The attic was a wedge of shadow and warped geometry, the beams above bending at angles that could not belong to any house built by human hands. Slanted rafters dripped with threads of mold the color of old blood, and the smell clung heavy. Wet wood, rust, and something sweet-rotten, like fruit left in the sun for weeks. The air felt thick with grit, sticking to lips and tongue until every shallow swallow tasted faintly of old paper and mildew.

Piles of warped furniture hunched beneath dust-heavy sheets, their outlines like shrouded corpses awaiting identification. The sheets sagged and quivered with the slightest draftless movement. From somewhere in the dark corners, something scratched. Not the nervous skitter of a rodent, but the slow, deliberate drag of claws across wood, the sound reverberating through the floorboards and up their shins.

Angela's flashlight jittered in her grip, its cone of light slicing through the dark and skimming over a wall mottled with stains that seemed to pulse faintly, like a slow heartbeat. She could feel her own pulse matching it, quick and erratic. "There," she said, pointing to a hatch wedged between two beams. Her voice sounded smaller in here, eaten by the attic before it could settle.

Bruce was already moving, shoulders tight, shoving aside a heap of broken picture frames. Glass tinkled across the boards, sharp and bright against the muffled gloom. Each step made the floor flex in unsettling, uneven ways, like the boards were quietly shifting under their weight.

Kristen knelt, metal scraping against metal as she worked the rusty latch on the hatch, the sound high and grating enough to make her head ache. Donna stood guard, both hands clamped around the jagged remnant of a chair leg. Her palms were slick with sweat, the wood biting into them.

The wall beside Angela rippled. It was not a hole opening. It was not something breaking through. The wall became a shape, swelling forward like wax pushed by unseen fingers. The plaster bulged warm with a clammy humidity she could feel even from inches away.

A face emerged, skin the same blistered paint as the boards, lips splitting in a soundless moan that carried a damp, metallic tang. The eyes were not hollow. They were deep pools of shadow, yet they seemed to watch her.

Arms followed, not separate from the wall but grown from it, smeared with curling paint and splinters that trailed down their length like veins. The grinding sound of plaster straining filled the attic, dry and wet at once.

"Move!" Donna's voice cracked against the walls.

The wall-face lunged, the cold of it radiating like damp stone. Its torso peeled forward, ribs suggested in warped lath. Bruce swung a length of broken pipe into its head. The blow landed with a dull crunch, cracking the plaster skin and releasing a burst of pale dust.

The smell hit them instantly. Mildew laced with copper, and the dust clung sticky against the tongue, making them gag. It staggered back, but only enough to let more shapes swell and tear free from the boards around it, the sounds of their emergence like wood tearing and something soft being pulled apart.

The new ones were worse. One slid from the wall like wet clay being squeezed from a mold, its arms far too long, knuckles dragging splinters as it hunched low, teeth forming in its paint-pitted jaw.

Another pressed forward upside-down, its face where its chest should be. A mouth wider than its head, the inside lined with slats of broken lath instead of teeth. A third was nothing but a cluster of reaching arms, their elbows bent at backward angles, fingers peeling away the boards as if the wood were only skin.

Kristen got the hatch half-open before something cold and damp coiled around her ankle. She looked down to see a hand—paint-flaked, knuckles like bent nails—pulling itself from the floorboards as if the wood were only a shallow pool. The sensation was both solid and surreal, fingers sinking slightly into her skin without breaking it. She kicked, hard, heel crunching into brittle fingers that cracked like dry twigs, and wrenched herself free, her stomach twisting in revulsion.

Two more hands shot up near Donna's feet, wrapping around her calf. She drove the chair leg down in a vicious stab, splintering it through a wrist. The arm recoiled, but not before the skin of her leg burned where it had touched her, as if something had been left behind.

From above, one of the beams split open, shedding paint flakes and dust. A head pushed through. Upside-down, with no eyes, its mouth gaping wide enough to reveal a darkness that seemed to recede forever. It dropped onto Bruce, the weight of it shockingly heavy. Its plaster-flesh was hot, almost feverish, and it clawed at him with nails like jagged strips of roofing tin. He slammed it against a post again and again until its head burst, spraying a foul, glue-like paste that clung to his hands.

Donna drove her chair leg into the throat of another wall-thing. The impact jolted up her arms, and the wood splintered in her hands, but the thing shuddered, chunks of plaster crumbling from its face. A thick gray ooze seeped from the cracks, smelling faintly of ash and wet cement. It reached anyway, fingers scraping her forearm and leaving a tacky smear that made her skin crawl.

The attic shifted. Not only the light, but the proportions. Beams seemed to press closer together. The boards underfoot softened in places, as though the wood was warming and giving way. A wardrobe that had been across the room now leaned behind Angela, its doors yawning wide. The inside was not dark. It was pale and clammy, lined with hands reaching out in silent, beckoning gestures.

Angela hurled a rusted toolbox into the open wardrobe. The clang was deafening in the enclosed space, and the impact scattered its contents—wrenches, nails, hammers—across the warped boards. She grabbed the hammer, its handle slick with decades of oil and dust, and drove it into the skull of the nearest thing clawing free of the wall. The head split with a damp crack, spilling dust that clung to her cheeks like cobwebs.

Behind her, another shape erupted from the wall. A torso entirely covered in plaster blisters, each one swelling and popping to reveal staring eyes. Its gaze followed her no matter where she moved. Angela swung her flashlight hard into its face, the lens shattering, glass slicing across its skin. No blood, just the same damp powder, thick and choking.

They moved together, hacking, shoving, and kicking. Fighting not to win, but to keep from being pulled into the house itself. Every strike sent tremors through their arms, every shriek from the wall-forms cutting high and sharp in their ears. Each blow bought a moment. Each moment made the shapes angrier, faster.

Kristen finally got the hatch open and shouted to the group.

They surged toward it in a rush, the attic folding inward like a mouth. Behind them, the beings pressed forward, their limbs stretching after them, fingertips just grazing clothing as the group shoved and scrambled toward whatever lay beyond the hatch, whether it was safety or something far worse.

CHAPTER THIRTY-SEVEN

Donna awoke in her own bed. In her own house. The sense of familiarity, safety, and comfort washed over her like the sun shining through her window.

It was all a dream. A bad dream.

She heard her husband and son downstairs, in the kitchen, making pancakes and laughing. She felt the warmth of her comforter on her. She had never been so happy to see sunlight.

She checked her phone, looking over the happy messages from Loretta, Phyllis, Kristen, and her friends. Saying how much fun the night before had been. Thanking her for the nightcap of grilled cheese and *Beetlejuice*.

She changed into jeans and a comfy sweater. She headed downstairs to see her husband and son at the dining room table, eating and chatting.

"Hey!" her husband said. "You were out like a light. We didn't want to wake you."

"Late night, Mom?" her son said.

She kissed both of the men in her life and sat down for pancakes. "Just an informal reunion. It was good to see everyone." The relief she felt was indescribable. The nightmare had felt so real, so vivid.

"Mom?" her son said as Donna poured maple syrup over her pancakes. "Mom? Do you know what happens when we die?"

"What? You don't need to think about that. You're going to live a very long time."

"They take your soul to a dark place. Where there is no sound or light. Where you can't feel anything but pain and suffering."

The syrup began to turn from golden brown to a thick, black color. The brightness of the dining room faded into a sepia tone, like someone had turned down the colors in the room.

"What?" Donna looked at her son and husband. Their faces were ashen, cracked like porcelain. Like puzzle pieces.

"Mom," her son said, his voice warping like a slowed-down cassette. "They take you to a place your imagination has never even considered. You can't even dream it up, it's so horrible."

Her husband and son's bodies shattered like glass. Their pieces crashing to the floor. No blood. Like they were hollow shells. Donna screamed.

Her eyes shot open. The fear and terror rushed back in an instant. She was on the ground, face down, on the dirty floor of The Faulkner House.

A pale-faced, sickly, inhuman, emaciated creature was kneeling over her, its hand pressed on her back. Its mouth next to her ear, whispering horrific words to her.

"You pray to a god that doesn't exist. Not in here. He doesn't hear any of your cries for help. You pray to a god who won't answer. There is no hope."

"Donna!" Angela shouted, swinging a wooden board at the thing. It cracked across the creature's back, splintering. The creature spun toward Angela, shooting out its clawed hand.

Its hand went completely through Angela, palm filled with her blood and viscous gore as it burst from her back. Angela slumped over on the floor, dead.

Bruce and Kristen helped Donna to her feet, swatting makeshift weapons at the thing as it approached.

The wood-paneled room groaned beneath the pressure. Thick velvet drapes, wine-colored and heavy with dust, quivered along their rods. An upright pipe organ in the corner, yellowed keys half-pressed as if mid-song, tipped an inch forward. Sheet music fluttered across the parquet floor like wounded birds. The wallpaper was gold paisley under a patina of nicotine. A sepia photograph swayed within its frame, its image water-damaged beyond recognition.

Kristen stumbled back into a side table, knocking over a ceramic lamp shaped like a swan. It shattered, the bulb sparking once. Donna, near the fireplace, clenched a fireplace poker like a lifeline. Bruce, back against the bookshelf, kicked away the remains of a chair. Shredded stuffing, cracked wood, iron nails slick with red.

The thing screamed. It was already in pieces. Not dead. Never alive. But coming apart. Its form flickering, unstable, some parts solid, others a suggestion. Sockets where eyes might have belonged tracked them, even as its limbs lost shape. It reached.

The walls exploded above them. Not in flame. Not with smoke. But with movement. They burst wide open. Plaster crumbling, wood beams splintering. What came pouring out was not fire or dust.

Bodies. Hundreds.

They fell with wet thuds and dry snaps, tangled limbs in coats and dresses, sneakers and bonnets, denim jackets and suspenders. A cascade of humanity, their skin pale and soft, their faces slack with that unmistakable

IT'S ALWAYS HALLOWEEN HERE

stillness. A teenage girl in a Nirvana tee. A man in Civil War gray. A nurse in a blood-smeared smock. Children in school uniforms. A woman with curlers, dragging a half-melted iron.

They tumbled over one another, rolled down into heaps, and stacked the room high. Bruce yelled. Kristen backed into Donna. The creature was gone, drowned beneath a sea of the unmoving.

Then came the light. Not from a lamp. Not from outside.

It poured down from nowhere, colorless, brighter than bone-white, and for an instant it erased shadow, shape, thought. No one screamed. No one moved. The light held everything in place like an insect pinned through its thorax.

The light vanished as fast as it arrived. The walls were whole again. The bodies had disappeared. The room was restored, down to the way the drapes hung. The creature was no longer present.

Donna lowered the poker, blinking. Bruce looked down at his shirt, blood-streaked. Kristen turned, eyes wide, and pointed to the center of the room.

Someone stood there. Disoriented. Dazed. But alive.

"Judy?" Bruce stepped forward.

She nodded slowly, eyes adjusting to the space. "I was—I was somewhere else," she whispered. "And then I wasn't."

None of them spoke. Not yet. The silence wasn't peaceful. It was temporary.

CHAPTER THIRTY-EIGHT

Loretta followed the sound.

It started low. A faint metallic *clink*, like someone dragging chains across the floor. At first, she thought it was inside her head. The house had been playing tricks on her since the moment they arrived. But not now. The sound had a direction, an echo, a pull.

She moved carefully through the darkened corridor, leaving the wall of mirrors behind her. Her flashlight beam swept over rotted wallpaper and warped family portraits with faces peeled away by time. The hallway narrowed and angled sharply, the ceiling dipping, the walls pressing closer. Eventually, she had to hunch.

The sound grew louder. Chains. Breathing. Whispering. Her own name, maybe.

The floor changed to tile. White and cold underfoot. The walls turned to pale stone, slick with condensation. It felt like she was walking into a mausoleum or a hospital built underground. The air had a copper tang to it. Blood. Or maybe rust. Or both.

She turned a corner. And there he was.

Drew. Or at least something shaped like him.

He knelt in the center of a stone cell, bound to the floor with heavy black chains. Ankles. Wrists. Torso. Neck. Each link was carved with faint, glowing symbols that pulsed red.

He looked up. Loretta froze.

"Loretta," he said, quiet and hoarse. Like he'd swallowed glass.

It looked like Drew. Mostly. But thinner. Eyes too wide. Hair longer, matted. Skin pale, almost translucent in places, like candle wax stretched too far. His breath came in shallow, tremoring gasps.

She didn't move. "Is it really you?"

His jaw trembled. "Yes. Yes. I think so. I—I think I still am."

"You think?"

He closed his eyes, as if the question hurt. "I don't know what I am anymore."

Loretta stepped closer, heart pounding. The room pulsed around her. A low throb beneath her feet, as if the house had veins. The chains vibrated slightly with every beat.

IT'S ALWAYS HALLOWEEN HERE

There were dozens of long, stone slabs spaced around the darkened room. On top of each slab was a dirty white sheet. Beneath the sheets, the shape of bodies. Unbreathing and unmoving. At least, they looked like bodies.

"What happened to you?" she asked.

Drew looked up again, eyes glassy and dark. "I got separated from you guys and it took me. When you couldn't find me, the house didn't kill me. It kept me. Changed me. I think it needed me to open the door."

Loretta crouched, keeping her flashlight aimed at the floor. "What door?"

"To it." His voice dropped to a whisper. "To whatever came before the house. To the thing that dreams it."

Her mouth went dry. "And what is that?"

He paused, then began to cry. Soft, shaking sobs. Not performative. Not theatrical. Just broken.

"I didn't want to help it. But it forced me. I opened something. And now it's wearing parts of me. Talking like me. Looking like me. But I'm still here. Buried. It made copies. Walked in my skin."

Loretta backed away a step. "Wait. You mean what we saw in the mirror, that wasn't you?"

"No." He looked up again. "And if it knows you're talking to me, it'll come for you next."

Behind him, on the far wall, a mirror shimmered. Dark glass framed in old iron. Something shifted behind it.

She squinted. The reflection showed her, but not in this room. It showed her in the hallway, talking to Drew. Except in the reflection, he was standing. Smiling. Unchained.

Loretta's stomach dropped. "Is that real?" she asked.

"No," Drew whispered. "But it might become real. If you trust the wrong one."

The real Drew slumped forward, exhausted. "I don't know how long I've been here. The others. Are they alive?"

"I don't know," she said truthfully.

He nodded slowly. "Then we don't have much time."

Loretta stared at the chains. The red symbols were beginning to dim, flickering like dying coals.

"I can try to free you," she said.

Drew flinched. "No," he said quickly. "Not yet. Not all at once. The

129

chains don't just bind me. They contain the thing it left behind."

"What thing?"

He looked her in the eyes. "You'll know it when it speaks to you in my voice and smiles like it loves you."

The air in the room dropped ten degrees. The lights flickered. The mirror darkened completely.

From somewhere in the house, a second voice. Identical. Warm. Friendly. Drew's voice.

"Loretta?" it called. "Are you in there?"

Loretta turned toward the door. Her hands shook.

Behind her, the real Drew whispered, "Don't trust him."

CHAPTER THIRTY-NINE

Loretta stood motionless. The voice came again, smooth and close now. "Loretta?" It rounded the corner.

Drew. But not the one in chains. The fake Drew.

This one walked upright. Perfect posture, rigid and unflinching. His clothes were dry, clean, unwrinkled. His hands hung at his sides, loose and gangly. His fingers bent slightly inward, like they were unsure how to behave.

His face was the worst part. A replica only from a distance. Up close, it was an imitation carved from memory and meat. The smile stretched unnaturally, peeling the skin at the corners of his mouth into thin, pink tears. His cheeks were tight, as though pulled inward by thread. His nose had a tremor, a subtle ticking motion, like something underneath was trying to push its way out.

His eyes were glass marbles floating in wet sockets. Off-center. Misaligned, shiny, still.

He spoke again, slower this time. "I was hoping it would be you."

Behind her, the Drew in chains rasped. "Don't let it talk."

Loretta didn't move. The standing Drew took a step forward. The floor creaked under him in a way that made her stomach flip, like his weight was wrong. Somehow light like air yet perfectly distributed. As if what moved inside him wasn't built for walking.

"You've seen things," he said. "I can see it in your face. You know how deep this place goes. How long it's waited."

Loretta backed against the wall. Her fingers brushed a jagged tile piece jutting from the wall. Cold. Sharp. Solid.

"I know what you are," she said.

The grin widened. The lips split further, almost to the cheeks. "Then you know what comes next."

"I don't think you do," she said.

It tilted its head, too far, until a tendon popped. A faint, wet *crack*.

"Don't be like the others," it said. "They screamed. You won't have to."

"I'm not screaming," she whispered.

The Drew clone, the thing, bent closer to her. His whole body tilted at an odd, unnatural angle. He whispered in her ear, but no breath escaped his soulless body.

"I remember being born yesterday, but my shoes were already wet."

"The doorknob told me your name, but it screamed when I asked again."

"My knees bend the wrong way when no one looks, just like the bird in the drawer showed me."

"I buried the sky under the floorboards so the ceiling could stop watching."

The thing lunged. Loretta moved faster. She grabbed the loose tile piece and stabbed.

The tile shard drove up beneath the Drew double's chin, through soft tissue, crunching into the base of the skull with a squelch that vibrated up her arms. It made no sound. Just shuddered once, like something flicked the spine of a hollow doll.

Its hands grabbed at her. Cold. Slick. The skin on its fingers sloughed off against her jacket. Wet, glovelike peels of flesh sliding to the floor.

Loretta yanked the tile free and struck again. This time across the jaw. A strip of cheek came loose. Something pale and stringy bulged from the tear.

It staggered back, gurgling, then began to change. The skin twitched. Buckled. Popped. The face split, not down the middle but from the temples, tearing open like overripe fruit. A second face pulsed beneath the first. Raw, faceless muscle trembling in the open air.

Through gurgled rasps, Drew's double spoke as he teetered, unable to regain the same posture as he had moments earlier.

"The shadows crawl out from under my skin and whisper secrets I can't forget."

"I swallow the night whole, but it scratches its way back up my throat."

"Sometimes my skin blinks before my eyes and peels itself away like forgotten paper."

"They told me to sleep, but the darkness keeps folding itself inside my eyes."

Its hands snapped backward at the wrists with a crunch of bone, then reformed. Longer, thinner, new fingers uncoiling from within the forearms like spider legs unfolding from a husk.

Loretta didn't wait. She grabbed one of the black chains anchored to the floor, and ripped. The symbols on the links pulsed red-hot, searing her

IT'S ALWAYS HALLOWEEN HERE

palms, but she didn't stop. She looped the chain around its neck and pulled.

It thrashed, clawing at its own throat, tearing off the false skin in strips. The mouth stretched wider, then split completely down the center. Inside was no tongue. No throat. Just a hole. Dark. Slick. Endless.

It convulsed. It howled without breath. A tremor rolled through the walls. Loretta pulled harder.

The skin boiled away. Muscles peeled back. Beneath all of it was something thin. Black as rotted wood, with long limbs that bent in the wrong directions. Its bones tried to escape its own body, snapping outward under the force of the chain.

It collapsed. Shivering, twitching, clawing at nothing. Then it went still. Not limp. Empty.

The flesh deflated. Cracked. And fell apart in crumbling, ashen flakes. Nothing remained. Not even heat.

Loretta stood over the scattered fragments, breath shuddering. Her hands were burned raw. Blood mixed with chain soot, dripping from her fingers in slow lines.

Behind her, the real Drew spoke. "You killed it."

She turned to look at him. He didn't meet her eyes.

"You don't understand," he said. "That was the easy one."

Loretta frowned. "What?"

He finally looked up. "The first copy is always crude. Too much guesswork. But it learns. Every time it fails, it sheds. It watches. Next one won't walk like a puppet. Next one might not smile at all."

A low sound vibrated through the floor. Not a noise. A presence. Like something enormous had shifted its weight far below the house.

Loretta stepped back from the chain. "Then what do we do?"

Drew closed his eyes. "You don't run."

"Why not?"

At once, like a horrific, synchronized ballet, each body on the slabs sat straight up. Their faces covered beneath the dirty white sheets. They rose, surrounding Loretta and Drew.

Loretta wasn't fast enough to stop what was coming. The things beneath the sheets ripped at Drew, tearing at his skin. Slashing, clawing at his body. Shredding Drew to mangled, mutilated pieces. Flinging Drew's flesh, limbs, and innards in every direction.

Loretta choked back her scream and ran away. Drew's screams rang in her ears.

CHAPTER FORTY

Loretta stepped through the narrow doorway and found herself in a room that looked as if it had been sealed away for a century. The wallpaper was a faded damask of deep burgundy, peeling at the seams in thin curls. An ornate clock on the mantel ticked in an unhurried, almost arrogant rhythm, its brass pendulum swaying in the half-light. Heavy drapes hung over tall windows, shutting out the world. A table at the center was set for tea, the porcelain painted with tiny roses, the cups rimmed with hairline cracks. The smell of dry wood and wax polish clung to everything. She felt as though she had stepped into a photograph that someone had forgotten to put away.

Then the lights went out.

The dark was sudden and complete, as though the room had been swallowed whole. Loretta's pulse quickened, the sound of it seeming to fill the space. She reached a hand forward and her fingers brushed a chair's carved arm. Smooth, cold, and slightly sticky with age. Somewhere in the blackness, the clock kept ticking, slow and deliberate. The silence around it seemed foreboding, ominous.

A harsh click. The lights flared again.

They were there.

Dozens of them. Men and women in clothing from another century. High collars and brocade jackets, long skirts and gloves the color of bone. Their faces were pale, their mouths slack but their eyes fixed directly on her. Not one of them moved. They stood as though they had always been there, placed exactly so, a human arrangement.

Loretta's throat tightened. She took a single step toward the far wall, keeping her gaze steady on the space between two women in matching feathered hats. The room felt narrower now, their bodies crowding it. Her shoulder brushed the sleeve of a man's frock coat, and she flinched at the faint rasp of fabric against her skin.

She moved carefully, her shoes clicking against the wood floor. Each step felt louder than the last. Out of the corner of her eye, the tilt of a head. Subtle, almost imagined. Another step. Fingers shifted at someone's side. A skirt's hem swayed.

They were following her without walking.

A man near the corner was suddenly closer, his shadow stretching in a way that did not match the light. A woman's gloved hand hung lower than it had a moment ago, as if reaching. Loretta threaded herself between them, heart hammering, keeping her movements small, deliberate. The exit was ahead, only a few more steps.

Behind her, the ticking clock faltered. Somewhere deep in the crowd, someone smiled.

Loretta hurried to the next doorway.

CHAPTER FORTY-ONE

Donna pressed her ear to the door, listening. Nothing.

No footsteps. No voices. Just the low groan of the old house shifting against time. She turned to Bruce, Judy, and Kristen, their faces lit only by the flickering oil lamp they'd found in the attic. The electrical lights had failed hours ago. Or maybe the house had simply taken them.

"I think we're alone now," she whispered.

Judy stood stiff near the window, watching the black yard beyond. "We're never alone in this place."

Bruce surveyed the walls. Bloody handprints dotted every inch of the wallpaper. He thought about his dog and cat at home, how much he wanted to get back to them. Who would feed and love them if he didn't escape this hell house?

Kristen sat in the armchair by the dead fireplace, rubbing her arms like she could shake the cold from her bones. "Something's changed. I feel it. They're coming."

"They?" Donna asked. Kristen didn't answer. The air suddenly turned silent. Not just quiet, but suffocatingly empty, like the house itself stopped all noise.

From the hallway outside came the first sound. A dragging noise. Heavy. Wet. Inhuman.

Another sound. Softer. A clicking. Like fingernails tapping along the walls. No rhythm. Just chaos.

Judy turned from the window. "We need to hide."

The door handle rattled. They all froze. Then, silence again. Kristen began backing toward the far side of the room, her eyes wide, mouth open. "We're too late."

The door slowly creaked open, but there was nothing there. At first. The shadows deepened.

They came. But not like anything they'd imagined.

The first thing crawled in on all fours, its joints bent the wrong way, long black hair clinging to its skeletal face like seaweed. Its mouth hung open in a drooping gape, unhinged like a snake, a tongue dragging across the floor. No eyes. Only two deep pits filled with writhing insects. It hissed as it moved, head jerking with every inch forward, bones snapping with each motion.

IT'S ALWAYS HALLOWEEN HERE

Kristen screamed and backed into the wall, tears streaking down her cheeks.

The second figure floated into the room like a ghost in a movie. Not walking, not flying, but suspended like a corpse underwater. A woman in a wedding dress, but the gown was wet, clinging to her skin, soaked in a spreading, dark stain. Her veil fluttered unnaturally, as if moved by an unseen current. Her mouth was stitched shut with wire, but her eyes burned with a grief so raw it seemed to peel the paint from the walls around her.

She drifted towards Judy. With every inch closer, the air grew damper, the scent of rot and algae clinging to their skin.

"I don't want to see this," Judy said, covering her eyes. It didn't help. When she opened them, the bride was upon her and inside her all at once.

She gasped and doubled over, vision splitting. She was no longer in the room but beneath water, sinking. Her lungs burned. Hands pulled at her dress, holding her down. Her screams bubbled uselessly into the void.

Across the room, a face, pressing against the wallpaper. Not just pressing. Stretching it, like flesh. Eyeless. Mouth moving, whispering things only she could hear. The wall split open like skin under pressure.

The child came out. A boy, barely seven. Head tilted unnaturally to the side, bones cracked. His eyes were sewn shut. Blood leaked from the stitches like tears. He held a spinning top in one hand and dragged a meat cleaver in the other. It left black scratches across the wooden floor.

He looked up at Donna and said, in a dry, rattling voice, "Where is my mommy?"

Donna shook her head, muttering, "No, no, no, no—"

The boy lunged, and Donna stumbled back, falling into the fireplace. Soot exploded around her. Hands reached from the ash. Dozens of fingers, burnt, bony, grasping. They clawed at her sleeves, her hair, her throat.

Donna scrambled to her feet and tried to run for the hallway. The first ghost, the crawling one, was already there, now standing. It towered over her, long limbs dragging on the floor, mouth unhinged and dripping something black and foul. Its tongue writhed like a parasite. It whispered:

"You were always going to stay." It bent backward in a grotesque arc, its body cracking with each unnatural movement, and screamed. The sound shattered the oil lamp, plunging the room into darkness.

In the dark, the walls began to bleed. The windows fogged over, runes etched from the inside. The ghosts gathered in a circle, waiting.

Donna searched for a weapon as the child pressed its face to hers. Kristen screamed as the crawler wrapped its limbs around her like a shroud. Bruce felt several hands envelope him, holding him down,

137

pressing against him.

Judy lay still, still trapped in the drowning bride's memory, her lips moving silently underwater.

The floorboards trembled beneath their feet, not with the casual groan of old wood, but with a shivering tension, like the house itself was trying to recoil from something rising deep within its bones.

Out of nowhere, a blaring, metallic howl tore through the walls. It wasn't just a noise. It was a laceration in the fabric of the air itself, a shriek so jagged and merciless it seemed to strip the skin from the world. It sounded like rusted steel being dragged across shattered glass, like air-raid sirens screaming through meat grinders, howling with a grief that felt ancient and furious.

Lightbulbs burst, showering the room in flickers of sparks and broken filaments. Paint blistered and peeled from the walls in sheets. The very skeleton of the house groaned. A low, tortured moan like timbers were being twisted, bones cracked by invisible hands clawing at the architecture of reality.

The entities—those long-limbed, twitching silhouettes that had lingered in corners like stains—jerked violently, as though caught in barbed wire yanked by some unseen force. They disintegrated. Not into smoke, not into air, but into splinters of shadow, shards of darkness whipped upward in tight spirals, vanishing through the ceiling like ash sucked into a reverse cyclone.

And then, nothing. No sound. No creak. No breath. Not even the soft hush of silence.

It was a void, an anti-sound that pressed against their ears with the density of drowning. It swallowed everything, even the notion of noise. Thoughts seemed to bend inward, muffled by the weight of that oppressive stillness.

The silence wasn't empty. It throbbed, a deep, suffocating pressure that made their hearts feel like they were beating out of time with the world.

They stood frozen.

The house had become a tomb, a mausoleum of warped geometry and still air. Wallpaper curled from the walls like the desiccated skin of something long-dead. A wooden chair sagged sideways, its legs bent at unnatural angles, as if it had melted under unseen eyes. Time itself felt misaligned. Stretched, thick like syrup, but their hearts pounded far too fast, too violently, in defiance of the slowness.

They couldn't speak.

IT'S ALWAYS HALLOWEEN HERE

Even their mouths felt sealed shut, not by fear alone, but by a deeper, more primal warning, that to utter a word might break something fragile and impossibly old.

Then, a scrape. Not loud. No. Barely a whisper against the silence. But real.

Donna turned. Her gaze locked onto a section of wall near the fireplace. Shimmering and vaguely distorted, like oil on water or heat rippling off metal. She stepped forward, trembling, reaching out with one unsteady hand.

The wallpaper was soft. Almost like skin. Her fingers sank into it like pressing into damp flesh, and then slipped through.

A hidden seam. Her hands shook as she gripped it and pulled.

The hatch peeled away from the wall like a scab from a wound. The opening beneath it exhaled a breathless darkness, pulsing faintly, like the echo of a reversed heartbeat, like something alive was watching from just beyond the veil. A tunnel stretched before her, narrow and glistening, its walls slick, its air warm and strange, and breathing.

She didn't speak. She couldn't.

She turned once, just once, to glance back at the others, frozen like statues in the overpowering silence. She screamed for them, but no sound came out of her mouth.

Her friends were like zombies. In a trance, their eyes milky white. Like their minds were in another world, an alternate universe, a completely different atmosphere.

She didn't know what to do. She shook them, but none of them snapped out of their trance. With a cry that couldn't be heard, she slipped inside the opening and crawled into the dark.

From the darkness, she screamed for Bruce, Judy, and Kristen, but she had no voice. No sound traveled. Her friends began to retain some semblance of realization. One by one, they turned to the hatch Donna had found. Saw her beckoning to them.

Regaining their senses, her friends locked arms and rushed to her. She pulled each one of them inside with her, thankful none of them were alone.

CHAPTER FORTY-TWO

Loretta awoke with a jolt, face pressed to cold marble, fingers twitching in her sleep. Her breath formed clouds in the air. *When had it gotten so cold?* She sat up slowly, every bone aching, every nerve lit with tension.

Around her stretched the ruins of what had once been a study. Its wood-paneled walls cracked like spiderwebs, the books melted into each other on the shelves like wax, as if they'd tried to flee the house's knowledge.

The chandelier above flickered erratically, as if disturbed by wind, though there were no windows. She had no idea how she'd ended up here. The last thing she remembered was following that sound. A song, sung in reverse, echoing down the long gallery, then darkness. Or was that a memory the house gave to her?

She stood. A low hum, like a heartbeat beneath the floorboards, began to throb in time with her own pulse.

She turned. The mirror above the crumbling fireplace was no longer reflecting the room.

It showed her, yes; but behind her, the walls were different. Clean. New. And something, someone, stood in the doorway behind her, just out of frame.

A woman in a mourning dress. Veil down. Silent.

Loretta spun. No one. The mirror version of herself remained, still staring into the glass. Frozen, as the woman behind her crept closer.

Loretta stepped back. The mirror cracked. From beneath the broken glass, paper spilled out. Pages. A map.

Written in frantic ink, the lines quivered like they had been drawn mid-seizure. Hallways that weren't part of the visible house. Hidden rooms. Dead-end corridors. Ghost doors.

In the center was a symbol carved in looping, ancient script. She didn't recognize it, but her body did. Her chest began to ache.

She pulled down her shirt collar, revealing the same symbol burned into her skin, right over her sternum. It pulsed faintly, like an infected wound.

Scrawled on the bottom of the map were the words, "To leave, one must unmake the rooms that made you."

IT'S ALWAYS HALLOWEEN HERE

Her hands trembled. "Unmake the rooms?"

The walls around her shuddered. The ceiling split. A voice, not a human one, whispered low in her left ear. "Every memory leaves a door. Every trauma, a lock."

Loretta followed the map through a narrow, hidden passage in the wall behind the fireplace. The air grew thicker as she walked, heavy with mold and whispers. The wallpaper peeled back like flesh. The light dimmed.

She entered a hallway lined with closed doors. Each had a name scratched into the wood.

One read, "Angela." Another, "Ionia." A third, "Reuben." She walked until she found her own. "Loretta."

The door was bleeding. Thick black ichor dripped from the keyhole. She braced herself and pushed the door open.

Inside was a hospital hallway. A mental hospital, for the worst offenders. The violent and dangerous.

White tile. Flickering fluorescents. The smell of antiseptic and something worse. Fear. Down the hall stood a girl.

Herself, at nine years old. Screaming. Crying. Doctors restrained her. Her father wept silently at the far end of the hall, unable to come closer. He was fitted with a dirty straitjacket.

Loretta clutched the doorframe, breath gone. That was the day. The thing she had buried. Her father's admission to The Calista Asylum for the Criminally Insane in Neve, Maine. Her family's shame.

Her father's breakdown. When he started "seeing" things. No one had believed Loretta when she told them something was wrong with Dad. No one had listened when she questioned why her father kept the basement locked.

It was her greatest fear. That whatever madness her father had would be passed down to her.

A nurse walked past her. She had no face. Just a mirror. In the mirror, Loretta saw something else behind her. A figure draped in chains, dragging itself across the floor.

It locked eyes with her. Not angry. Begging.

The scene shattered.

Loretta stumbled back into the hallway of doors, gasping, trembling. She understood. The rooms weren't rooms. They were memories locked away.

She had to face each memory, each pain the house had latched onto,

141

and "unmake" it. To break the house's grip on her.

And maybe, just maybe, she could do the same for the others. As she turned to find the next door, she saw it.

Something was following her. A figure wrapped in funeral veils, dragging a hand that ended in rusted keys, thousands of them, rattling like bones.

Its face changed every second. Donna. Kristen. Helen. Judy.

It was them. Twisted. Possessed. Calling her name from mouths full of static.

The figure cloaked in veils dragged itself down the corridor, keys jingling in rhythm with her heartbeat. Its body barely moved, but it grew closer, the air thickening with a reek of rusted metal and forgotten tears.

Loretta ran. The map in her hand twisted. Ink bleeding into new paths, hallways folding like origami around her. She passed doors with unfamiliar names. "Bridget." "Desmond." "Mother." They pulsed faintly as she ran past, as if aware of her.

The house wanted her to open them. To look. To remember. To break.

She slid around a corner and into a different corridor. One where the wallpaper had peeled to the bones of the house itself. Support beams like ribs, floors groaning like strained cartilage beneath her steps. At the end stood another mirror, but this one wasn't cracked.

It was waiting. In it, she saw a different version of herself. Not younger.

Older. Frail. Skin paper-thin and pale. Sitting on the floor of a locked room, whispering to herself, rocking, as hundreds of tiny black insects swarmed over her bare arms and face.

Loretta reached for the mirror. The glass turned to liquid.

A voice came from inside. "You saw what they wouldn't. You opened the wrong door. That's why the house chose you."

She pulled away. Behind her, the figure of veils had caught up. It stood inches away.

Loretta gasped as a decrepit hand, trembling with urgency, emerged from beneath its shroud. The figure didn't speak.

She didn't wait. Loretta dashed from the room, not looking back.

CHAPTER FORTY-THREE

Frannie, Ionia, and Marti had descended to the lowest level of the house. The basement door had sealed shut behind them with a thunderclap. What had once been servant quarters, now warped into something labyrinthine and diseased.

The narrow stairwell was damp, its stones slick with green-black moss. With every step, the air grew colder and heavier. A dripping sound echoed from below, though no one could find the source.

"Are you okay?" Marti said.

"I think I might have cracked a rib or two," said Frannie. "I'll live."

"We're all going to live," said Marti. "We're getting out of this godforsaken house and having waffles at the diner again."

"Do you think everybody else is okay?" said Ionia.

"I hope so," Frannie said.

"You know, I survived two alcoholic parents who told me I was worthless and would never amount to anything," said Ionia. "I made a good career for myself and raised awesome kids. I fought hard for everything I have. I survived a nasty divorce, health scares, the economy, and lecherous bosses to make something of myself. And now we're going to die in this house."

"No, we're not," Frannie said. "We're not."

"Maybe crazy, old Mrs. Tipton was right about Halloween," Ionia said, with a humorless chuckle.

"I used to worry about getting older," said Marti. "The gray hairs, the wrinkles, the new aches and pains I discovered every day. Now we might not have the chance to get old. I just wanted to have one night where I felt young again."

"Is this karma for all the bad things we've done? Like leaving bags of flaming dog shit on people's porches on Halloween?" said Ionia.

Frannie, Ionia, and Marti burst out laughing. A release. They held each other's hands.

The trio paused. Frannie read a plaque on the wall. "The Feeding Room."

Inside was a nursery. Dust hung in the air like ash. Cradles lined the walls, each gently rocking, though no wind stirred.

Above them, the ceiling sagged like something moved just above the plaster. From the walls hung portraits of infants, but each painting was surreal. The babies' eyes were abnormally large and knowing, their mouths curled into gnarled smirks. And all of them were painted with mouths open, as though they were screaming, but the sound had been stolen.

The rocking stopped. Marti approached a cradle. Inside lay a bundle of rags. No baby.

The moment she touched it, the rags latched on, thin strips wrapping around her wrists like snakes. She screamed, falling backward, and the cradle levitated slightly, as if something inside it had woken.

The ceiling cracked. A long, skeletal hand punched through, fingers like spider legs. It began to pull itself down.

"Run!" Ionia yelled, grabbing Marti and yanking her out.

Frannie sprinted ahead. The hallway shifted. Walls extending, doors elongating, as if the house didn't want to let them escape.

Behind them came the cradle-creature, now fully emerged. Its form a coagulation of many limbs, crawling atop one another in a nightmarish tower. Its face was a blank porcelain mask, split down the middle, revealing a red void.

It let out a horrible gurgling shriek, and the hallway tilted downward, turning into a slope.

The group slid, screaming, as the creature pursued on the walls and ceiling.

They crashed through a rusted metal door at the bottom and tumbled into a chamber lit by a sickly green glow.

In the center of the room was a pedestal. Upon it, a glass sphere.

Inside it was a miniature model of the Faulkner House. Within the model, tiny moving figures. One of them was Loretta.

"She's in there," Ionia whispered.

Frannie nodded. "We all are."

Around the pedestal, symbols etched into the stone pulsed in rhythm with their heartbeats. They stepped closer and saw words written in reverse: "Abandon all hope."

Marti looked up and saw that each of their shadows had begun to twist on the walls, becoming distorted reflections of themselves. They were moving independently.

"There has to be a way out," Marti said.

Behind them, something was climbing down the walls. A creature shaped like a man, but with no skin, only sinew and pulsing veins. Its eyes were clusters of black splotches and blots. It grinned, extending its arms, its voice a wet, gurgling whisper.

"Your story ends here. Unless you rewrite it."

CHAPTER FORTY-FOUR

Loretta sprinted through the narrowing hallways, the walls seeming to swell and pulse, like veins fed by some hidden, malevolent heart. Her breath tore through her lungs, but she kept running.

Behind her, it was coming. She didn't dare look.

The map had folded back into silence. No more shifting corridors. No more twisted ink paths. The house wanted her still. Waiting. Loretta had seen too much. She knew the rules weren't as fixed as they seemed.

She skidded into a corridor lined with oil paintings. Every canvas bore faceless versions of herself, posed in violent or submissive scenes. Tied to chairs, submerged in water, missing limbs. Her reflection stared back from the painted eyes.

She turned the corner and saw them.

"Loretta?" Kristen gasped, racing forward, arms flung around her. Donna, Judy, and Bruce weren't far behind.

"Jesus, you're alive," Donna whispered.

"I—I didn't know if—" Loretta began, but her voice cracked. She looked ragged, lips cracked, eyes wide with new knowledge. "I found something. Or I think I did."

They moved quickly into a small room and barricaded the door with a dresser. Inside, faded wallpaper peeled in long curls from the walls. A stained crib rested in one corner, and from the ceiling, a child's mobile spun slowly, though there was no breeze.

Loretta pulled out the warped, twitching map. She spread it on the ground.

"I think there's a way out," she said. "Or a way to break it. The house. It feeds on us. On trauma. On guilt. It replays things. Twists them. It wants us to believe we're powerless."

The truth was that Loretta had no idea if her theory was correct. She had no actual proof. The house didn't have rules, as far as she could tell. She was grasping at straws, desperately attempting to make sense of something senseless and beyond the scope of what she'd ever experienced.

She showed them the marked locations. The map bled slightly at the edges, oozing faint black ink.

"There are pieces of something. Some structure that holds this place together. I think if we find them, break them, we might be able to end this.

IT'S ALWAYS HALLOWEEN HERE

Or weaken it."

Bruce crouched beside her, staring at the map. "What do you mean, pieces?"

"Altars. Memories. Something buried."

Kristen's voice was barely audible. "I think I saw one upstairs. A room full of clocks that didn't tick. And a child crying through the walls."

"The house shows us things that aren't real," said Bruce. "It plays tricks on us, gives us clues that are lies. We're just here for the house's amusement. Like it's playing with its food. That map is useless. There is no layout to the house."

"You could be right," Loretta said.

"Maybe, if we make it until sunrise, the house will let us go," Judy said.

"Maybe," said Donna. She walked over to the window and stared out. There was nothing except deep, dark blackness staring back at her. Like she was staring into the deepest parts of outer space. "I keep waiting for a vampire or werewolf to burst through one of those doors."

"I think I could take down a mummy if I had to," Bruce said, hoping for a laugh. "Jason, Freddy, Michael Myers, Leatherface? They sound like a picnic compared to what we've seen tonight."

"I know this isn't the right time," said Kristen. "But Phyllis and I have tickets to The Bangles' reunion show next week. And I just keep thinking, we have to get out of here. We have to make it to that show."

Donna put her hands on Kristen's shoulders. "We will get out of here. You will go to that concert. You will walk like an Egyptian again."

Kristen smiled and laughed, despite her worry. "Okay."

"From here on out, keep your mind clear," Loretta said. "A blank space. Only focus on survival and the tasks at hand. Getting out of this house. Any memories, any fear, any guilt, push it down as far as you can. Maybe we can starve the house."

"Or maybe we just have to fight our way out," Bruce said.

Thump.

They froze. Listening.

Thump.

The walls trembled. Plaster cracked above the doorframe. Then again.

Thump. Closer.

Loretta turned slowly to the others. "I didn't come alone. It followed me."

147

A low scraping sound began to echo, like talons dragged across stone. From the far corner of the room, a section of the wallpaper bulged outward, as if something behind it was pressing through. A shredding sound. A long tear in the paper.

Five long fingers broke through the wall, each one blackened and jointed like a spider's leg. They flexed and peeled the wall back like wet paper. A head emerged. It wasn't human.

Its skull was elongated, slick with glistening tissue. The face was a mass of shifting, inverted human features, like someone had taken a face and folded it inside out. Eyes turning inward, mouth stretched across the brow, veins protruding from its cheeks.

It screamed. The sound was not from its mouth, but from every pore of its body.

Loretta grabbed the map and ran, pulling the others through a door on the other side of the room that had not been there seconds ago. The house was giving them a chance. Or setting a trap.

They raced down the new corridor, the walls groaning. Lightbulbs burst overhead in a shower of glass. Behind them, the thing gave chase, limbs smashing through walls, tearing chunks of plaster, pushing its body through spaces too narrow for any living thing.

Kristen suddenly screamed. A second head had grown from the wall beside her, eyes rolling, crying with her voice. It snapped its teeth, moaning *"Help me..."* as it split open into hundreds of beetles and vanished into the molding.

They crashed through a final door into a library. Books exploded from shelves as they entered, flying through the air like wings of black paper. The windows had no glass, only dark water behind them, as though the house now floated underwater.

Donna slammed the door and shoved a chair beneath the knob. "That won't hold it long."

Bruce looked around, trembling. "Then we have to go. We can't keep running. We're breaking. It's eating us one memory at a time."

Kristen turned to Loretta. "Is there even a real way out?"

Loretta met her gaze. "I don't know. But I think if we destroy enough of what keeps this place alive, it'll collapse."

"Fuck this house," Bruce said.

CHAPTER FORTY-FIVE

The door Loretta unlocked fought against her weight as she opened it. Not with a click but with a shudder, like it resisted remembering what lay behind it.

The hallway beyond was narrow and slanted, walls pressed too close together, coated in a waxy, uneven material that stuck to their sleeves when brushed. Faint vibrations pulsed through the floor beneath their shoes. No rhythm, no logic. The map had gone still again, its ink frozen in a new configuration.

Bruce walked ahead with a lantern they'd found. Its light sputtered and hissed, casting shadows that moved faster than they did.

"This place hates light," Donna whispered.

They passed a series of paintings. Each one a portrait of a figure with no face. Just gray, stretched skin where features should be. The figures were posed in different emotional states, like laughter, agony, and boredom, but all the same blank canvas for a head. One portrait slowly tilted as they passed, a wet, sucking sound following its movement.

Kristen clutched Loretta's hand tightly. "Why does it feel like this hall knows us?"

"It does," Loretta whispered.

They reached a door that had no handle. Just a narrow slit in the center, as though the door wanted to watch them.

The door sighed open. The room beyond was circular, impossibly large, like a cathedral turned inside out. High overhead, a chandelier of body parts spun slowly in the dark. The walls were shelves, floor to ceiling, lined with jars.

Each jar held a memory. They could feel it before they even approached. The contents pulsed, and sound came with them. Not echoes. Moments.

Loretta stepped toward one jar. Inside, a sliver of film fluttered in syrupy fluid. Her fingers grazed the glass.

"Don't cry, Loretta, you're stronger than that."

"I'm not ready for the casket to close."

"You should have said goodbye."

Her mother's voice. Her voice. Her childhood bedroom.

Kristen reached for a jar marked with a blue ribbon. "This is mine."

"No!" Donna yanked her back. "That's the trap. That's how it gets in."

At the center of the room stood a massive stone slab. Slick, black, carved with sigils that hurt the eyes to look at. The surface had deep indentations, as though something had once been chained there.

Loretta circled it, heart pounding like fists against a locked door. There were three bizarre, abstract symbols engraved on the edge.

"I don't understand what any of this means," said Kristen.

"I don't think we're supposed to," Donna said.

"How do we destroy it?" Bruce asked.

Before anyone could answer, a low hum filled the room, coming from the jars. The shelves began to tremble. One by one, the jars cracked. From inside, something emerged.

The figures were shaped like the people in their memories, but twisted and abnormal. Mottled, pale skin, with wide mouths, burned-out eyes, and dripping black fluid. One of them had Kristen's mother's face. Another wore Loretta's old prom dress, but its legs bent backwards and dragged nails along the floor.

They hissed. Not in anger, but in recognition.

"They're made from us," Donna said, backing toward the slab.

Loretta ran her fingers over the carved indentations on the slab. None of the symbols or words meant anything to her.

The room screamed. Every jar shattered at once. The air shook with whispers, a hurricane of voices and sorrow and everything they had buried.

Silence. The slab cracked down the center. A new door opened behind the slab. Another path.

"Follow me!" said Loretta.

Something watched them through the chandelier. Its eyes older than the house, blinking once, then vanishing.

CHAPTER FORTY-SIX

The hatch groaned as they hauled themselves through, the wood splintering under their hands. Kristen was first, dragging herself up onto a floor that felt like soil. Soft and uneven, like thick flesh under a thin carpet of boards. Her knees sank slightly with every movement, and the faint vibration of something shifting beneath her made her skin tighten.

Loretta followed, yanking Judy by the arm until she was clear. Donna shoved Bruce upward, then scrambled after him, hammering the hatch shut just as a hand burst through the opening, nails raking against her boot. The sound was sharp, like claws on slate. She stomped down hard, feeling the give of brittle bone, before the wood warped inward, sealing over the opening like a scab knitting over a wound. The sealing wasn't just silent. It was final.

They stood in a room that had no shape. The walls sloped and curved, melting into each other as though the architecture had been left too close to a flame. Colors bled together in sickening patterns. Dull red sinking into black, with strange green veins pulsing just beneath the surface.

The smell clung thick. Old rot, copper, and the rank sharpness of something long dead but not gone. It coated the back of their throats until each swallow brought a ghost of bile.

A single doorway gaped ahead, leading into a corridor that bent sharply after only a few steps. No windows. No familiar attic rafters. No hint that they were still inside the same house at all.

They moved as one, weapons ready, their footsteps making faint, sticky sounds against the floor. The texture underfoot was unsettling. Like walking on tightly stretched leather, with something faintly giving under every step, as though the floor breathed.

A noise came from above. A wet drip, then another. Something pattered onto Kristen's shoulder, cold and viscous. She froze, the skin at the back of her neck prickling, and looked up.

The ceiling was alive with movement. Shapes pressed against it from the other side, distorting the surface in fleshy bulges. Something pushed close enough to reveal a face; its features melting, sliding over themselves like hot wax before reforming into something worse. The eyes were all pupil, no white. It lingered just long enough for her to see its mouth open in an almost-smile before it slipped away, rippling through the bulges overhead.

"Keep moving," Loretta said, though her voice had gone thin. She kept glancing upward as if expecting the ceiling to drop on them at any moment.

They entered the corridor. The bend came quickly, and when they turned it, the space opened into a long, low hall lined with framed portraits on both sides. The frames were heavy, ornate, their carvings worn to almost unrecognizable shapes. twisted vines, bones, and strange spirals. Each canvas was coated in a dull layer of grime, but faint human shapes could be seen beneath.

Donna wiped one with her sleeve. It was Kristen.

Not as she was now, but hollow-cheeked, her skin almost gray, eyes black from corner to corner, her lips slightly parted as if in mid-whisper. The longer they looked, the more the painted eyes seemed to follow.

Kristen staggered back, slamming into the opposite wall, where her own portrait stared at her again, this time with half her face peeled away, skin gone and the inner layer of the wall exposed in place of bone. Her stomach lurched, and she swallowed hard to keep from retching.

The floor shifted beneath them. The boards rose in jagged ridges, splinters jutting upward in sharp spears. From the tips, pale fingers uncurled, knuckles cracking wetly.

Bruce brought his pipe down hard, snapping the knuckles that reached for him, but more hands sprouted further ahead, blocking the corridor. The texture of the wood changed. No longer dry, but slick and warm, as if alive, stretching and tearing with every grasp.

Loretta hurled her flashlight at the nearest ridge. It spun wildly, the beam flaring across the corridor. In that fractured light, shadows revealed the wall-forms from the attic following. They crawled without legs, dragging themselves forward with long, scraping pulls. Their lower halves trailed into splintered roots that left streaks on the floor.

The portraits began to weep. Dark, viscous streaks slid down the glass, thick as oil. Drops splattered onto the floorboards, where they hissed and bored holes straight through. The smell that rose from the holes was chemical and choking, stinging the inside of their noses.

"Run!" Donna shouted, voice breaking.

They barreled forward, stomping over grasping hands, ducking as the ceiling sagged so low it brushed their hair. Behind them, the dragging, wall-born things scraped along faster now, their limbs jerking in unnatural spasms.

The corridor didn't end. Every sprint made the next bend drift farther away, stretching as if the space itself was resisting them. Through the dim ahead, they heard a voice.

IT'S ALWAYS HALLOWEEN HERE

It was soft, curling through the dark like a caress. It whispered their names one by one. Kristen's first. Then Loretta's. Bruce, Donna, Judy.

The sound was warm and intimate, almost loving. Yet every nerve told them to stop. They reached the next bend in the hallway.

The hall turned and then widened into a round chamber whose walls seemed to be made of stretched canvas, each one breathing slowly, the surface shifting under the weight of something moving behind it.

In the center stood a figure.

It was tall, though it bent itself low as if bowing in welcome. Its skin looked like paper that had been soaked and left to dry, sagging in places, tearing in others to reveal a slick blackness beneath. Its arms were long enough to rest both hands on the floor without bending its knees. The fingers were multiple jointed, curling and uncurling in restless motion.

Its head tilted. No eyes. No mouth. Yet its voice filled the room as if whispered directly into each of their ears at once.

"You've come so far."

Something rippled beneath its skin. Faces pressing against the surface from within, their mouths opening in silent screams before sinking back into the black beneath.

Bruce gripped the pipe tighter. "We're not staying."

The thing took a step forward. The floor under them quivered as though reacting to its movement.

"You are already part of me."

From the walls, the skin-like surface began to split. Long black arms emerged, fingertips hooked into claws, reaching for them from every side.

The figure lunged. It moved faster than anything that size should. One moment, it was several feet away, its long arms dragging like dead ropes. The next, its paper-skin face was inches from Donna's, the faint smell of damp ink wafting off it. She swung the broken chair leg up hard, driving it into where a throat should have been.

The wood pierced. For a moment, it felt like stabbing into soaked cardboard. It sank deeper with a sickening tear, the surface parting around it as though swallowing the weapon.

A sudden jolt wrenched the chair leg from her grip. Black fluid welled from the wound, but instead of dripping, it crawled upward, tendrils snaking toward her arm.

"Down!" Loretta shouted, slamming into Donna's side. The two of them hit the floor as Bruce brought the pipe around in a wide, brutal arc, catching the thing square across the head.

The impact caved half its skull inward with a crunch like crushing a thick wad of paper. Instead of falling, it straightened, the caved section inflating again from within as dozens of small, pale hands pressed against the skin from inside, reshaping it.

From the walls, the black arms were closer, claws scraping long, dry streaks into the floor. They moved without sound, except for the low vibration in the boards that thrummed underfoot with every grasp.

Loretta smashed the rusted hammer into the nearest wall-arm. The blow cracked the claw in half, sending shards skittering like broken nails across the boards, but the arm didn't retreat. It only reached with the stump, wrapping around the hammer's handle and yanking her toward the wall.

She screamed, boots scraping the slick floor as Kristen lunged in, stabbing the sharp end of a picture frame into the arm's joint. The skin split, releasing a burst of stench so strong it coated her tongue. Rotted meat mixed with burning glue. The arm recoiled at last, slithering back into the wall's surface.

The thing in the center laughed without a mouth. The sound was layered, dozens of tones stacked at once, each voice just slightly off from the others.

Loretta raised a jagged piece of splintered beam and charged. She drove it deep into the creature's chest, feeling the resistance shift halfway in, as if she had pierced one layer and struck something harder beneath. The thing grabbed her wrist, its too-many-jointed fingers locking tight.

Her skin crawled where it touched her. Literal movement under her flesh, as if the thing's touch sent something living racing into her veins. She wrenched herself free, leaving behind a streak of pale handprints across her arm that throbbed faintly.

Bruce swung again, this time aiming for the creature's knees. The joint bent the wrong way, snapping like wet kindling, but it stayed upright, supporting itself with those long arms.

From its split knee spilled a torrent of black fluid. Only this time, the fluid rose in the shape of small, human figures, no taller than a child. Each one had the face of someone they recognized—neighbors, friends, strangers they'd passed on the street—faces they should not be seeing here.

The shapes darted forward on all fours, their limbs bending with insect quickness.

Kristen smashed one flat with her frame-shard, the crunch underfoot too soft to be bone. Donna grabbed another by the head and slammed it into the wall, but the wall caught it, absorbed it, swallowing it in a single ripple.

The thing's head tilted again. "You tire yourselves," it whispered, its voice inside them, pressing against their thoughts like fingers probing for a way in.

The walls convulsed. The black arms doubled in number. The floor began to sink under their feet. They were being drawn into it. Into all of it.

Loretta looked at the others, breath harsh, eyes wide. "We kill it now, or we don't get another chance."

Bruce gritted his teeth, pipe raised. Kristen gripped her shard. Donna and Judy tightened their hold on the hammer and splintered beam.

The thing leaned closer, the movement smooth and predatory. "Then come into me," it said.

They attacked, hitting it all at once.

Bruce's pipe came down on its shoulder with a shattering crack, the force denting the paper-skin deep enough to tear open a hollow beneath. From the hole, black fluid gushed in an upward stream, defying gravity, splattering across the ceiling in writhing shapes that stuck there like shadows come alive.

Donna swung the splintered beam low, stabbing deep into the side of its torso. The wood punched through the papery flesh with a sharp rip, and something beneath it flexed in answer. A coiled muscle not meant for human anatomy. The thing bent toward her, the tear widening to reveal a dark corridor inside its body, walls slick and pulsing as though it were hollow all the way through.

Kristen darted in and drove her picture-frame shard deep into its spine. The sensation made her stomach lurch. It was like pushing metal into wet fabric over stone, the shard grinding on something hard inside.

The creature's head snapped backward with a sound like paper tearing. Faces bulged beneath its skin, their mouths moving in silent cries, their eyes rolling wildly before sinking back into the black beneath.

Judy lifted the rusted hammer and brought it down on the joint of one arm. Bone, or something like it, crunched under the impact. The limb dangled for a moment, twitching, then dropped to the floor with a heavy slap. The severed arm twitched on its own, claws scraping against the boards until they carved deep grooves.

From the walls, more black arms erupted. This time, tipped not with claws, but hands shaped like human faces, mouths stretched wide. They clamped onto the floor, leaving puckered, wet marks wherever they touched.

Loretta grabbed one and wrenched it hard, feeling the skin give before tearing it loose. The moment it hit the ground, it liquefied into a pool that surged toward her boots, forcing her to leap back.

The creature slithered, both hands outstretched. Its fingers split lengthwise, opening into strips of paper-like flesh, each strip curling inward like a leech's mouth. Loretta sidestepped, then shoved the jagged beam into its chest again, deeper this time, until she felt the wood catch on something that pulsed beneath the surface. She twisted hard.

The thing screamed.

It wasn't a sound. It was a vibration, a shock through the floor, the walls, their bones. The stretched-canvas walls split wide in places, and from behind them came a cyclone of movement; other shapes, half-formed, clawing to escape.

The floor buckled. Kristen hacked at the child-shapes that darted between them, their tiny bodies bursting into damp tatters when struck. Donna stomped one flat, its face still staring upward, eyes tracking her as it dissolved.

The creature reared back, its paper-skin sloughing away in sheets. Beneath was a writhing skeleton of black limbs and wet cords that pulsed like veins. The face was gone entirely, only a void where its head should be, inside which something moved, as though a larger form were turning slowly in the dark.

Judy swung the hammer into that void. The moment the metal passed the edge, it vanished, pulled inside, and a spray of black fluid shot back out, splattering her arms and face. It was hot, almost burning, the smell like scorched hair and spoiled meat.

The room convulsed.

The portraits on the walls peeled from their frames, the painted figures stepping out, their movements jerky and stuttering. Each one turned toward the group, their own faces painted over theirs, mouths opening in unison.

Bruce roared and charged, swinging for the creature's knees again. Kristen slashed upward along its arm, peeling the paper-skin in strips. Loretta drove the beam straight into its torso until she was shoulder-deep, then ripped it sideways.

Something inside tore.

The entire chamber screamed; walls, floor, and ceiling. The black arms shot upward, flailing, before retracting into the walls all at once. The portraits convulsed, their figures collapsing into smears. The floor sagged in the center, opening into a hole that yawned wide beneath the creature's feet.

IT'S ALWAYS HALLOWEEN HERE

It toppled backward into the hole, its many hands grasping at the edges, dragging splinters and fragments of floor down with it.

Loretta didn't hesitate. She grabbed the jagged beam, jammed it through its chest again, and kicked hard.

The thing fell.

For a moment there was only the sound of it receding into the dark, its many voices fading into whispers. Then, silence.

The floor beneath them gave way. They dropped, all of them, into a blackness that felt too thick to be empty. They fell without wind, without weight.

One by one, they landed on something that wasn't floor so much as an endless surface; smooth, cold, and faintly slick. It reflected nothing, yet it shimmered faintly, as if something beneath it moved in slow currents.

CHAPTER FORTY-SEVEN

Loretta pushed herself up, palms leaving pale handprints on the surface before they faded. Her heart hammered hard enough that she felt each beat in her jaw. This wasn't falling into another part of the house. This was somewhere else. The airless void pressed in on her thoughts, making it hard to tell where her mind ended and the place began.

The space around them stretched forever, yet every step in any direction kept the others just a few feet away. Above, there was no ceiling, only a vast, dim void, broken in places by faint shapes hanging far overhead like fragments of the house suspended in the dark. A doorframe here. Part of a window there. The crooked peak of the attic roof, dangling upside down.

Tools and discarded junk scattered everywhere. On shelves, in between doorways, mixed with antiques, knickknacks, and people's long-forgotten belongings.

Bruce took a step forward, grabbing a pipe that was wedged between a curly-haired doll and a broken compass. He froze. Directly ahead stood another Bruce. Same clothes, same weapon in hand. It stared back at him with eyes like still water. His stomach turned; it felt like staring into a version of himself that had already given up.

"Bruce, don't," Kristen said sharply, her voice shaking. "It's not—"

The other Bruce opened his mouth, and the sound that came out was not a voice but the slow creak of a door opening. The noise rolled over them, deep enough to rattle their ribs, and with it came movement beneath the slick surface at their feet. Shapes turned lazily below. Pale, boneless things drifting upward, their faces pressed flat against the underside of the floor as though trying to look in.

Donna's skin prickled. She turned and found herself face-to-face with herself. This double had no mouth, but its skin was cracked from chin to sternum, and inside the crack was nothing but slow, twisting black cords. A shiver ran through her, not just from fear but from a strange, sick familiarity, as if she'd seen that image in a nightmare years ago and had been trying to forget it ever since.

The floor flexed.

Kristen looked down. Her reflection was gone. In its place, something long and narrow stared up from beneath the surface, its body coiling endlessly out of sight. Its head was featureless except for a single, round

IT'S ALWAYS HALLOWEEN HERE

opening lined with bristling teeth that clicked gently in anticipation. She swallowed hard, forcing herself to stand her ground. Her knees wanted to buckle, but giving in meant going under.

"We need to move," Loretta said, gripping the jagged beam tighter. She hated how her voice shook. How small it sounded against the sheer size of the place. She refused to let them hear doubt.

Moving didn't take them anywhere. The space folded. One step forward and the doorframe above was suddenly at their feet, lying sideways, its edges dripping with something like melted paint.

Donna's pulse pounded in her ears as she reached out to test the frame. The moment her fingers touched it, a cold pressure hit her chest, hard and sudden, as if someone had shoved her into icy water. She yanked her hand back with a gasp and found it wet. Not with liquid, but with something that crawled against her skin like hundreds of tiny legs before evaporating. She clenched her fist to stop the shaking.

A sound rippled through the void. It was the same voice as before, the one that had called their names in the corridor, but now it came from everywhere. It spoke in a language they couldn't understand, yet each of them felt the truth of it settling in their bones. It was describing them. Not their bodies, but the parts of themselves they never said out loud.

Loretta's stomach twisted, and she had to fight the urge to cover her ears. Bruce bit down on the inside of his cheek until he tasted blood, using the pain to block the words.

The shapes above began to lower. The attic roof drifted down slowly, tilting, until its warped beams nearly touched the surface they stood on. From behind it, something impossibly tall began to step into view. Long-limbed, black as ink, with its head bowed low.

The head lifted. It was the thing they'd fought. Stripped of skin now, nothing but wet, knotted cords for muscle and branching limbs that moved like spider legs. In its center, where a heart should have been, was a yawning hole lined with hundreds of whispering mouths.

Every instinct screamed for them to run, but there was nowhere to go. Donna's throat went dry, Kristen's jaw locked so hard it ached, Judy's hands tightened until her knuckles burned.

From those mouths came one word, over and over, in every tone it had ever stolen. "Stay."

The doubles moved closer, slow and deliberate, their twisted faces contorting with cruel delight as they fed on the tremors of dread rippling through the group. Their eyes gleamed. Not with light, but with the shadows of every failure, every whispered shame the real ones had buried deep inside, the darkest fragments they refused to face.

Donna's double leaned in close, voice a serpentine hiss spilling secrets she'd never dared confess, words curling like smoke around her chest, tightening until her limbs trembled uncontrollably. The air around her thickened with a sickly-sweet stench, like rotten sugar melting in the heat.

Her vision blurred. Nausea clawed up her throat. The thing smiled, lips peeling back to reveal cracked teeth, sharp and glittering like broken glass, ready to cut.

"No," Donna spat, voice rough and ragged. Her eyes fell upon a crowbar leaning against the wall. She reached for it.

Her fingers clenched the cold, unyielding metal. It was real, solid, a lifeline against the choking illusion. She swung with all her strength, the bar smashing into the double's cheek.

The face cracked with a high, sharp snap, fracturing like a porcelain mask worn thin by age and grief. Cracks spread like spiderwebs, edges curling and lifting like brittle paper in a faint, ghostly breeze.

As Donna reached to tear it away, the double's hand shot out with unnatural speed, fingers like blackened vines snaking forward to latch onto her skin.

Kristen's hand closed over Donna's wrist, yanking her back with a harsh grunt, just as the mask began to crawl, writhing with a terrible hunger, whispering, *"You belong to me."*

Loretta's beam cut through the darkness like a shard of truth. She jabbed it fiercely into the chest of her own twisted mirror, which hissed and writhed but recoiled from the strike as if burned.

The doubles snarled, a chorus of broken faces folding and unfolding like nightmarish origami. Their too-many-jointed limbs reached hungrily for the group, mouths opening wide with whispered lies and cruel doubts, seeping poison into the space between them.

Judy faced her double, whose mouthless grin stretched impossibly wide, eyes hollow yet filled with cold accusation. It stepped closer, hand reaching out, lunging to tear its mask free.

Her heart thundered in her chest as she snatched the mask between shaking hands. It writhed and pulsed like a living thing, desperate to slip onto her own face, to claim her identity.

"No," she screamed, muscles burning as she yanked the mask down into the ground. It shattered with a scream that echoed inside her skull like a breaking bone.

"Fight the part they show you!" Loretta urged, her voice breaking but steady. She turned toward Kristen.

IT'S ALWAYS HALLOWEEN HERE

Kristen locked eyes with her double, which whispered a poison so intimate it clenched her chest. A memory of failure, a friend lost to silence and shadow.

"No," Kristen breathed fiercely, voice fierce and unyielding. "I am not her."

Kristen lurched forward, shoving the double into a sharp beam jutting from one of the walls. The beam pierced through the double's chest, a violent tearing sensation that made the creature twist and shriek. A sound like ancient paper ripping apart under endless strain.

She grabbed the cracked mask and ripped it free with a desperate roar. The double trembled violently, shuddering like a candle flame caught in a storm, before collapsing into shards of shadow and bone that scattered like dark ash in the cold void.

One by one, the group took up the terrible work, confronting the darkest parts of themselves, wielding real weapons that still held the weight of the world outside this nightmare. They tore off cursed masks that clung and fought to possess, shards of paper flesh cracking and falling away.

The doubles fought with animal desperation, feeding on fear, on doubt, but each act of refusal weakened them, every strike from something real shattered their illusory forms further.

Bruce met his double's gaze, eyes hardening as he spoke softly, "You don't own me." His pipe slammed down with brutal force on the double's skull, splintering it like dry wood. Only when Bruce stepped forward and ripped the mask from its face did the creature scream and dissolve into nothingness.

The last double screamed. A terrible, echoing howl filled with rage and sorrow. Loretta drove her beam through its twisted form, heart, or whatever black pit it hid within, tearing the mask from its face with trembling hands and watching as the twisted version of herself tore apart, leaving behind only flickers of black smoke that drifted away like dying embers.

When the last shards of shadow vanished, silence poured over the void like a cold tide. The endless surface beneath their feet stilled, and the terrible voice that had called their names faded into distant memory.

They stood there. Shaking, breath ragged, bodies battered but unbroken. Together.

CHAPTER FORTY-EIGHT

Marti led the way, each step heavier than the last as the ancient door groaned open on rusted hinges, revealing a room swallowed by shadows so dense they seemed to absorb the weak light from their flashlights. The stale, choking scent of burnt herbs mingled with a sour, metallic tang, like the sharp stink of blood left to rot in damp earth, seized their nostrils and clawed deep, stirring nausea and dread.

The floorboards, slick with a dark, viscous residue, squelched beneath their feet, sticky and cold as if soaked in old, congealed blood. Each step sent up a faint, sickly-sweet odor of decay, like forgotten fruit fermenting in the dark. Flickering candle stubs—half-melted, blackened, their wicks snapped or charred—clustered in uneven, broken circles upon the floor. The shadows between the flickers seemed to twist and breathe, shifting into grotesque, impossible shapes that crawled just beyond the edge of vision.

Tattered scraps of brittle parchment lay scattered like fallen leaves, their edges curled and stained with age and something darker. Smears of rust-colored stains that glistened wetly in the dim glow. Inked sigils and symbols writhed unsettlingly across the pages: tangled knots of lines and spirals that pulsed like veins beneath the skin, as if alive and hungry.

The walls themselves were carved deep with crude, furious etchings. Contorted faces frozen in silent screams, spiraling tendrils reaching outward, knotting and twisting endlessly. The wood seemed swollen and warped, the grain shifting as if it were breathing, convulsing with silent agony. Every glance sparked the maddening feeling that the room was watching them, waiting for a moment's weakness.

Ionia's fingertips brushed an iron chalice resting on a low altar. Cold, heavy, stained with dried crimson that flaked and cracked like old leather. A chill shot through her as she lifted it. Somewhere beneath the rotten floor, a slow, relentless pulse throbbed like a buried heart, hammering to be heard beneath layers of rot and silence.

Frannie's hand trembled as she picked up a weathered, leather-bound book, its cracked spine barely holding the fragile, yellowed pages together. She opened it cautiously, breath hitching as her eyes met line after line of names. Names of people who had died within these walls, stretching back to the mid-1800s and crawling toward the present like an endless litany of sorrow and death.

The ink twisted and smeared, the letters bending and doubling, some

IT'S ALWAYS HALLOWEEN HERE

names crossed out and rewritten in a darker, almost bleeding script. Strange symbols sprawled beside the entries. Circles enclosing crosses, inverted triangles, lines that seemed to crawl off the page like black, writhing worms.

Marti's voice broke the silence, brittle and raw. "These are all victims." Her hand trembled as she traced a name dated 1847, the letters curling like sinister vines that threatened to reach out and strangle her. "Every death recorded here. All of them." Her gaze flickered over the dates. Dozens, centuries of horror marked with terrifying precision. The weight of it settled like a stone in her gut.

Frannie crouched by the altar, fingers trembling as she lifted a brittle scrap of parchment, its surface mottled with ash and dried blood. The scrawled words were neither prayer nor curse, but something warped and knotted in meaning, as if pleading with and damning powers unseen. The script twisted on itself, a dark hymn to darkness.

The room seemed to pulse with a sinister energy, pressing in on their minds, tugging at the edges of their sanity. The flickering candlelight twisted wildly, shadows undulating and crawling along the walls like hungry things reaching for flesh and bone. Whispered names brushed against their ears. Soft, unintelligible voices skimming just beyond comprehension, drowning in static and echoes.

A sharp, scraping sound echoed. A frantic, desperate clawing. Something just behind the walls, scratching and scraping as if desperate to break free.

The group froze, breaths shallow and hearts pounding in wild staccato. Eyes darted frantically, scanning every inch of the room's rotting darkness. The walls seemed to pulse, the shadows deepening as the air thickened with unspoken menace.

The room itself felt alive. Closing in, swallowing the flickering light, the fragile hope, and any lingering sense of safety.

They had found a ledger of death, and the house was far from finished with them.

Frannie's fingers trembled as she flipped through the brittle pages of the weathered book, eyes scanning the dense, looping script etched in ink that had darkened to the color of dried blood. Names stretched endlessly down the yellowed pages. Faces erased by time but immortalized here in ink, a ledger of death and despair.

Her breath caught when her eyes landed on three names clustered together, each marked with dates that sent chills racing down her spine.

Jerry—1923

Suzanne—1978

Drew—2005

The dates felt like wounds reopened, fresh and bleeding. Their friends. Were they alive? Did death in The Faulkner House mean death in the real world?

"This makes no sense," said Ionia. "The dates are all wrong. Jerry, Suzanne, and Drew aren't dead. Are they?"

"Time has no meaning in this house," said Frannie.

Marti traced Drew's name with a shaking finger, the ink beneath seeming to ripple like a disturbed pool. "They're here," she whispered. "All of them."

Ionia's eyes darted nervously between the names and the twisting symbols beside them. Sigils of binding, death, and eternal torment. The weight of centuries pressed down on them, suffocating and absolute.

Frannie closed the book slowly, the scratch of the brittle pages echoing like a death toll in the oppressive silence. The house had kept its secrets, but now the ledger was clear: their friends had become part of its unending horror.

The candle flames flickered violently as if disturbed by unseen breath, shadows crawling nearer. The whispers returned. Soft, cold, insistent.

They're waiting. They're not gone.

A sudden scraping noise rose from the walls once more, urgent, desperate. The house was alive with its terrible hunger, and their names were carved into its endless, dark appetite.

CHAPTER FORTY-NINE

Somewhere else in the house, Donna's fingers trembled as she pressed them against the wallpaper. The pattern was shifting again. Once roses, now rows of open eyes.

Loretta, Bruce, Judy, and Kristen stood behind her in a cramped corridor, where every light bulb overhead had long since melted, leaving only the dull flicker of Bruce's lighter.

"We've been walking in circles," Kristen said, voice flat but shaky. "That's the third time we've passed the window with the doll's head jammed into the sill."

Bruce wiped his hands on his jeans. They were sticky with something that hadn't been there moments before. "This place loops. It mirrors our panic."

Loretta looked at them. "Maybe we should stop playing its game."

"How?"

"We pick a direction and destroy what we find."

They turned down a new hallway. One that hadn't been there a heartbeat ago. This one was made entirely of doors. Every wall surface, every inch of ceiling and floor was lined with them. Hundreds. None repeated. Some were wood, others glass, and some iron. Some bled. Some wept.

From behind each, they could hear scratching. Or laughter. Or themselves, whispering.

They stopped before a large steel door marked, REMEMBERING ROOM: DO NOT ENTER ALONE.

"Well, that's inviting," Donna said. She turned the handle.

Inside, the room was blinding white. At the center sat a large, round table, set for guests. Plates of food sat steaming. Fried chicken, mashed potatoes, peach cobbler.

The seats were labeled with all of Loretta's friends' names. A phonograph in the corner played old gospel music. Loretta's throat went tight.

"My father used to sing that when he was happy."

They stepped forward, hesitant. The lights flickered. All the chairs were suddenly occupied.

Each one held a version of themselves. Older, hollow, skin hanging loose. Their eyes were all white. The versions began to eat, shoving food in with mechanical jerks. The food spoiled as they touched it, gravy turning black, meat crawling with wriggling things.

Bruce backed away. "We gotta go."

His older self stopped chewing and looked up. "You already did. You never left. You belong." It grinned. The room imploded. The walls crushed inward.

"We tried to hide," Bruce said. "But it always finds us."

"What does?" Donna asked.

The room imploded. The walls crushed inward. Screams. Loud and close. From the ceiling, something fell.

A thud, then another. A low gurgling laugh. The first creature burst from the dark like a smear of shadows pulled into the shape of a man, but inhuman. Its limbs were unnaturally long, its face stretched thin and eyeless, and its mouth was vertical, splitting its head in two. It dropped onto all fours and galloped, fast and spider-like, straight for Bruce.

Loretta swung a chair. It shattered. The creature didn't stop. It screeched like a boiling kettle. Donna tackled Bruce out of the way.

Two more shapes poured in. Smaller, shrieking with children's voices. They crawled on the walls, slapping the stone with hands that left behind burning sigils.

The creatures lined up, as if blocking their path. Without hesitation, Loretta directed her friends to an exit. Now, they were running, screaming. Loretta pulling Kristen out by the arm, Donna smashing her shoulder into the doorway just before it collapsed into a howling throat of bone.

They landed in a hallway that hadn't existed seconds earlier. Behind them, the door screamed shut like a severed nerve.

Silence. Bruce sat up. "No more games. We find the others."

The friends checked themselves for wounds and cuts. Their activity was halted when Kristen let out a whimper. Bruce, Donna, Judy, and Loretta turned to her. Kristen was frozen still, her eyes fixed on the ceiling.

Faces. Ghostly white, angry visages piercing through the dark, watching them. Eyes that glowed silver. Bending all laws of physics, as if the beings had pushed their faces through the floor above them to stare, to menace.

As quickly as they appeared, they vanished.

"I hate it here," said Donna.

Judy looked down. Her hand was shaking. She was still holding the napkin from the table. It had her name on it.

It was soaked with blood.

CHAPTER FIFTY

The floor moaned underfoot. Not creaked. Moaned, like something beneath it recognized the weight of their bodies and didn't want them to leave again.

Loretta stepped into the room first. A cathedral-sized space with walls that shifted as you looked at them. Some moments stone, other moments shimmers. At the center stood a cruciform of mirrors, floating in midair, arranged like a broken compass. Each reflected the room differently. One showed it upside-down, one pulsing like a heartbeat, one drenched in fire, one choked with mold.

"Where are we?" Donna asked.

Kristen moved slowly, her hand brushing against the veined wall, which pulsed in response. "It feels like this is the stomach. The center. The part of the house that digests."

Bruce nodded toward the other side of the chamber. "There's someone there."

Shapes emerged from the far shadows. Frannie. Ionia. Marti.

Their clothes were torn, their eyes red from seeing too much, but they were alive. A collective gasp and brief sense of relief and happiness shared, coursing through their veins.

Marti ran forward first, colliding into Loretta. "I am so relieved to see you."

The moment swelled. Hope tried to crawl in. The mirrors began to spin, slowly. A dry grinding sound echoed through the room, like flesh dragged over stone.

The mirrors sang. Not melody, but voices. All their voices, warped and layered.

"She was dead when I found her, but she asked me not to tell anyone until after dinner."

"Every night he eats more of the silence, and now the house can't breathe."

"The moon won't stop laughing, and now the baby's learning how to peel its own shadow."

"I stitched your voice into my coat so it could keep whispering when you finally rot quiet."

Loretta stepped closer to the mirror marked in inked cracks. Her

IT'S ALWAYS HALLOWEEN HERE

reflection didn't mimic her. It moved slightly too late. The eyes were wrong.

Inside the mirror, the reflection's chest bulged, and something moved under the skin. She pressed her hand to the glass.

The surface melted, slick and warm, pulling her in. Bruce and Ionia grabbed her shoulders and yanked her back just before her whole face disappeared inside.

"What did you see?" Frannie asked.

Loretta wiped her face, fighting nausea. Her mouth tasted like rusted coins and something sickly sweet, like overripe peaches turned to rot.

"He's here," she said. "Drew. He's part of the house. Or it's part of him."

The mirrors stilled. The room changed. A grinding sound above them, like someone cranking a rusty winch, followed by a wet slap. The walls peeled away.

Behind them stood a colossal figure, fused with the stone. Its body was hunched, lumpy, stitched to the structure. Not just trapped but incorporated.

One massive eye twitched open. It was Drew's. His voice rasped from every wall, from the cracks in the floor, from the flickering lights.

"They put it in me."

"I was just the vessel."

"I tried to hold it. I tried to keep it from spreading."

The mouth was just a hole in the torso, stretched wide and rimmed with bleeding roots, as though the house had grown from inside him like a tumor.

Ionia gagged, covering her mouth. The smell was unbearable, like burned oil mixed with spoiled meat and formaldehyde. She stepped forward, rage and pity twisted across her face. "What is it? What's in you?"

Drew's form rippled. From the gash in his chest, arms spilled out, dozens, maybe hundreds. Differently-sized, twitching, reaching. They waved blindly, mouths opening and closing where hands should be.

"It's not just ghosts," Drew said. "It's not just spirits. It's a pattern. A sickness that started as a thought. A thought that learned how to live."

Kristen backed into Donna. "Why didn't it kill him?"

"I think it did," Donna said softly. "But it also wanted to use him. And now it wants to use us."

A rumble echoed from behind the walls.

Drew's voice cracked. "If you sever the loops, you cut off its memories. You starve it. You starve it, you kill it."

One of the limbs grabbed at Marti. Its hand fused briefly with her skin, burning her, then let go.

Loretta turned to the group. "We need to go. Now."

The cathedral shuddered as the mirrors cracked and the ceiling began to bleed. The entire structure was trying to reject them now.

In the chaos, no one noticed Drew back away from the group, shielding his ears from the onslaught of sound. A shrill, insectoid whine filled the space, followed by a ripple in the wall.

Not metaphorical. The bricks liquified. Drew turned toward the others to shout. A gray and impossibly long hand shot out of the wall and clamped around his wrist. Then another. And another.

"Drew!" screamed Donna.

He thrashed, clawing at the brick and mortar, but they were like mud now. The wall opened like a hungry mouth, and he was dragged inside, screaming, kicking, begging. His fingers left bloody streaks on the wall.

Kristen lunged, grabbing his hand, but it peeled away from hers. Drew's final scream twisted into something inhuman. He was gone. The wall re-solidified. Clean. Dry. Silent.

Loretta, Frannie, Bruce, Ionia, Kristen, Marti, Judy, and Donna ran together through a hallway that had not been there seconds earlier. The walls were lined with knickknacks that clicked in rhythm as they passed. None of them looked back.

They could still hear Drew screaming. And something inside him was screaming louder.

CHAPTER FIFTY-ONE

They entered a corridor they hadn't noticed before. The walls throbbed gently, alive beneath the faded floral wallpaper. The pattern itself seemed to shift when they weren't looking, petals curling into mouths, stems into slithering veins. The sconces lining the walls flickered with cold, pale light, casting warping shadows that never stayed in place.

Kristen gripped Donna's hand. Bruce stayed in the back, turning every few seconds. Loretta walked ahead, her jaw tight, heart pounding in her ears like war drums.

Ahead, a door. Carved from wood too dark to be natural. It creaked open on its own. Inside was a long chamber of filth and splendor.

Pews lined the room like a chapel, each one filled. Not with people, but figures sewn together from remnants of the house itself. Porcelain doll faces embedded in walls of stitched clothing, eyes stuffed with buttons, mouths sealed with thread. Every time someone stepped forward, the floor groaned, and the figures shifted.

Loretta's foot sank slightly into something soft. She looked down. A patch of scalp, complete with brittle hair, half-buried in the rug. A shudder rippled through her.

They reached the altar.

Atop it sat a book. Bound in leather that looked disturbingly close to human skin, its spine stitched shut with thick black thread. The script inside was unreadable. A language that shimmered and resisted focus, as if the letters crawled when looked at directly.

Donna pointed to the far wall. "That's the thing following us."

The mural wasn't a painting. It was flesh, fused into the plaster. A screaming face pressed forward. A man's, or something that once had been. One eye open, leaking black fluid. Lips cracked into a permanent grimace, as if it had just understood its fate.

"Drew?" Bruce whispered.

"No," Loretta said. "A part of him."

"I don't understand," Marti said. "Why does the house like Drew so much? Why him?"

"I don't know," said Loretta. "The house picks certain people, I think."

The figures in the pews began to hum. A dissonant chorus.

Somewhere beneath the room, something enormous shifted. The walls shook. The figures stood. Their mouths unthreaded, their skin tore slowly, impossibly. The sound that came out was wrong. Not words. Not screams.

It was like a voice being born.

They were not going to stay to see what it was. Loretta grabbed the book as they exited.

CHAPTER FIFTY-TWO

Ionia led the others down a spiral staircase slick with residue that clung to the soles of their shoes. Bruce slipped once and didn't speak for ten minutes after. Marti wouldn't stop shaking. Judy kept glancing behind them, whispering, "I saw something. It's coming."

The basement opened into a chamber of pulsing ivory. It looked almost skeletal. Arches like ribs, walls glistening as if wet, pulsing slightly with each step. In the center stood a cage. Mechanical in nature but organic in design, it looked woven from bone and brass. Tubes slithered into it from the ceiling.

Inside was a human shape, unmoving. Covered in wax. Eyes closed. Mouth sewn shut. Bruce stepped closer. The thing twitched.

Bruce screamed and stepped back. The wax cracked. It was a doll, and also not a doll.

Ionia moved to a table at the back, fingers trembling as she leafed through crumbling documents. Ink bled across the pages.

She read aloud. "The house requires tethering. Sacrifices in flesh, memory, lineage. Terrors hidden in plain sight."

They didn't notice the figure forming behind them until it stepped from the wall. Not a ghost. Not a creature.

A twisted version of themselves. A warped reflection of all of them, melted together. Ionia's eyes. Bruce's jaw. Marti's hair. Donna's hands.

The amalgamated creature stepped toward them, dragging a broken statue, whispering, "Let me out. Let me out. Let me out."

They ran, slamming the door shut behind them.

CHAPTER FIFTY-THREE

The house creaked and groaned, as if in physical pain.

Its walls bled from every seam. Screams came from the pipes. The chandeliers dripped hot wax that sizzled as it hit the floor. Yet, the central chamber remained unchanged.

They found Drew again. Or what was left of him. His form was smaller now, curled, half-submerged in a cradle of bone. The skin hung loose. The chest cavity had split wide, exposing nothing inside.

The voice remained. It came not from his mouth, but from everywhere at once. "You've come to finish it."

Loretta stepped forward. "What does that mean?"

Drew's mouth moved in jerks. "You're the story. The house doesn't just want to live. It wants to collect. Loop. Endless rooms. Endless pain. And it needed people with pain to do it."

Drew's body convulsed. "You broke the pattern. I couldn't. I held it too long."

Loretta stared at the wound in his chest. "What was inside you?"

Drew didn't answer. But they saw. A mass in the corner. A squirming ball of limbs, mouths, and eyes blinking memories. It shivered as they approached.

Each mouth opened and whispered parts of their lives. Entire conversations. Sobs. Apologies. Laughs. Regret. It had eaten everything they were.

Kristen stepped forward. "If we kill it..."

"We'll lose the memories," Donna said. "All of them."

Ionia's eyes narrowed. "But we'll get to be ourselves."

Marti raised a shard of mirror. Bruce held out the book, torn and burning.

Loretta nodded. "No more loops."

They stabbed the creature at once with whatever they could find, and whatever weapons they'd held on to from the attic. Mirror shards, pipe, hammer, wooden slats. Their strikes were fueled by their own memories and fear.

The creature didn't scream. It sighed. A deep, relieved sigh that shook the walls.

IT'S ALWAYS HALLOWEEN HERE

The house fell silent.

"Is everybody okay?" Loretta asked.

Judy gasped. "Where's Donna?"

CHAPTER FIFTY-FOUR

Donna pushed the door open, and the glow of dusty indicator lights blinked in the dark like distant stars. The room was cramped, walls lined with shelves sagging under the weight of old electronics. Dozens of televisions—fat, boxy sets with convex glass—were stacked three and four high. Between them, radios sat in neat rows, their metal grilles rust-speckled, knobs dulled from decades of use. On the far wall, a bank of security monitors huddled together, their screens dark, cables snaking down into a tangle that looked almost organic. An oscillating fan, unmoving, sat in the corner, its blades coated in a fur of grey dust.

Donna stepped inside, running her hand over the edge of a heavy cathode-ray set. The glass was cold and slightly sticky. She caught the faint metallic, acrid scent of scorched wiring.

A low *pop* sounded somewhere in the room. One television blinked on without warning, its screen a murky blue static that writhed and snapped. The static parted for a moment, revealing a grainy image: a hallway she didn't recognize, its walls trembling faintly, as though filmed through water. A single figure stood at the far end. Thin, motionless, facing the camera.

Another television came to life beside it. This one showed a close-up of a mouth. Dry, colorless lips moving soundlessly, protruding jaw. The image flickered and cut to black, then returned closer, the lips now glistening as if wet.

From somewhere low on the shelves, a radio crackled. Its speaker released a thin, quavering voice. Not quite male, not quite female.

"You've been walking here much longer than you think."

The voice paused, static crawling in the silence.

"We already know which door you'll choose."

Donna froze. She turned toward the sound, but the voice seemed to slide to another radio, then another, shifting its location in the room like a predator circling prey.

The televisions kept lighting up, one after another, each screen showing a different scene.

A child's bedroom with the wallpaper peeling upward, revealing a pulsating black wall beneath.

A kitchen table covered in plates of food, each dish crawling with pale, segmented shapes.

IT'S ALWAYS HALLOWEEN HERE

A close-up of her own face, filmed from just behind her shoulder.

On the security monitors, the darkness broke with a sudden flood of impossible images. One camera showed the very room she stood in, but there was someone else in it. A tall, shadowed figure standing directly behind her. Another showed a vast, rotting field where shapes twitched beneath the soil. A third revealed a narrow staircase descending endlessly into blackness, small hands clinging to the banister just out of sight.

The radio's voice returned, low and deliberate:

"Don't look behind you. If you do, you'll see who's holding your hand."

Donna's skin prickled, her knees locking in place.

From the corner of her eye, one of the televisions shifted its image again. It showed her, right now, in that very moment, standing in that exact spot, surrounded by screens. But in the image, every single television and monitor was off. Only her own reflection in the dead glass stared back.

On that same screen, the reflection smiled.

The smile in the reflection lingered, too wide, the skin at the corners of its mouth stretching in unnatural creases. Donna's chest tightened, and without meaning to, she took a step backward.

A low hum swelled in the room, deep enough that it rattled in her bones. The televisions flickered in unison, their glow sickly, each one stuttering through images faster than she could register: open mouths, blank eyes, hallways collapsing in on themselves, flashes of her own hands held against walls she didn't remember touching.

One of the radios let out a single, sharp burst of static. Then every radio in the room clicked on together, dials twitching on their own. The speakers whispered in dozens of voices at once. Some were high and childlike, others guttural and strained, muttering words that were almost familiar, just shy of making sense. Her ears strained to catch them, but every time she thought she understood, the voices bent the syllables into something alien.

The security monitors changed again. Now, every single feed showed her back, filmed from inches away, as though something was pressed against her spine holding the camera. The angle didn't move, didn't sway. It just stayed fixed, while the shadow behind her in the footage began to lengthen, its head stretching upward until it grazed the top of the frame.

The hum deepened. Several screens began to bulge outward, glass bending toward her as if the images themselves were trying to push into the room. The glow from the screens thickened, oily, casting shifting shadows across the floor that didn't match her movements.

One radio crackled louder than the rest, drowning out the whispers.

"They'll open their eyes now."

Immediately, the televisions stopped flickering. Every screen showed a face, dozens of them, pressed right against the glass from the inside. Eyes shut. Foreheads leaving foggy marks. Their features were pale, lips slack.

Then, in perfect unison, the eyes opened. They stared straight at her.

The screens shuddered violently, rattling on their shelves. The glass bowed outward another inch, spiderweb cracks racing across the surfaces. A thin black fluid began to seep from the edges of some, trickling down the cabinets, leaving streaks that smelled metallic and rotten.

From the security monitors, the shadow in the feed lunged forward. Its movement was jarring and jagged, as if frames had been skipped. The camera view slammed into static.

The radios screamed at once, a single blaring note that made Donna stagger.

Something inside the largest television was pushing harder now, the screen distending like stretched skin. Elongated fingers pressed from the inside until the glass began to split with a slow, high-pitched squeal.

The last thing Donna saw before the first hand broke through was her own reflection in the corner of the screen. It wasn't watching the hands. It was watching her.

The first hand punched through the glass, spraying her with sharp flecks that bit into her cheek. It was bone-pale, the fingers unnaturally jointed, nails yellowed and hooked. It gripped the edge of the television, pulling at it with jerks that made the entire metal casing groan.

Another screen shattered beside it, and a second arm slithered out, black liquid dripping from its wrist. Donna's pulse roared in her ears, but she wasn't frozen. She moved. Her gaze swept the room in a single, frantic scan until she spotted a metal rod on the floor. A piece of shelving that had come loose.

She lunged for it just as a third television burst, the face inside forcing itself halfway out, jaws unhinged far wider than human. The thing's teeth were small and numerous, like a shark's, clacking together in anticipation.

Donna swung the rod in a brutal arc. The impact rang like a church bell, caving the face sideways into the jagged edge of its own shattered screen. Black fluid sprayed across the cabinet and floor. The voice from the radio shrieked in something between rage and pain, and for a moment, the other hands faltered.

The security monitors lit again. Every feed showing her swinging the rod. In each, the things on the screens were closer to her than they were in reality.

A wire from somewhere in the dark mass of equipment lashed out like a whip, curling around her ankle and yanking her off balance. She hit the floor hard, vision rattling. Another hand clawed at her calf, cold and wet.

Gritting her teeth, she kicked savagely, the rod clattering out of her grip for a second before she caught it again. She drove the end down on the hand until its fingers broke away like brittle twigs, retreating with a hiss.

The radio's whispers turned into rapid, urgent chanting. The televisions flickered with new images. A door behind her, shown from the outside, slamming shut on its own. A hallway full of shadows was converging toward where she was now.

Something inside the largest television forced itself farther out. Its shoulders popping through the torn glass, shards embedded deep in its pale flesh. Its head turned toward her, neck cracking in slow increments.

Donna didn't wait for it to crawl free. She charged.

She slammed the rod into the base of the screen with all her strength. Sparks erupted, and the figure inside convulsed violently before collapsing backward into the dark void beyond the glass. The static surged so bright it bleached the whole room white for a second.

The hum faltered. Several hands withdrew at once. The chanting broke into scattered, panicked murmurs.

Donna spun toward the door. It was closed, just as the monitors had shown, but she didn't hesitate. She rammed the rod into the old brass handle, twisting and forcing it until the metal screeched and gave way.

The moment the door cracked open, the televisions howled. The sound was low and deep, vibrating in her ribs. The wires lashed in all directions, but she ducked under them, shoving the door wide and diving through.

Behind her, the room snapped into silence.

When she looked back, the doorway was just a plain wall. No door. No sign of anything.

Only the faintest sound slid into her ears. A single, tinny voice, impossibly far away.

"We'll find another screen."

In the dark silence of the room that no longer had a door, something stirred.

One by one, the televisions blinked back to life, the static slow and steady now, like deep, measured pulses. The broken glass on the floor slid inward across the boards, pulled back into the jagged mouths of the screens, as though time were rewinding.

The radios clicked on together, dials twitching in unison. A faint, warbling hum filled the space. Low at first, then swelling until it seemed to shake the shelves.

On the security monitors, Donna appeared again. She was walking quickly down a hallway, glancing over her shoulder. The camera angles shifted, following her in perfect sync, even though there was no one holding a camera.

The largest monitor zoomed in on her face, the image sharpening until the color drained away, leaving her skin the same pale grey as the hands that had reached for her. Her mouth opened slightly in the footage.

From the speakers, her own voice came through. Soft, slow, but not her.

"She'll look again. They always look again."

The static hissed approvingly.

In the farthest television, deep in the black beyond the glass, something vast moved forward; its edges indistinct, its weight unmistakable. It stopped just at the surface, as though listening.

From every screen, every radio, and every monitor at once, the same whisper slithered out:

"Soon."

The lights in the room snapped off.

CHAPTER FIFTY-FIVE

Donna was missing. The house had taken her, like it had taken the others.

Loretta stayed in front of the line, leading her friends. She saw the front door. It was only hundreds of feet away from them.

"We have to get out," Judy said. "We get out, we call the police, we come back and rescue everybody."

"If we get out of this, I'll never go into a strange house ever again," said Marti.

Nobody was celebrating yet. They still had to get out of the house. There were no guarantees the door would open for them.

The floor was slick beneath their feet. Not wet, but greasy, as if coated in the remnants of something long-decayed and still listening. They moved through a narrow corridor that shuddered with each step, the walls pulsing faintly, like tissue around a wound. Loretta kept the half-burned book close. Its pages were rearranging themselves. Words crawled across them like insects trying to escape.

Ionia was the first to speak. "Something's wrong. It's too quiet."

"I was just thinking that," Marti said.

"I want to see my family again," Kristen said quietly.

Kristen moved beside Bruce, and Loretta caught it. The brief glance, the worried kind. Bruce noticed, gave a small smile.

The smile didn't last. The wall split open. Not with noise. There was no cracking, no tearing. One moment Bruce stood beside them, and the next he was sinking into the wall as though it were made of tar.

"Bruce!" Kristen shouted, grabbing for him. He reached back, his arm disappearing to the elbow.

"Don't let go!" Ionia cried.

They all pulled but it was no use. The wall closed like a mouth, folding in on itself with a soft, sick kiss. Bruce was gone.

"No!" Kristen pounded the wall. "Bruce!"

"Go to the door!" Loretta ordered. "Get out!"

Her friends rushed past her. Loretta touched the surface of the wall. It was warm, faintly pulsing, like a heartbeat hidden under layers of skin.

Frannie backed away. "It's still hungry."

The corridor behind them twisted. The path they'd come through was gone.

The screaming began again. First just one. Then dozens.

The ghosts came pouring through the cracks, their mouths stretched wide, filled with endless rows of teeth. Their faces had changed. They were angrier now, more defined. They didn't just want release. They wanted companions.

Demons came behind them. These were bigger, limbs bloated and dragging, voices like insect wings. One walked on arms alone, its legs curled up like a dead spider. It hissed from a headless neck.

"We have to move!" Judy shouted.

Loretta grabbed Frannie's hand. "Where?"

Marti and Kristen pounded at the door. It wasn't moving. They saw the greeter outside, the woman from earlier in the night. There was nobody outside, nobody waiting in line to get inside the house. She simply stood on the porch, staring into the distance, unmoving.

"God, I want to punch that bitch!" Frannie snarled.

Loretta turned, feeling something pull inside her chest. The book. It pulsed with heat. She followed it, leaving her friends in the hallway.

"Loretta," something from down the hallway whispered.

She passed under an archway of bone and into a chamber that wasn't on any floor plan. An impossibility made real by hunger and ritual.

It was circular, lined with shelves full of jars containing tongues, each labeled in a language no one could read. The walls were covered in scripts made from skin, stitched together with hair.

In the center was a figure.

It sat cross-legged, wrapped in funeral shrouds. Its face was a blur, as if painted over, and where its eyes should have been, there were tiny hands, twitching. It did not look up, but it spoke.

"You've come far, Loretta."

She stopped cold. "How do you know my name?"

"The house knows what you fear. I know what it is."

She stepped forward, still trembling. "Are you part of it?"

The figure made a motion. Half shrug, half dismissal. "I was once like you. Then I learned to listen. Now I keep the book of open mouths."

Loretta frowned. She was done. "What the hell does that mean?"

"It means I catalog what the house consumes. It has eaten families, cities, churches, wars. But only a few ever make it to this room."

IT'S ALWAYS HALLOWEEN HERE

"Are my friends still alive?"

The figure's hands spread across its lap. "Alive? Possibly. Yours? No."

Loretta stepped forward, anger sharpening her voice. "What is the house? Where did it come from?"

The figure finally raised its head. The hands where its eyes were opened, revealing darkness that wasn't just absence but depth.

"A mistake. A hunger given a body. The result of a spell cast backward. Blood magic that tried to reverse death but opened something else instead."

"Who cast it?"

"Many did. Over centuries. But we made it stick. Fed it. Tried to contain it. But it fed too long, on too many souls. Now it cannot stop unless it is cut from its foundation."

"What about our friends?"

"If they still live, they will be part of it. The legacy. The whispers in town." The figure pointed behind her.

A door had appeared. Heavy. Carved. Waiting.

"You must go now. The house has found you."

The room began to tremble. The jars rattled. The tongues inside them twitched. The shadows peeled from the walls.

Loretta didn't hesitate. She ran. The door swung open on its own. The house howled behind her.

CHAPTER FIFTY-SIX

Frannie, Ionia, Judy, Kristen, and Marti stood at the front door. The wood beneath their feet felt soft, as if the boards had been soaked in something long since curdled.

"Look!" said Frannie. She pointed to the ground.

A trap door. Marti gripped the rusted iron ring in the floor and pulled. The door opened with a shrill creak.

"We are right by the entrance of the house," Frannie said. "We can dig our way out if we have to."

Stale rot wafted from below, thick with something metallic and unnatural. The steps leading down were slick, uneven stone. Some crumbled completely, others sagged like damp tongues. A long-forgotten lantern on the dirty ground burst to life. The flickering light trembled across the walls, revealing roots. Hundreds of roots.

They were everywhere. Coiling out of the stone, hanging like veins from the ceiling, slick and pulsing faintly. They looked more like muscle than plant. The further they descended, the more the roots began to quiver. Not in response to wind or movement, but as if aware. As if reacting.

At the bottom, the cellar opened into a wide chamber, unnaturally round. The walls were slick and glistening with sap or blood, or both. In the center, suspended by root-like tendrils from every angle, was a chandelier of bones and silver.

Kristen clutched Ionia's arm. "What happens when we go down there?"

"Something wakes up," Ionia said. "Or something dies."

"I don't want to die," said Kristen.

"We're not going to, Kristen. We're going to ditch this shitty party and fucked-up house."

Judy stepped forward, holding her flashlight high. The light cast strange refractions of faces across the walls. Shadows distorted, howling, reaching. Marti saw her father. Kristen saw herself. Frannie's face twisted into her sister's. Each hallucination clawed at memory and guilt.

Ionia had held on to the hammer they'd used in the attic days ago. Or was it just hours? "We can't wait."

She struck the chandelier. It didn't fall. It writhed, every bone shifting and breaking as if fighting to stay whole. Roots snapped back violently, spraying black fluid that hissed when it touched their skin. The silver caught fire without flame.

The house shook.

Not like an earthquake. Like a living thing convulsing in pain.

CHAPTER FIFTY-SEVEN

The dim lights flickered violently, casting shadows that didn't align with their movements. The roots in the cellar curled inward. A deep voice—not human, not quite language—chanted from nowhere and everywhere at once.

They fled deeper into cellar, regrouping in yet another part of the house they didn't recognize. A crumbling drawing room lined with broken portraits. Some had no faces. Others had too many.

For a moment, they sat in silence, bloodstained, trembling, trying not to break. The door they stumbled through should've led to another hall, but instead it opened into a long, rectangular room lined with windows.

"Light!" Judy shouted. The faintest glimmer of a sunrise.

The windows weren't normal. They faced out into a world that shouldn't exist. Not the street. Not the sky. Not even the forest.

Beyond the glass was a storm unraveling in reverse. Rain ascended in glistening ribbons. Lightning crackled upward into the clouds. Trees leaned backward, their leaves retreating into branches. A deer ran in reverse, movements jerky and unnatural.

Inside the room, it was still. Quiet. Safe, for the moment. They collapsed in a corner. No words. Just the sound of their hearts thudding in their skulls.

Marti stared at her hands, then at the glass. "I just wanted to go home," she whispered. "My family. I should've been waking them up right now. I wonder if they miss me. If they're scared."

No one else spoke. Kristen sat beside her, staring out the window at the impossible landscape. Her voice was barely audible. "I think, even if we do escape, no one will believe us."

"If we don't make it," Marti said. "Will anyone even know where to look for us? How to find us? Will we be forgotten in this house, like everything else here?"

Frannie leaned her head back against the wall. "We are going to make it," she said, smashing her fists against the windows. The others joined in.

"We're so close," Ionia said. She closed her eyes, lips moving silently, perhaps praying, or trying to remember the sound of her husband's voice.

A cold rush, like movement that didn't pass through the room but underneath it, around it.

IT'S ALWAYS HALLOWEEN HERE

The windows fogged. The glass cracked. A whisper filled the space, speaking names none of them had given. The door they came through was gone.

The spirits did not rise. They grew. Swelled out of the wood, pulled up like rot through grain. First, thin hands. Then bodies without mass. They had faces stolen from memory, mouths too wide, eyes too many. Or none at all.

One spirit crawled on inverted knees, its jaw opening like a drawer. Another hovered with empty sockets from which worms dripped like tears. A third whispered with a dozen tongues, flicking in and out of slits across its torso.

The demons followed. No two alike.

One was a mass of mismatched body parts on legs, each of its limbs different. Another slithered, made of hands sewn together, clutching and weeping and pulling itself forward by grabbing its own spine. They hissed, chanted, screamed, but without air, without sound. Only the pressure of their presence could be felt.

They descended upon the group. Marti went first. Dragged into the wall, kicking, her last scream muffled by hands. Ionia tried to hold her. The spirit grinned through her face as it tore her away.

Kristen ran toward the window. She screamed as something crawled down from the ceiling and wrapped around her face.

Frannie fought with whatever she could find. Anything among the ruins of the room that could be used as a weapon. Ionia swung the hammer wildly.

Frannie fell. A demon grabbed her by the shoulders and peeled him backward, folding her body like a ribbon.

Ionia turned, blood running from her arms. The ghost of a woman with no lower jaw climbed inside her, mouth first, and she fell without a sound.

Judy was alone. Surrounded. Everyone else was gone. They had fought as hard as their bodies allowed. It wasn't enough. One by one, they were taken away.

She was the last. Standing in the center of the room, her hands trembling, blood on her face, she watched her friends disappear into the shadows, screaming and convulsing.

Then stillness. All gone.

They took her next.

CHAPTER FIFTY-EIGHT

Loretta stumbled into the next room. She didn't have time to take in her surroundings.

A figure emerged from the far corner. Not from a door. Not from shadow. It just was.

A person. Or something dressed in the echo of one. Skin like waxed parchment. Its voice came from behind its face.

"You've tasted the marrow of the house. Now it knows you."

"Who are you?" she demanded.

"I was once the house's guest. Then the historian. Now the host. I don't remember my old life."

"What is this place?"

"A vessel," the thing said. "For a god that never sleeps. A monument built on ritual and pain. The Faulkner family wanted power. The house grew from their pact. Flesh to stone, soul to room."

"And the demons?"

"Remnants. Guardians. Trapped hunger."

"How do we escape?"

The historian smiled wanly. "You don't. The house needs new blood." A pause. A weight.

"God, you talk like such an asshole," Loretta said.

The historian smiled wider, as if mimicking a human. Loretta saw it. The subtle twitch of its left eye, the way its hands pulsed like hearts. Something about it was off, more so than anything else in the house. Not because it looked unnatural, but because it looked like it was trying too hard not to.

"No," she said. "You're lying." Loretta stepped forward, staring down the waxen figure. "There's no deal. No choice. You're just trying to trap us here permanently. You want a sacrifice because it's how you feed."

The historian's mouth twisted, not into a frown, but a smirk. A warped, amused expression that tore at the corners of its cheeks.

"Clever girl. But too late."

It raised both arms. The walls peeled away, revealing rows of figures nailed into the beams behind them. They were screaming silently, eyes sewn shut, tongues hanging loose. The room shifted like a throat swallowing.

A candle on a wall sconce, encased in glass, flickered in the breeze. Loretta didn't wait. She hurled it straight into the thing's face.

It ignited. The figure shrieked in a frequency that bent its spine and made the walls shimmer.

The historian's voice burned through the floorboards as it collapsed into itself, limbs twitching, face melting like wax over embers.

She was done running. Blood soaked her sleeves. Her lungs burned. The room warped behind her, growing longer the more she looked.

Behind her, the demons gave chase.

The last stand. I tried. I fought. It wasn't enough.

The sounds were not of footsteps, but of wet dragging, of clicking, of laughter layered with gargling sobs.

She turned, swinging a shattered chair leg like a club, smashing it through the face of something with spindly arms and no torso, only a yawning ribcage filled with eyes. It recoiled, shrieking.

Another creature lunged. Its mouth was vertical, splitting its entire body.

Loretta rolled, scrambling into a narrow doorway, slamming it behind her. Darkness. Stillness.

Click. Gaslight sconces along the walls flickered to life.

She was in a parlor, though not like any she'd seen before. Everything was preserved in deep sepia. Not just color, but mood. Velvet furniture that hadn't aged. A fireplace with coals that glowed faintly without heat. Paintings that followed her with their real, blinking eyes.

She felt it. The weight. The absence. She knew that everyone else was gone. She dropped to her knees, her hands pressed on the warped floorboards. Bruce, Donna, Kristen, Ionia, Virgilia, Marti, all of them. All taken. All absorbed.

Something deeper sank into her chest. The realization. They weren't just dead. They were inside the house now. Bound to it. Digested by it.

Pieces of them would whisper through its walls, rattle through vents, cry through doorframes for eternity.

She screamed. A deep, ragged, animal scream. Not out of fear, but rage. The house had stolen everything.

"I'm getting out," she gasped, standing. "You don't get to keep me, too."

"Oh, I wouldn't be so hasty." The voice oozed coolly from behind her.

She turned. Standing by the fireplace was a man in a brown wool suit. He looked out of place, like a photo come to life. High collar, waistcoat, silver watch chain. His beard was trimmed in a stiff Victorian fashion. A bowler hat rested in his hand.

His skin was grayish-pink. Alive, but not quite. His eyes twinkled, as though lit from within. He smiled, far too easily.

"Miss Loretta, is it? You've done quite a bit of stomping through my house."

She knew instantly who he was.

"Faulkner."

He bowed low, theatrically. "Mr. Alistair Faulkner, at your cursed service."

Loretta took a step back. "You're dead."

"Oh, yes. Several times. Depends on how you define it." His grin widened. "This house is me now. And I must say, you're the most troublesome intruder I've had since those nuns in '43."

She didn't answer. Her hands balled into fists.

"You know, it was never meant to be this big," he continued. "Just a few rooms. A few experiments. A few souls. But the house grew hungry. So, I fed it. You understand, don't you?"

Loretta glared. "You killed them."

Faulkner laughed. "I invited them. They just didn't read the fine print." His eyes darkened.

"And now you're the last. The house likes you, Loretta. It thinks you'd make a fitting seed."

Loretta flung the chair leg like a spear.

It passed through him, but the illusion didn't break. Instead, he winced in mock offense.

"Temper, temper."

The fireplace roared to life, flames rising unnaturally high.

"You've one chance left, girl," he said. "You can offer yourself. End the line. Become part of the story. Or try to run. But I warn you, the house doesn't like runners."

He tipped his hat. "Tick-tock."

With that, he vanished. The room groaned.

Behind her, the door slowly creaked open into blackness.

CHAPTER FIFTY-NINE

Though the room did not contain a door, it became one.

Loretta stepped forward. The walls pulled back like meat from bone, revealing a hallway that hadn't been built. It had been remembered. Faded wallpaper throbbed gently, like a dying pulse. The floor was lined with dust that wasn't just dust. It was ashes, gray and clinging, coating her boots and the ends of her fingers.

Each step forward tightened her chest with something that wasn't fear, exactly. It was something older. Like shame wearing a mask.

She saw it. A door on the right opened without a sound.

Inside was a room from another century. Candles, stone walls, a crude operating table, rust-colored tools aligned in perfect rows. And a woman. Bound, eyes gouged. Still alive. Faulkner was there, in memory form, whispering Latin into her ear as her body spasmed. He cut into her chest with loving precision.

Loretta staggered back. She turned and was suddenly somewhere else.

A long dining room. Dozens seated. Dead faces sewn with smiles. They turned in unison to look at her.

She blinked. A classroom now. Children with moth wings for eyes and split mouths, reading from leather-bound books that wept. A teacher moved among them with scissors for hands.

Another blink. A nursery. Crib mobiles made from finger bones. A baby crying, its mouth filled with black feathers. In the corner, a rocking chair moved on its own.

The house wasn't done. It dragged her through itself. It showed her what it was, what it had been. The soul-furnace of Alistair Faulkner, who had turned grief into fuel, magic into meat. The house fed on memory, and now it wanted hers.

She was back in the parlor again. No time had passed. Or maybe all of it had.

A breeze, like movement. Not through air, but space. Loretta turned and Alistair Faulkner was right behind her.

His smile was a slit, his eyes sharp and inhuman, sparkling like stars seen from the bottom of a grave.

"What did you think you'd find, my dear?" he murmured. "A way out? There is none. You're in me now. You are me now. There's a house like this in every neighborhood. There is no why. No reason. It just exists."

She staggered back but didn't run. Not this time. She reached into her pocket. The tile she used to kill Drew's double was still there.

Faulkner reached out, his hand brushing her cheek. "People will forget. You'll be erased. You'll make such a lovely fixture."

She drove the tile into his throat. Hard. Twisting. His eyes widened. No rage, no pain, just surprise.

Loretta pushed deeper. The tile burned white-hot in her grip, and Faulkner began to crack, his flesh splintering like old wood. Dark steam hissed from his mouth and nostrils. His voice gurgled out in dozens of different languages at once, until there was nothing but the hissing of dissolving bone. The tile was lodged in his neck.

He collapsed. Not into dust, not into ash, but into fragments of light, like shattered memory.

Behind him, where he'd stood, a door appeared. Black. Smooth. Waiting.

Loretta stepped forward, alone. She stepped through the black door, into what the house had been hiding all along.

The Keeping Room.

It was vast, cathedral-sized, but felt buried, like it had been sunk beneath time. The walls were carved with thousands of names, some in English, some in jagged runes, some in languages not made for mouths. In alcoves along the room's perimeter, sat chairs. Each one crafted of twisted bone and iron, shaped like thrones. Each one occupied.

Her heart sank. They were all there. Angela. Bruce. Callie. Donna. Drew. Frannie. Helen. Ionia. Jerry. Judy. Kristen. Marti. Phyllis. Reuben. Suzanne. Virgilia.

Virgilia sat against the far wall, her hair streaked with grime, her knees drawn up. Suzanne stood beside her like a statue, eyes rimmed with red. Callie was pacing, mumbling numbers under her breath, her fingers twitching like she was still holding a knife.

For a moment, no one moved.

Angela raised her head. "Loretta?"

Loretta reached out to embrace her. "You're alive."

"No," Angela said. "We're just not dead yet. They've collected us."

Kristen turned slowly, and Loretta saw it. Burn marks on her arms in the shape of fingers. Helen's mouth trembled. "They've been watching us. Crawling on the ceilings. Talking behind the walls."

IT'S ALWAYS HALLOWEEN HERE

The room was deathly quiet, like a church where every prayer had been denied.

She ran first to Judy, who looked up at her slowly, eyes muddy but open. "Loretta, is it really you?"

Phyllis was emaciated, her body pale. Her lips cracked as she tried to speak. "We've been waiting."

Jerry and Bruce sat to her right, fused to their chairs, hands rigid in positions of prayer. Their eyes were gone, long dissolved.

Donna was on the far side, barely holding on. Her fingers twitched, and her lips moved without sound. Her face was partly fading, like a painting left out in the sun.

Drew sat in a broken throne, slumped forward. His chest was open. Hollow, as though whatever had possessed him had finally used him up.

Reuben was gone. Only his clothes remained, draped over a skeletal frame. A plaque above read simply, "Willing Sacrifice."

Marti and Ionia were dead. Their bodies still, but not empty. Their eyes blinked occasionally, as if remembering how.

Loretta staggered back, stomach threatening to wrench itself inside out.

The house hadn't killed them. It had kept them, like trophies on display in a tomb made of memory.

At the center of the room was a pedestal. On it, a mirror, framed in roots and fingernails. The mirror was liquid-like, swirling. A portal. It shimmered with the shimmer of escape.

"The house is alive, though everything inside it is dead," said a voice. "You'll be dead soon, too."

Mr. Faulkner stood at the edge of the room. Not a ghost. Not an illusion. Real. Somehow real again. The wounds from the tile shard were gone. He stood before a decrepit, withering portrait of himself.

"You can't just walk out," he said. "There's a price. You know that now. One soul must pay for another."

Loretta didn't speak. She walked toward him slowly. He opened his arms, mock-welcoming.

"I am eternal. Neither alive nor dead. The house chooses who remains. You? You're special. The house wants you to stay. Forever." His expression didn't change. "But you already know that, don't you?"

In that instant, everything became clear to Loretta. Everything inside the house had been set up to confuse them. Tricks and subterfuge to deceive them. There were no rules. The house was lawless. Nothing they'd been told, or had seen, mattered. Everything had been created to keep them confused and distracted, to keep them from thinking clearly. From leaving.

She nodded. She was thinking clearly now. The house. It knew she had grown up familiar with madness because of her father. That's why she was still standing.

Faulkner held his hands out toward her, beckoning her to take them. Loretta slowly reached out, eyes fixed on the painting behind him.

Loretta tilted her head. "Not today, bitch."

She pushed him out of her way. Snatched the painting off of the wall. Smashed its brittle frame against the wall, sending wooden shards flying in every direction. She gripped one of the sharp, broken pieces of the frame.

She thrust her arm forward and stabbed Faulkner with the shard. Again and again. He tried to back away, but Loretta's rage was in a bloodlust, a frenzy, a hatred she had never felt before.

She had him backed against the wall, his breath only bloody gurgles. His eyes draining of what little life the house had allowed him.

This time, she used the shard to cut. She jammed it into his cheek and dragged it across his face, splitting it from temple to jaw. He screamed, but it didn't echo. It stuck, thick and wet.

She peeled the mask of his face free. It squirmed in her hands, still warm. Loretta put his face over hers.

The flesh clung to her own, reshaping itself. Her body shifted subtly. Limbs lengthened, skin sagged, hair grayed and thinned.

She became Alistair Faulkner. The room paused. The mirror glowed.

You must trick the house. That's what she had been told.

Judy watched, barely able to sit up. "Loretta?"

"Still me," she rasped, voice sounding like pebbles under ice. "I'm getting us out."

She dragged Judy from the chair. Judy reached out, grabbing the crumpled portrait of Faulkner. She threw it over his skinless face.

Frannie blinked, eyes open. Loretta and Judy turned toward her. Loretta grabbed Judy with one hand and Frannie with her other.

Loretta knew she couldn't save everyone. There wasn't enough time. She felt the house ticking the seconds down, felt it inside her bones. Despite the pain in her chest at not being able to rescue all of her friends, she was determined to save who she could.

The room shrieked. Ghosts emerged from the walls, shadow-thin and serpentine, all of them weeping black fluid and screaming in every language of death.

The mirror vibrated angrily. Once. Twice. Loretta, wearing the mask of Faulkner, pulled Judy and Frannie into it.

The house howled, as if dying.

The portal snapped shut.

CHAPTER SIXTY

Loretta awoke on the grass. Cold. Damp. Under a sky revealing a rising, yellow sun. Rain fell, but in reverse, upward into the clouds.

Loretta sat up. Judy and Frannie lay beside her, breathing shallow but alive.

She was still wearing Faulkner's face. She tore it off with shaking hands and cast it aside.

The house behind them was gone. Nothing but a flat field of blackened soil.

Loretta knew it was a trick by The Faulkner House, hiding itself from them. She felt its presence, even if she couldn't see it. Loretta didn't care. They were out. Free.

Judy stirred and whispered. "We made it."

Loretta reached in her pocket, pulling out the rotted tooth she had been given. She threw it at the empty space where the house should have stood.

She looked back one last time. No wind. No whisper. But she felt them. The ones lost. Held forever in The Faulkner house.

No one but them would ever know what really happened.

CHAPTER SIXTY-ONE

ONE YEAR LATER

The envelope was heavy.

Thick parchment. Black wax seal, unbroken. Loretta's name and address handwritten in calligraphy, etched into the page as though pressed by bone.

Judy and Frannie received envelopes, too.

They hadn't spoken of the house in months. Not since the first nightmares. Not since the marks appeared, just under their skin, like ink bleeding from memory.

They knew. When the letters came, they didn't ask why.

They packed water bottles and coats. When they arrived at the iron gates of the Faulkner Estate, they found a single sign nailed into a crooked wooden post.

ONE NIGHT ONLY

Faulkner House Halloween Walkthrough

October 31st

Midnight to Sunrise

Admission by Invitation Only

Loretta's throat tightened. The gates creaked open as they approached, without being touched.

They didn't enter the house. They walked the long mile, past gnarled trees and empty statues, past rustling leaves that made no sound.

The house stood just as they remembered. Looming, timeless, watching. It pulsed faintly at the edges, as if alive again.

Candles flickered in each window. Laughter echoed from inside. Something that sounded like a string quartet played out of tune.

People were going into the house. Excited. Laughing. Curious. Naïve.

Frannie, Judy, and Loretta stopped just shy of the porch. That's when they saw her.

Standing at the door was a woman in a 1900s satin evening gown, dusty blue, with a brooch like a tiny screaming face.

This year's greeter.

She handed candy to guests. Tilted her head in an almost-human way. She was smiling. Polite. Calm.

She looked exactly like Donna.

Not just similar. Exactly.

Same dimple on the left cheek. Same mole near the right brow. Same blue-gray eyes. Only now, something deeper, more sinister, flickered behind her smile. Like she was pretending to be Donna. Like she was imitating human behavior, but not fully human.

Donna turned her head toward Loretta, Frannie, and Judy.

Her smile remained.

She raised her hand and waved.

THE END

ABOUT THE AUTHOR:

Matt Forgit lives and writes in New England. He is the author of *It's Always Halloween Here*, *How to Be a Professional Mourner*, *The Felicitous*, and *You Better Watch Out*. His interests include spending time with friends and family, annoying his better half, trying to be a cool uncle, scary stuff, movies, television shows, music, reading, eating, board games, final girls, creepy folklore, urban legends, spooky history, abandoned places, castles, islands, cabins in the woods, being near the ocean, and the 1970s, 1980s, and 1990s. He is terrible with social media, dreams of owning a haunted bed and breakfast atop a cliffside overlooking the sea, hopes that someday *Chopping Mall: The Musical* becomes a reality, and doesn't normally talk about himself in the third person.

For signed books, merchandise, convention and event appearance news, updates, random thoughts, horror recommendations, and general nonsense, scan here:

ABOUT THE ARTIST:

Matthew Keller is a Boston based artist who is active in various artist communities across New England. Drawing from his small-town upbringing, his art explores the contradictions between societal norms and personal beliefs that exist in various methods of communication. His work evokes feelings of alienation, guilt, and duplicity, challenging both himself and his audience to question moral understandings. Find more at matthewkellerart.com.

ACKNOWLEDGEMENTS:

Lisa, who is a queen, icon, hero, goddess, and inspiration, but above all, a genuine friend.

Meg, James, Brandon, and Matt, who really, truly went above and beyond for me on this book, and in so many other ways. It's never forgotten or lost on me.

The amazing, incredible, wonderful, brilliant people who give me their time, love, encouragement, and support—Amanda, Eric, Pearl, and Cora Pray; Andy and Mary Ann Forgit; Anna Maria Skiotis, Steve Galuna, Sofia Maria and Diana; Colin and Olivia Capelle; Dad and Kay; Danielle, Harry, and A.J. Providakes; Drew, Kassie, Carver, and Sailer McConville; Erica and Brian Sheldon; Gina Newell; Jake, Dory, Jasper, Isla, and Gus Forgit; James Sanguinetti; Jared, Sophie, and Simon Rohrer; Jessica, Andy, Leah, and Naomi Simon; Julie and Jake Forgit; Katie, Gavin, Owen, and Simon Allen; Kerri Allard; Lisa and Logan Stout; Maribel Palin; Matt Keller; Megan Ruggiero; Meghan and Paul Buckley; Melissa, Phil, Poppy, and Bowen Capezio; Mia Turner; Nancy Dorr; Phoebe Sexton; Roberta Townsend; Ryan, Sara, and Emerson Hastings; Shannon, Ryan, and Ryder Vogt; Shannon White; Stephanie Iscovitz, Frank Valdez, Frankie, and Cece; Tami, Travis, Mirren, and Porter Harless; Toni and Steve Weymer; my game night, movie date, and Friendsgiving crew; my hometown friends; The Forgit and Luoma clan; and my friends, family, friend family, and friends' families.

The authors, artists, and creators who befriended, welcome, and include me—Brandon Perras-Sanchez, Ryan Miller, Donna A. Latham, Karen Oldman, Amanda Warner, J.J. Salas, Erica Summers, Laura Bilodeau, Katrina Thornley, Victoria Dalpe, and more

Joshua Dahlin at Horror Depot, and Dave Lizotte and Brandin Whetstone at PVD Horror, for giving us Boston boys a home at the Providence events.

My beta readers, editors, and readers; the readers who have become friends; every person who takes time out of their day to post kind words about my books; and everyone who includes me in their cons, events, podcasts, interviews, spotlights, blogs, stories, reels, videos, posts, groups, and bookshelves. Huge shoutouts to Kyla Webber, Brigit at Brooklyn Attic Books, Chana Odom, The Ashaway Free Library Book Club, Jessica Diner, Jeff Bailey, Kim Ray, Erin Pritchard, Laura Roberts, Christine Cole, and more, for their support.

My favorite final girls—Ripley from *Alien*; Kit from *April Fool's Day*; Jess from *Black Christmas*; Kelli and Leigh from *Black Christmas '06*; Buffy from *Buffy the Vampire Slayer*; Alison from *Chopping Mall*; Sarah from *The Descent*; Stevie from *The Fog*; Alice from *Friday the 13th*; Ginny from *Friday the 13th Part 2*; Chris from *Friday the 13th Part 3*; Trish from *Friday the 13th: The Final Chapter*; Micki from *Friday the 13th: The Series*; Laurie from *Halloween*; Rachel from *Halloween 4*; Marti from *Hell Night*; Julie from *I Know What You Did Last Summer*; Vivia and Phoebe from *Killer Party*; Nancy Drew; Regina and Samantha from *Night of the Comet*; Judy from *Night of the Demons*; Nancy from *A Nightmare on Elm Street*; Alice from *A Nightmare on Elm Street 4*; Yvonne from *A Nightmare on Elm Street 5*; Maggie from *Popcorn*; Meagan from *Prom Night 4*; Grace from *Ready or Not*; Daphne and Velma from *Scooby-Doo*; Sidney and Gale from *Scream*; Lisa from *Scream Blacula Scream*; Maggie from *Severance*; Randi from *She-Wolf of London*; Sally from *The Texas Chainsaw Massacre*; Stretch from *Texas Chainsaw Massacre 2*; Michelle from *Texas Chainsaw Massacre 3*; Selena from *28 Days Later*; Scully from *The X-Files*; and Erin from *You're Next*—for being the smart, strong, capable, resilient, resourceful, and brave icons who bring me comfort, inspiration, and courage.

Mozzarella sticks, for being beautiful, delicious, and comforting.

IT'S ALWAYS HALLOWEEN HERE

HALLOWEEN MOVIE RECOMMENDATIONS

Are you looking for the perfect scary movie to watch at your next Halloween party? Or is spooky season all-year round in your house? I asked my wonderful, awesome, smart, thoughtful, and way-cooler-than-me, horror movie expert pals Swizzle Stick, Flapjack, Shecky, Curly Sue, Hot Rod, Disco Johnny, and Nickels to choose their all-time favorite horror and horror-adjacent movies (note: not necessarily the "best" or most technically well-made, but their personal favorites; the ones that hold a special place in their hearts, for various reasons). This is our final list, from us to you!

*Alien (1979) * Aliens (1986) * American Psycho (2000) * An American Werewolf in London (1981) * Annihilation (2018) * April Fool's Day (1986) * Army of Darkness (1992) * Banshee Chapter (2013) * Barbarian (2022) * Beetlejuice (1988) * Black Christmas (1974) * The Blair Witch Project (1999) * The Blob (1988) * The Cabin in the Woods (2011) * Candyman (1992) * Carrie (1976) * The Changeling (1980) * Chopping Mall (1986) * Cold Prey (2006) * Companion (2025) * The Conjuring (2013) * The Cottage (2008) * The Craft (1996) * Critters (1986) * Dead and Breakfast (2004) * Deadstream (2022) * Deathdream (1974) * Demon Wind (1990) * The Demon's Rook (2013) * Demons (1985) * The Descent (2005) * Doom Asylum (1987) * The Evil Dead (1981) * The Exorcist (1973) * Final Prayer (2013) * The Fly (1986) * The Fog (1980) * Friday the 13th (1980) * Friday the 13th Part 2 (1981) * Friday the 13th Part 3 (1982) * Friday the 13th Part 4: The Final Chapter (1984) * Fright Night (1985) * Funny Games (2007) * The Gates of Hell (1980) * Get Out (2017) * Gremlins (1984) * The Grudge (2004) * Halloween (1978) * Halloween 5: The Revenge of Michael Myers (1989) * Halloween: H20 (1998) * Haunt (2019) * Hell House LLC (2015) * Hell Night (1981) * Hellbound: Hellraiser II (1988) * Hello Mary Lou: Prom Night II (1987) * Hellraiser (1987) * Henry: Portrait of a Serial Killer (1986) * Hereditary (2018) * Heretic (2024) * The Hills Have Eyes (1977) * Hocus Pocus (1993) * The*

*House of the Devil (2009) * The Howling (1981) * I Know What You Did Last Summer (1997) * I Still Know What You Did Last Summer (1998) * Imprint (2007) * The Incredible Melting Man (1977) * Insidious (2010) * Invasion of the Body Snatchers (1978) * The Invitation (2022) * It Follows (2014) * It: Chapter One (2017) * Jaws (1975) * Just Before Dawn (1981) * Killer Klowns from Outer Space (1988) * Killer Party (1986) * Lake Mungo (2008) * Let the Right One In (2008) * Let's Scare Jessica to Death (1971) * Longlegs (2024) * The Lost Boys (1987) * Madman (1981) * Martyrs (2008) * M3gan (2022) * The Menu (2022) * Messiah of Evil (1974) * Midsommar (2019) * Misery (1990) * My Bloody Valentine (1981) * Night of the Comet (1984) * Night of the Creeps (1986) * Night of the Demons (1988) * Nightbreed (1990) * A Nightmare on Elm Street (1984) * A Nightmare on Elm Street 3: Dream Warriors (1987) * Nope (2022) * Oddity (2024) * The Orphanage (2007) * The Others (2001) * Outpost (2008) * Pan's Labyrinth (2006) * The People Under the Stairs (1991) * Poltergeist (1982) * Popcorn (1991) * Prey (2022) * Prom Night 4: Deliver Us from Evil (1991) * The Prowler (1981) * Psycho (1960) * Pumpkinhead (1988) * Pyewacket (2017) * A Quiet Place (2018) * Ready or Not (2019) * [REC] (2007) * The Return of the Living Dead (1985) * The Ring (2002) * Savageland (2015) * Saw (2004) * Scarecrows (1988) * Scream (1996) * Session 9 (2001) * Seven (1995) * Severance (2006) * Shaun of the Dead (2004) * The Shining (1980) * Shock Waves (1977) * The Silence of the Lambs (1991) * Sinister (2012) * Sinners (2025) * Sleepaway Camp 2: Unhappy Campers (1988) * Spookies (1986) * The Strangers (2008) * Student Bodies (1981) * The Taking of Deborah Logan (2014) * Talk to Me (2022) * 10 Cloverfield Lane (2016) * Terror Vision (1986) * The Texas Chainsaw Massacre (1974) * There's Nothing Out There (1991) * The Thing (1982) * Tourist Trap (1979) * 28 Days Later (2002) * Us (2019) * The Village (2004) * Waxwork (1988) * Weapons (2025) * Wes Craven's New Nightmare (1994) * When a Stranger Calls Back (1993) * When Evil Lurks (2023) * The Witch (2015) * You're Next (2011) * The Zero Boys (1986) **

IT'S ALWAYS HALLOWEEN HERE

Printed in Dunstable, United Kingdom